PRAISE FOR MARTIN SHANNON

Tales of Weird Florida is pure fun!

— KAT STILES - INTERNATIONAL BEST SELLING
AUTHOR OF MODIFIED

Martin hits the weirdness that is Florida right on the nose. The magick is clever, the laughs are big, and these people are my neighbors.

— G. MICHAEL REYNOLDS

You will love every crazy minute.

— KA MILTIMORE - AMAZON BEST SELLING
AUTHOR OF BURNED TO A CRISP

FREE STORIES

Pixies, Shades, and tribal Magick—having a baby is hard enough, but having a Magician's baby is in a league all of its own...

Sign up at www.martin-shannon.com to get "Danderous Delivery," the Tales of Weird Florida short story only available to newsletter subscribers.

DEAD SET

MARTIN SHANNON

To the most Magickal people in my life, my loving wife and daughter, for their understanding, love, and industrial-sized outpouring of patience, to my parents, who never stopped me from imagining Magickal things—even when I should have been weeding the hedge— and to my grandmother, for her unceasing encouragement and a lifetime of Sunday conversations.

PART I
DEADSTINATIONS

RIDING THE PINE

*S*mall beads of sweat joined forces on my forehead, coming together in a sign of unity before sliding into a defenseless eyeball.

What the hell am I doing?

Cathy, my lovely yet ill-inspired teenage daughter, beamed at me from a few rows over, her once-white jiu-jitsu gi now crusted with sweat and a few drops of someone else's blood.

That's right, I'm being a good dad—and trying to lose a few pounds in the process. Yay me.

Cathy turned away to listen to the instructor, a tall and well-built Brazilian kid fresh off the boat. I might have been passable in the low speech of demons, but this guy's Portuguese accent was giving me fits.

I wiped more sweat off my face with the cardboard sleeve of my loaner gi—a five-pound, white, Japanese looking suit that soaked up sweat like a shammy—and tried to focus on the instructor. His scrambled accent droned on, so I took a moment to survey the hotbox-turned-dojo. Cathy's love affair with martial arts meant I'd been to a few of these places over the years, and as dojos went, this one wasn't half-bad. It was clean and reasonably well laid out, with dense red mats covering the floor and walls—more than enough padding to take the impact of thick-skulled older guys like myself. The only real problem, aside from our instructor's befuddling accent, was the heat; air conditioning was clearly not something martial artists put much thought into.

Cathy and I knelt together with a dozen or so men and women on the lava-hot mats while our instructor stepped through a simple yet hard-to-follow escape. It all had to do with someone pinning you down—school-yard-style basic self-defense. Every few minutes Cathy would lean over and assure me I'd be able to handle it just fine.

Hardly.

As far as my daughter and the rest of the world knew, I was middle management for a local builder—keeping the workers working and the projects on track. It wasn't glamorous, but it paid for a life with two kids and a loving wife. All of this was great, but the real reason I took the job was the flexibility; it gave me the time I needed for my second life.

Magick.

My daughter didn't know it, but I was actually here as much for her as for the crash course in how not to get beaten up by some Demon of the unspeakable darkness. The terrifying denizens of the netherworld weren't up on Brazilian Jiu-Jitsu yet, so I took every advantage I could get.

Our instructor rounded off the demonstration with what I guessed must have been a perfectly delivered joke in Portuguese, then sent us off to pair up. I wasn't keen on seeing strange, sweaty men climb on top of my baby girl, but I got the impression many of them weren't keen on it either. Cathy might have been a little on the small side, but what she gave up in size she more than made up for with wild energy.

A couple of the guys had started calling her 'little twister,' but somewhere along the way that got twisted itself, and now she was 'tiny twister' and every inch of her five-foot-tall frame loved it.

"Hey, I'm Mike," my randomly assigned partner said, extending a sweat-soaked hand my direction.

"Eugene, but everyone calls me Gene."

We shook hands and sized each other up; it's just what men do—especially men with a little gray in their hair. Mike offered to play the victim first, which was fine with me. It gave me a few extra seconds to watch my daughter girl-handle another would-be attacker.

In the natural world I had nothing to worry about with Cathy—she was more than capable of taking care of herself. But it wasn't the natural world that kept me up at night, it was the supernatural one.

I went through the motions of an attacker and Mike demonstrated his basic understanding of the technique. He succeeded in tossing me off and gaining the upper hand, but I wasn't really trying, I was distracted by something sparkling on the bench.

Cathy had taken off her necklace.

Any normal parent wouldn't have had a problem with this, but I was far from a normal parent, and that was far from a normal necklace.

One of the problems with being a Magician was that you had a tendency to make a lot of very scary things quite angry with you. I didn't mind, it was all part of the process—can't make omelets without breaking open a few monster skulls and all that —but what about the family?

Mike climbed on top and pinned my arms down just like we'd been taught. I tried to remember the right sequence of moves but couldn't shake the visual of my daughter's necklace casually discarded.

She took it off! She took the necklace off!

My brain was having a difficult time reconciling the

complex set of leg movements required to escape thanks to the terrifying realization Cathy was completely unprotected.

"No, you have to shift your hips more," my well-meaning partner said, trying to keep me from embarrassing myself further.

The necklace, a powerful Lenar's Logic Loop that I'd spent over a year painstakingly creating, lay like a discarded sock on the bench.

"I got it." I pushed my hips out and struggled to free myself from an overzealous Mike. It worked, but not without a little give from the larger man—Cathy wouldn't be pleased, but hell, neither was I.

A Logic Loop was Deep Magick: important, powerful, and altogether representative of thousands of hours of work—yet there it was, lying on the bench, leaving my beautiful daughter completely exposed to the supernatural world. Yeah, she might be able to fight off angry men, break arms, and put people in choker holds, but with the necklace off, she was powerless as a newborn kitten against the hordes of unfathomable evil.

Mike and I switched positions and the big man went to work on another escape.

"Think you could make it a little harder this time?"

Sure.

"Grauior..." I mumbled under my breath. It was a simple bit of Magick, but one I loved using to play tricks on the nurse at the doctor's office. It took me right up to 250lbs without changing my actual size—yeah, physics can suck it.

"Oof—" Mike said, no doubt feeling the sudden change in weight distribution rather keenly. "That'll work..."

"Great..."

I all but ignored my half-crushed partner and instead put all my energy into willing Cathy to look this way.

Come on, sweetheart... Damn it, Cathy.

Back when Porter and I were new parents we'd had 'the talk.'

For most couples, that conversation was about how to split up activities: child care, diapering, feeding, etc. For us that conversation centered around how to keep our newborn safe from my world. The night she'd been born, Cathy'd almost been ferreted off by Pixies, eaten by a Shade from the second circle of Hell, and sacrificed to a self-aware Tocobaga burial mound—it was an important discussion.

Magick was in my blood, but not my wife's. My little Midwest transplant was about as normal as apple pie. That didn't make her any less beautiful, but it did make her far less likely to borrow a grimoire or show me up with her own evocations. Still, our early marital years hadn't been without their challenges, the biggest of which being how we would protect our children—should we have had any—from the terrors that existed just beyond the visible world.

In the end we'd settled for serious Deep Magick, a big fat lump of it in fact—a talisman that would make Cathy all but invisible to the things that go bump in the night. It had taken all I had at the time to build it, and even more weeks after had been spent recovering from the making, but there it was, one of the most powerful Magickal items I'd ever created—now keeping that bench perfectly safe from the forces of evil.

My partner struggled to free himself from heavy Eugene Law, giving me ample time to try and get Cathy's attention, but she wasn't having anything to do it with. That diminutive grappler was too busy twisting arms and wringing necks to pay attention to her old man.

Mike shifted under me and I adjusted my position. In doing so I caught a blast of hot air from one of the fans, and with it a scent I wasn't expecting. It wasn't the smell of the loaner gi, or the caustic stench of bleach our instructor used to clean the mats; this was something far worse.

New Dead.

Not every soul ended up in a better place when they died—

not by a long shot—and some of them were willing to do damn near anything to find a way back.

Florida's problems with New Dead were well documented, if not well understood. There was even a whole Twitter account dedicated to the antics of 'Florida Man,' an amalgamation of all the terrible and inane crimes perpetrated by individuals in the Sunshine State. I just happened to know more than half of them were the work of New Dead.

How did they get here? That's what wasn't well understood. Through some twist of fate Florida happened to exist at that geometric vertex where the natural and supernatural collided with high frequency—plus we had 'Thinnings.'

Those threadbare sections of the veil that kept the supernatural world far away from the real world grew like stink on a dead rabbit down here in the orange juice capital of the world. When they popped up, bad things came through—our tourism board worked so well even the damned like to visit.

Still, there was one here now, in Cathy's jiu-jitsu class—how had I missed it? While the telltale signs of the possessed were impossible for a normal person to see, Magickal blood meant I got the benefit of seeing all sorts of things you can't un-see: Dragon egg fever, Alligator Men, murderous wraiths on I-75, and even the ashen bodies of the damned.

Mike's weight shifted underneath me—somehow my partner had found a way to dislodge all 250 lbs of Magickally enhanced Eugene Law and send it tumbling to the mat. My body hit the rubber with a resounding thump, drawing looks from more than half the class.

That was when I found it.

If the eyes really were a window to the soul, then this young man's body was running a double-occupancy special. Black as coal with burned edges, they sank deep into the crumpled paper of his ashen cheeks ringed with tar.

Yep, New Dead—damn it.

A smile split his face, knocking free large flakes of withered lip that tumbled away like ash from a spent cigarette.

I could see him, but he hadn't made eye contact with me yet —instead, he'd found something far sweeter to feast upon.

Cathy!

2

DOMINOS

*T*he New Dead licked its lips, sending a blackened tongue to peel off flakes of ash and rotting skin in a single pass. Like a lone wolf spotting its prey, it had zeroed in on my daughter.

Evil loves innocence—it's the caviar of the supernatural world.

The possessed was on top of its partner, but I had to move fast, all it took was close proximity or touch for the New Dead to keep moving. Old Dead had it easier, they could do all manner of unspeakable horrors without the need to touch you —New Dead were still just learning the ropes.

Mike had pinned me down again like we'd been instructed, but now I found myself working the technique with new determination. My daughter didn't know it, but she was in the crosshairs of New Dead, and the one protection she had was lying like an old jock strap on that bench—I had no time to waste.

"That's it," Mike said, guiding my arms a little. "You're getting it, now you shift your hips like—"

I threw my hips and pulled Mike's arms, using the new-found momentum from the weight-increasing spell to slam him against the mat.

"Nice work!" my partner grunted out after his diaphragm worked his lungs over like a cheap squeeze ball.

I found the New Dead a few grapplers over, the noxious damned riding a heavyset older gentleman. The old guy flipped his partner and flashed a snake-like black tongue at me.

I tried to get up, but Mike had me upended again.

I don't have time for this, I've got to get that necklace back on Cathy—now!

"You okay?" Mike asked, wiping beads of sweat from his face.

'Why, no, Mike, I'm not okay. There's a terrifying Hellspawn trying to ride my daughter like a plow horse, so would you mind if I got up to go protect her from the forces of darkness?' is what I wanted to say, but just like the stage magician's secrecy, Magick was best left unspoken. So instead I settled for a less flattering yet all together highly effective response.

"No... I'm not feeling so good," I said, putting a hand on my gut. "Where's the restroom?"

Bathroom troubles—the most powerful escape technique.

Mike quickly pulled himself off me.

"It's over in the corner," he said, pointing to a narrow door hanging open a crack. "I'd put on some sandals before you go in there, though."

My bare feet agreed, but I wasn't going to the restroom. I had to get the necklace back on Cathy, then deal with the New Dead.

Yo ho, yo ho, it's a Magick life for me.

I released the mass-increasing Magick, not interested in carrying any extra weight with me while I scanned the studio for the New Dead.

11

He must have gone to ground and slipped beneath the skin. He'd surface again, but first I needed to get Cathy safe.

The necklace glittered from atop the bench just beyond the mats. Its bright silver shone in the industrial fluorescents that hung high above our heads. Cathy's necklace was a custom design. I knew an old Magician out west in Nevada who excelled at those sorts of designs, and who had been more than happy to fabricate it for me. The hard work was in the enchanting.

The necklace had started as a bracelet, sized for my baby's wrist, but as she got older it got a lot harder to keep it on her. Porter and I tried longer chains and better clasps, but nothing worked for long—*you* try keeping jewelry on a toddler—go ahead, I'll wait.

I tried to slip past a couple of middle-aged women working their way through the escape when I caught the stench of New Dead. It was a vile, rotting aroma that made the Law family compost pile downright heavenly in comparison.

An arm shot out from that twisting mass of femininity and reached for my leg. I pulled my foot out of the way, but not without losing my balance on the sweat-soaked mat and crashing headlong into another set of students.

"Okay. We stop for a new technique, yes," our instructor said, his bellowing voice momentarily overtaking that dense accent.

Like a fountain bubbling apologies, I untangled myself from the crash pad of students I'd just landed on and got to my feet— along with the rest of the class. Salvation in the form of Cathy's necklace disappeared behind the sweat-covered masses.

"Okay, so now we are gonna to cover a new escape. I show you. First, I need a person."

Please don't be Cathy.

My daughter launched herself to the front of the class, jockeying her tiny frame in front of the instructor.

And so much for that...

The young Brazilian grabbed my daughter's wrists. "Okay, so now we pretend they grab your wrists—like this."

All eyes were on the instructor—all eyes except one set. Blackened sockets sunk deep in the face of a middle-aged woman twisted around to face me. She smiled, showing me the withering remains of her rotted teeth—the New Dead were not without dramatics.

Bingo.

I pushed my way through the mass of students, but the spirit was faster. It shifted bodies like falling dominos, each one touching the next, and sending the monster surging toward my daughter.

"Yes, now how you would escape? Don't answer, Cathy," the instructor said, turning to face the sweat-laced students.

The New Dead was gaining, manipulating skin-to-skin contact and working its way through the crowd at a blistering pace. It would reach Cathy in seconds if I didn't stop it.

I slipped off the white belt holding the folds of my gi together and twisted it into a loop. I was out of options for exorcisms—I didn't carry a full kit around with me, even though Porter thought I should.

Magicians do not wear fanny packs.

Still, there had to be something—something salty that wasn't rolling out of my pores. A shiny green can of energy drink beckoned to me like a siren's call from just off the mats. I scooped it up and poured a little on my loaner gi belt.

It's not salt from the dead sea, but I'm sure there's enough heart-stopping sodium in here to do the job.

The New Dead shed its latest ride and washed over a gangly teenager only a few feet from Cathy. The kid's newly burned and blackened hand reached for Cathy—his fingers mere inches from my beautiful daughter's wrist.

"Coercere," I whispered to the twisted loop of energy-drink-soaked white belt, sending a bit of the Magick swirling around in my chest into the soaked fabric, then hooked the wide loop around his blackened hand.

Ride em, cowboy!

3

OCCUPADO

The Magick wasn't perfect, but you did what you could with what you had available—in this case that meant restraint.

"Dad!" my easily embarrassed daughter cried as I dragged the white belt loop down the young boy's arm. To her—and everyone else in the room—I was just a strange old duck, but to the New Dead I was an infuriating mallard.

There's a difference!

The New Dead's ghostly hand was now cinched in a loop of Magickal white belt—and it hated every second of it. The monster tore at the fabric and reached for Cathy, those blackened digits straining against the belt, but coming up short.

"Sorry, honey. Just need to hit the restroom," I said, doing my best to keep the New Dead from making contact with my daughter or the young Brazilian instructor.

The instructor nodded, pointing to the same narrow doorway my partner had indicated earlier.

"Thanks, sorry."

The New Dead flailed wildly, and like an angry pit-viper it lashed out at both of them. Not wanting to draw any more attention to myself, I did my best to keep the twisted loop tight, but casual. This proved to be a tall order with an overly aggressive Hellspawn doing its damnedest to joy ride your daughter.

"Okay. So I show you the escape, yes," the instructor said, with a hint of frustration in his voice. I'd love to have watched, but I had an escape artist of my own to deal with.

Keeping my arms low and as nonchalant as possible I dragged the cursing spirit to the bathroom door.

Locked?!

"There's somebody in here," said a voice behind the paper-thin wood.

"Do you think you could—"

The New Dead switched tactics and didn't give me time to finish my sentence. The Magick I'd laid on the belt gave the spirit mass—enough to catch it with a loaner gi belt—but that also meant it had enough mass to take me down.

Somewhere physics was grinning at my self-inflicted predicament.

Black and twisted fingers wrapped my neck, and I fell backward against the hard concrete—we were well off the mats, but thankfully obscured by a long counter. I was already in enough trouble with Cathy, and having her dad grapple with some invisible monster was not going to improve my polling numbers.

The ghost squeezed, cutting off the air to my lungs and reminding me just how bad an idea it had been to give him solid form, but if I dropped the Magick now I'd have to fight off a possession at close range, and I was just too damn tired to even consider that.

I grabbed the spirit's wrists and tried to pry its hands from my neck. They might as well have been steel rebar for all the give I could muster. The monster squeezed harder, and the edges of my vision darkened. Sulfur mixed with the rotting stench of New Dead filled what little air passed through my nose. Was this how it was going to end? Florida man, found dead on the sweat-stained floor of a shopping mall dojo, looking to all the world like yet another victim of heart disease.

The instructor's booming voice broke through my pity parade. "Don't forget now you have two escapes. I wanna to see both ah them."

The escape!

I shifted my hips and changed hand positions, hoping to God I wasn't missing anything, then threw my weight into it. The effect was immediate. The New Dead flipped, and I landed solidly on top of it.

So, Brazilian Jiu-Jitsu works on corporeal spirts of the damned—who knew?

Flush.

The New Dead's fingers clawed at my face, but I pushed them aside. The door to the bathroom opened and a rail-skinny old geezer stepped out.

"Might want to wait a minute or two," he said, running a hand over his bald head and thankfully ignoring the fact that I was on the ground looking for all the world like I was practicing mount escapes on myself.

"Ah, okay…" I said, swatting away the New Dead's arm and reaching for the discarded white belt.

"Yeah." He opened and closed the door a few times, sending a potpourri of concerning odors washing over us. "I lit a match…"

"Thanks," I said, getting a hand on the belt, but not before the New Dead's rotten teeth bit down on my wrist; that wasn't part of the escape—I might have to bring it up later, 'cause it was highly effective.

"Damn it!" I shouted, practically leaping off the beast and opening up a lasso of Magickal gi belt.

The old guy shrugged and fanned the door a few more times.

"I know. Sorry, man," he said, leaving us with only the scent of his passing.

The New Dead changed tactics—seeing a ride so close must have been too compelling. It ignored me and scrambled after the old man.

"Oh no you don't." I tossed the large loop of belt around the creature's neck and yanked it back like a yoked horse.

The New Dead's fingers scraped at the edge of the old man's gi pants, but came up short.

I dragged it toward the bathroom, twisting the belt like a bag tie and squeezing the monster's neck. The dead don't breathe, but the idea that having your neck squeezed is a bad thing doesn't go away the instant you die—you have to be Old Dead to not fall for that trick.

Shrieks, screams, and then a litany of curses flowed out from the New Dead's peeling lips. I just had to get it to the bathroom —I had an idea, but it was more than a little dicey.

Beggars can't be choosers.

"Dad?"

Cathy!

I looked up from the New Dead to find my daughter leaning over the counter and staring down at her father. A dad presently in the midst of pulling an invisible Hellspawn into the half-open bathroom door, looking for all the world like he'd gone bat-shit crazy.

"You okay, Dad?"

You bet, I do this all the time.

4

AW HELL

*T*he New Dead clawed for my daughter, its charred fingers swinging wildly. I pulled the ends of the belt out to either side pretending to stretch but actually cinching down on the monster's neck.

"Sorry, honey," I said, pulling the ends taut. "My back's tight. I think I might have pulled something."

"Really? Does that mean you won't come back again?" A frown crept up around the edges of Cathy's lips.

The New Dead snarled and clawed at the belt loop, dragging me across the polished concrete.

"No!" I shouted, pulling the rotting spirit back harder. "No, I can come again. Sure. Just need to loosen up better before I get here."

Cathy smiled and her eyes lit up; even covered with sweat and other people's funk my daughter was beautiful—how on earth does one say no to that?

"Thanks, Dad!"

Cathy's heart-shaped face disappeared behind the counter, and the New Dead turned its attention back to me.

"Time to go," I said, yanking the beast back into the broom-closet-sized bathroom with me.

"You say something, Dad?" Cathy's voice asked from somewhere on the other side of the counter.

"Nope."

I hooked the door with my foot and closed us in—one sweaty middle-aged Magician and a scrappy, and hellish New Dead.

Definitely need to loosen up more next time—provided there is a next time.

Mercifully the owner had installed a motion-sensor light because I didn't have a spare hand to locate the switch. The phone-booth-sized bathroom had a narrow pedestal sink, a toilet that had been around the block the hard way, and an impossibly tight set of utility shelves holding all manner of supplies.

"Clauditis," I shouted, using my head to whack the door—when both your hands are full of belt you use whatever is available.

Click.

Magick flowed over me like a cresting wave and locked the door. We were in this together now—two things enter, one thing leaves.

Welcome to Thunderdome, New Dead.

I found the utility-sized box of matches the old man had mentioned on the shelf.

That'll do. I hope.

I slammed the monster's face against the sink and smiled at the wet, cracking sound of contact—the dead are much easier to handle in corporeal form.

I switched hands with the belt and reached for the matches. If I could get enough sulfur, there was a chance I could punch this bastard's ticket and send him home—straight back to Hell.

The trick would be not joining him, or bringing back any souvenirs.

No sooner had I got a hand on the box than the New Dead latched its fingers on my neck. It was the spirit's turn to yank me against the wall, and not to be outdone; my own head provided an equally nice thump as it made contact with the drywall. "Aargh!"

The inner tray of the match box shot out into the air, knocking into the wall and sending a confetti spray of precious sticks into the air.

Plink. Plink. Plink.

Wet matches weren't going to do me a damn bit of good, and now the toilet bowl held at least half of those drowned soldiers.

The New Dead tossed me to the floor. I tucked my head to my chest to avoid a second brain-jarring impact. The New Dead turned its attention to the tangled belt wrapped around its neck, clawing at the enchanted fabric.

"Oh, hell no."

I yanked down on the belt edge and dragged the foul-smelling spirit on top of me for the second time tonight.

Knock. Knock.

"Dad? You okay in there?" Cathy's sweet voice asked through the door.

I kicked my legs around the New Dead's neck and grunted in pain as its claws tore at my sides.

"Uh. Yeah... just give me... a... second."

The New Dead screeched and bit down on my thigh, only scant inches from my man parts.

"Son of a bitch!" I shouted, swinging a fist and making contact with the creature's torched face.

"You sure?"

"Uh-huh."

Just fighting off a New Dead spirit, honey. In a second or two I'm going to open a portal to Hell and toss it in—can I get you anything?

"Okay, but if you need something we've got a doctor here. She said it's okay, that sometimes guys your age—"

"I'm fine, Cathy!" I shouted, kicking off the New Dead and scrambling backward.

"Okay..." said a clearly concerned teenage voice on the other side of the door.

Nice work, Gene. This was supposed to be a daddy-daughter bonding session.

The New Dead clawed at the belt loop, its scorched fingers tearing on the once-white fabric.

I didn't waste any time. I scooped up as many matches as I could locate on the floor. Once I had a fist's worth, I turned to face the beast.

"It's time to go back in—you look a tad under-cooked," I said, grabbing the box sleeve and striking the bundle against it.

Nothing.

"Come on!"

I struck the bundle again.

Still nothing.

The New Dead tore at the belt loop, widening it until the last bits of Magick fell away.

"Dad, I know you said you were okay, but I'm starting to get worried. Doctor Judy is here—"

"Hello, Mr. Law."

"She says if you need her to come in she will..."

"I'll be right out, Cathy!"

The New Dead smiled, its withered lips cracking. It was non-corporeal again, and that meant Cathy was fair game. It had only to pass through the door and it would take my daughter, one leg of the three-legged stool that made life worth living, away from me.

"Portae Inferni!" I shouted, ripping the matches across the box sleeve with all my might and sending my Magick into those wooden sticks.

Whoosh!

The fistful of fire roared to life and filled the tiny bathroom with the acrid scent of sulfur.

Time to get you back in the oven, you undercooked ash clown.

The New Dead scrambled for the door, clawing at the painted wood. I traced a sigil in the air with my bundle of brimstone, and in an instant my window to the inferno was open.

The swirling ring of fire between us was a portal to a nightmarish Hellscape—it was 'the bad place,' after all—lakes of roaring fire, boiling pools of magma, and souls by the thousands writhing in agony. Screams of pain and terror washed over me and the hot wind singed my eyelids. This was the hard way to take out your dead, and more than a little reckless, but at this moment it was that or risk Cathy—easy decision.

Across the bathroom, the New Dead scrambled for the door, but it couldn't fight the pull of the gate.

There's no place like home.

A rocketing roll of toilet paper shot past my head and into the great sucking void, soon to be followed by half the contents of the utility shelf. A plunger, paper towels, and a jug of hand soap toppled in from behind me and burst into flames in the fires of Hell.

My window to Dante's summer home was wide open and with each new item dragged in it burped up hot blasts of fiery embers. At least, I thought they were embers until the first one landed on my cheek and bit down.

Hell Fleas!

Hell was the epitome of all things evil and malevolent, the antithesis of life and love—of course it had fleas.

The spirit clawed at the sink, its blackened fingers sliding over the smooth porcelain, but the yawning mouth of Hell only drew it closer. I took my eyes off the Hellgate to swat at the swarm of infernal insects staking out their claims to my skin. The New Dead was already halfway through the portal, its charred fingers clinging to the edges, and its limbs stretched taut.

What remained of the spirit wailed as flakes of its undead flesh burned away.

"I'll be back—"

I kept swatting at Hell Fleas while holding up the still smoldering bundle of spent matches.

"Come on, that's the best you have? 'I'll be back' is so overused."

"Dad?" Cathy said, her voice faint through the bathroom door.

"I'll be back, for her!"

"Like Hell you will!"

I rammed my fist into the toilet water, matches and all. The portal collapsed, taking with it the New Dead and leaving a faint hint of brimstone, a few falling embers, and a cyclone-wrecked bathroom as the only evidence of its passing.

"I'll be right out, Cathy," I said, pulling the spent matches out of the toilet and tossing them in the trash, then admiring the many dollars of damage I'd just done.

"Just give me a second to clean up."

5

MOVING DAY

I ran a towel over my face and put the key in the ignition. The old Mazda hatchback's engine roared to life and belched out a blast of lukewarm AC that hit me square between the eyes.

Good old Dad Wagon.

"I said I was sorry, kiddo."

Cathy wasn't having anything to do with my apologies. The post-bathroom event had been far too traumatizing for my teenager to fathom. At present she was doing her best to remind me just how much she resembled her mother—sitting in the passenger seat and staring out the window with arms and legs crossed.

I dropped the shifter into reverse and backed out of the parking space, wondering who would cool off first—the car or my teenager.

At least she's got the necklace back on—small victories.

It'd been a heck of a time working up an explanation for the minor cyclone that had destroyed their bathroom. In the end it had taken a promise from me to never come back to allow

Cathy to return—that and a considerable advance on the next few months of lessons.

I wasn't sure I'd get off as cheap with my daughter.

The tiny twister uncrossed her arms and played with the sleeves of her bright red rash guard.

That's a start, but I'm holding out for eye contact.

The Mazda hadn't gotten around to blowing cold air yet, but at least it was working. We rolled slowly through the parking lot, giving me an opportunity to put a few things together. While it was true that Florida had a New Dead problem, they didn't tend to travel far, and they certainly didn't typically show up with that much power. This wasn't a random possession. For starters, they don't just appear out of thin air, they tend to congregate—like pack hunters and labor unions—the good ones organize and work together. Tonight's lone wolf was an abnormality, but not unheard of. The real question was, where had it come from?

I reached the edge of the parking lot and rolled to a stop. A couple of oversized gentlemen were wrangling an ornate couch out of the back of a truck and across the parking lot. I waved them past and waited for the AC to start blowing something that resembled cool air.

There's the Veteran's Cemetery on Kennedy...

While space-time laws didn't really apply to the recently departed, I was reasonably sure they wouldn't travel that many miles.

What about that new mega church?

I shook my head and chucked. The mega church had a latte machine, an ATM, and Jesus Pale Ale on draft—nothing that even remotely resembled a cemetery.

The monster couch crawled past, and I made sure to perform the sacred manly-man head-nod back to the movers. I'd started to roll forward, when a second piece of furniture snaked its way past us and forced me to hit the brakes.

It was a brand-new, shiny, state-of-the-art aluminum casket.

It took my New-Dead-rattled brain a few seconds to register it, and by then I'd missed the obligatory return nod for this new set of movers. I followed the casket as it made its way into what appeared to be the newest addition to the home-town renovation scene, the Brighton 8 Movie Theatre.

Never one to miss an auspicious opportunity, the Dad Wagon choose that moment to start blowing icy-cold air.

"I need you to stay in the car," I said, pulling the Mazda into one of the open spaces.

"Why? Wait, what happened to your arm?" Cathy said, pointing at the tiny burn marks left by the Hell Fleas.

"It's nothing, just a chemical burn," I lied, rubbing a hand over the reddened skin. I'd been bitten by Hell Fleas before, but these must have been an industrial-strength variety—they still hurt.

I'll feel better after a shower.

I rubbed my back against the seat, scratching an itch that had been driving me nuts ever since we'd gotten in the car.

Must have bit my back too—damn it.

Cathy leaned forward and unzipped the gym bag at her feet. She pulled out her phone and aimed it at my arm.

Click!

"What are you doing?" I said, keeping one eye on my daughter and the other on the blinding late-day sun.

"Taking a picture of it," my daughter said, like she was sizing me up for some science project. "Maybe there's something on it on the internet. I bet if you put the right stuff on those they'll go away faster. You know, Tristan got burned the other day and I found just the right thing to help him heal up faster—trust me, Dad."

Tristan?

I could almost hear my wife's sigh.

Boyfriend of the month, Gene. You've gotta pay attention to these things.

I leaned over her screen. "Find anything?"

'Cause craft beer comes to mind...

"It takes a second, but a new phone would really—"

"Nice try," I said, pressing my back against the seat—whatever was itching me was doing a remarkable job of finding that unreachable spot in the middle of my shoulder blades.

"Could be all sorts of things—have you been to a military base?"

"Nope," I said, dropping the visor down to shade my eyes, then giving my back another vigorous rub.

"Well they look like Tristan's burns, but his came from sparklers."

"Huh? It's November, what's he doing with sparklers?"

"He said he was just fooling around with them."

This kid doesn't sound too bright. Mental note—talk to Mom about Tristan.

"You like this guy?"

I don't really want to know the answer; I would just prefer you to stop staring at the Hell Flea bites.

My daughter squirmed in her seat, uncrossing her arms, then crossing them again. "Kinda."

Oh boy.

"What's he do again?"

"Dad, he's in high school—he doesn't do anything... yet. He said he might have a part-time job soon though..."

"So you're dating someone on the unemployment line?"

That coaxed a smile out of Cathy.

"He's got good grades and is super smart—like you, Dad."

Smart move, kiddo. Pulling from your mom's playbook. Buttering up the old man any chance you get makes it easier to slide things past him in the future.

"Oh yeah? What makes him like me? Is he devilishly handsome with a taste for khakis?"

"Dad!"

"What?"

Cathy fixed her ponytail, and as she did, it was hard not to think of a young Porter. Cathy had a lot of her mom in her. She was a spirit of justice with a passion for life, but heaven help you if you made her angry.

Look out, Tristan.

Cathy's phone chirped and drew her attention, giving me a chance to put the Mazda in park and give my back one last vigorous rub against the seat. Just when I thought it wouldn't stop, whatever was itching me disappeared.

"I'll be right back," I said, leaving the engine and AC running while I paid a visit to the partially remodeled Brighton 8.

My daughter didn't respond; my spirit of justice was too busy updating the internet on her father's latest antics.

6

THE SILVER SCREAM

*T*he movers had a second casket at the door by the time I arrived.

"I got you." I grabbed the entrance door and held it wide so they could maneuver the space-age steel coffin past the ticket counter and into a cramped concession area.

After a perfunctory grunt of thanks, the movers set the coffin down and headed back to the truck. I slipped in behind them to get a look at the latest addition to the neighborhood.

The Brighton 8 was a never-ceasing remodel job that my boss had stayed away from for years. Each new owner seemed to go broke trying to get the theatre back up off the ground. Even I had to admit, bringing in a few coffins was an odd way to start. Years ago, the theatre had been a stalwart fixture in the community, but neglect, streaming services, and good old-fashioned mismanagement had brought it to the brink countless times since.

It was clear the new owners were trying their best to get the projectors rolling—they'd replaced the worn out floor inside the lobby with a deep-red, smooth-cut carpet, that while my firm would have counseled them to stay away from long term, it sure looked good right now. I also counted more than a couple new pieces of furniture still wrapped in the original plastic. It wasn't hard to imagine how they wanted the pre-movie waiting area to look, but it still had a long way to go. The walls were recently painted, a nice muted gray with a few different gold-leaf framed paintings leaning against them waiting to be hung up. The Brighton 8 had gotten a decent upgrade, at least on the front side of the house. My question was whether that upgrade included an unhealthy dose of New Dead.

The lobby opened up on to a wide concession counter, also in a half-assembled state. Tall popcorn machines sat empty, still positioned on pallets and butting up against coolers, which were dark and suspiciously bereft of sugary soda. I took a deep breath—no New Dead, only the smell of fresh carpet, shipping supplies, and an undercurrent of popcorn oil.

"Pardon me," an elderly woman's voice said. "We aren't open yet, but we plan to run a special for all the neighbors here in the mall. I'm going to bring tickets down myself next week. Are you from the karate school?"

I turned around to find a small, elderly woman, not much larger than Cathy. She wore her hair short, a boyish cut that lay tight against an aging head. Glasses dangled from a thin chain around her neck.

"I'm sorry, I guess I got ahead of myself. I saw those coffins and I just sort of followed them in," I said, extending a hand. "I'm Eugene Law—with Kinder Construction. I'm a sucker for a good remodel. I held the door for the movers and couldn't help but get a look at the interior. I'm sorry, I didn't mean to come in before you were open."

It's easier to attract flies with honey than it is with vinegar— slather it on.

"Oh, sweetheart, that is so nice of you to say. I couldn't be happier with how it's come out so far. The coffins are some props one of the kids I hired thought would help sell people on the new 'Demon High' remake."

"Props..." I said, running a hand over the brushed-steel caskets and not picking up a single hint of Magick. "They look pretty real to me."

"Well they are, but they're just on loan. I've poured enough money into getting the theater open, I hope I don't need one of these myself when it's all done."

"Well you should be proud," I said, stalling for time. If there had been some Magicking in here, it wasn't in the lobby, or the concession stand. I needed to go deeper. "How about the individual theaters? I remember coming here before our daughter was born and being very afraid of the pooling mass of soda runoff down near the screen—in hindsight it made the movie that much more frightening, as you were afraid to put your feet down."

The old woman smiled, showing off a tiny array of near-perfect teeth. "All part of the process—like I said, I'm committed to a better moviegoing experience," she said, taking my hand and shaking it. Her fingers were soft and well-moisturized, and there wasn't a hint of Magick on them.

"It's great to meet you, Mrs..."

"Sorry, it's Ms. Wilson. Mr. Wilson has moved on."

"I'm sorry to hear that."

"That's sweet of you to say, but he's been gone a very long time. Please, call me Claudia."

"Well, I'm sure he'd be impressed with what you've done here, Claudia. The theater is really coming together."

The petite Ms. Wilson nodded, directing me back toward the entrance. "It will be once I'm done fixing it up."

"Still, you've done great work so far," I said, stalling for an opportunity to get to the back side of the house.

"Yes," my gracious yet rather direct host agreed, herding me like a lost sheep toward the exit.

"Is there any chance you could get me the remodeler's phone number? Or email, perhaps? We sometimes have to sub work out and it would be good to know who you used."

Claudia paused, and while I was sure she wanted me out of her theater, I could also tell those latent southern hospitalities were tugging at her just the same.

"Hm, I believe it is on my desk," the elderly proprietress said, again waffling between leaving me on my own in the lobby, or bringing me with her to the office.

"I can stay here if you would—"

"No, come with me. They did a very nice job on my office as well."

Damn.

Claudia's busy feet shuffled along the carpet and led me to a sliding pocket door off the main entrance I hadn't noticed before. She slid the door open to reveal a very impressive and ornate oak desk with painstakingly organized papers and a small lamp. Two well-cushioned leather chairs sat opposite the desk, still partially wrapped in plastic.

"Give me just a minute," my host said, sorting through the papers on her desk.

"Certainly. I appreciate you doing this," I said, extending my Magickal senses and taking in the room. Unlike the foyer, Claudia's office had its pictures hung, two beautiful watercolor paintings of the Gulf with sandpipers racing away from the foamy surf, and a multi-colored starfish with long arms radiating out from the center.

Nothing...

Neither the pictures, the chairs, nor even the desk itself held anything even remotely Magickal.

"Here it is," she said, pulling a business card out from her stack of papers. "I knew I'd find it—Gulf Remodeling and Restoration."

She paused, then tore the top sheet off a pad on her desk and put it under the stack of papers. "I might need to call them, but I'll copy the number down for you," Claudia said, writing the phone number down, then tearing that top sheet off and handing it to me.

"Thank you," I said, accepting the paper and finally letting Ms. Wilson guide me to the front door.

"Oh, my pleasure, sweetheart." The genteel woman ushered me out into the parking lot. "It was very nice to meet you Mr. Law; if you come back again before we're open I'm going to call the police."

"I—"

Claudia Wilson smiled again, those perfect teeth flashing in the setting sun, then slammed the door shut.

I could have sworn the blast of air that followed held a hint of New Dead, but if so, I'd lost it in the smell of plastic and fresh carpet. I gently folded up the paper she'd given me and placed it in my pocket. Something told me I hadn't seen the last of Claudia Wilson.

* * *

I PUSHED DOWN on the accelerator and the Dad Wagon's engine grumbled along the thin ribbon of asphalt toward home.

I didn't yet know what to make of the newly remodeled Brighton 8, but I did know one thing, I'd been lucky—very lucky—in that martial arts class.

Cathy wasn't getting any younger. She was sixteen now and while we had driving lessons, a boyfriend-of-the-month with questionable firework hobbies, and all the other things that came with being a high-schooler to worry about, it was the thought of her potentially becoming a Magician that kept me up at night.

Porter didn't have a lick of it in her blood. God bless my wife and her unwavering normalcy, but Cathy and Kris were a crap-shoot.

At five years old, Kris was still far too little. He still had a decade of blissful ignorance ahead of him, and even after that he might not develop a lick of Magickal talent—he did have his mother's eyes and all.

Cathy, on the other hand, was too much like me. She had my stupid blue eyes and angled jaw—both looked far better on her —and along with them she'd gotten a solid case of the 'cares too much.' If that girl had Magick in her she'd become a magnet for every unspeakable terror in the known and unknown world. The things that dwell in the dark just love succulent, juicy, and caring souls.

I pulled off the main road and noticed the check-engine light had popped on.

And now I have a new task for tomorrow…

At least Cathy hadn't developed any Magickal senses yet—those came first, and shortly thereafter came the spontaneous bursts of Wild Magick. She could think what she wanted about her old man, but I was happy knowing I didn't have to explain the horrifying things that prowled the shadows to my baby girl just yet.

"Dad?"

"Yeah?"

"Did you smell something really strange at class tonight?"

Crap.

7

MARITAL ARTS

I pressed my forehead against the shower wall and let the hot water beat down on my back. Each droplet that rolled over the Hell Flea bites was a sobering reminder of just how painful those little buggers could be.

Steam filled the bathroom, covering the glass shower doors and giving me an excellent finger board for writing down my thoughts for tomorrow.

1. Investigate Claudia Wilson.

2. Keep an eye on the daughter.

3...

The bathroom door swung open and slammed shut again before I could mark down 'take the car in for service.' After eighteen years of marriage it didn't take me long to figure out when Porter was angry.

"Magick at karate class, Gene! Really?!"

Yep, angry. I am a master at detecting subtle human emotions.

I slid the shower door open enough to flip the vent on. A loud fan hummed above our heads, taking away some of the precious steam I'd built up, but also assuring us of a little privacy.

"It's jiu-jitsu, and I didn't have a choice," I said, working up a lather with the soap.

Porter slammed the toilet lid down and took a seat. She had her rail-straight brown hair pulled back in a loose ponytail, which was good, cause with the steam I'd built up in here she'd go full frizz in seconds and be even more angry.

Some guys like to say their wives look cute when they're mad—I was *not* one of those guys. Don't get me wrong, Porter was the love of my life, but when she's had her mad on, it was safer to have the solid glass shower door between us.

I closed my eyes and rubbed the soap over my face to avoid my wife's death-stare.

"Didn't have a choice? What the heck happened to 'I've made them special jewelry, it'll hide them from the bad things, honey.'" Porter held up her engagement ring; it was the first Logic Loop I'd ever made. Only two stones remained from that three-stone setting. They weren't real diamonds—I was a Magician, not a lawyer—and the gold was plated on, but the real power wasn't in how it looked, it was in the Magick I'd packed inside.

Porter's ring and all the Logic Loops held a tiny piece of me locked inside them, and as Magick went it was pretty damn potent.

"She took it off," I said, turning my face into the cascade of water.

"Damn it."

I let the water soak my hair. "Yeah, she left it on the bench. For twenty minutes or so, that was the safest piece of group seating in the supernatural world."

Porter stood up and prowled the tiny bathroom like a jungle cat.

"Gene, we've gotta come up with something better. The kids aren't going to keep jewelry on indefinitely—they're kids. They'll take them off."

"I can't enchant her phone, honey."

That wasn't technically true, but I wasn't great at mixing Magick with high-tech gizmos.

Calling them gizmos is probably why...

"I wasn't asking you to enchant her phone—but that would be helpful—that girl's phone is just an extension of her arm."

"I won't argue that point."

Porter rolled her eyes. "Or you could just enchant Tristan. She spends *far* too much time with him as it is."

"Who? Oh right, our daughter's super-genius boyfriend who burned himself with sparklers."

Porter shook her head. "The girl can pick 'em. Still, he's better than the last guy, who I swear only showered once a month."

"How did I forget that one?" I said, reaching for the shampoo. Porter waved me off what was sure to be a rabbit-hole conversation. "Still, Kris keeps his charm on, right?"

"He's five—do you know what I have to do to keep it on him?"

No, but I know better than to ask.

"That's why you are such an amazing wife and mother."

Nice one, Gene.

"Stow it, naked man. That's not going to work on me tonight. Tell me what happened."

I worked the shampoo in my hair into a glorious soap-mohawk and checked my reflection in the shower glass; instead of my goofy head all I got was Porter's laser-eyes.

"Right, so... there was New Dead."

My wife's face darkened. She may not know everything about Magick, or the rest of the world I inhabit, but she knew about the dead, New, Old, or otherwise, and that they were a serious problem.

"How bad?"

"Bad."

"Did it go after you?"

"No…" I said, letting the word hang in the air, knowing what she would say next and hating it just the same.

"Why would it go after Cathy? Did it know you two were related?"

"I don't think so."

That was technically a lie, but if Cathy had smelled the New Dead then she just might have Magick in her blood and it was starting to show up.

One problem at a time, Gene.

My wife had enough to deal with right now with Kris in kindergarten and Cathy's boyfriend of the month—I didn't want to add Magick to the ever-growing list of worries.

"Damn it, Gene. What did you do?"

I rinsed the shampoo from my hands and avoided Porter's eyes. "Opened a portal to Hell."

"You what?!"

"It was a small one," I said, holding my hands roughly a basketball's width apart. "Tiny, barely there, *minuscule* by Hell-hole standards—"

"Of all the reckless, stupid things you could try. There was no salt? Didn't I tell you to bring some anti-possession supplies? Is it really so hard to wear that fanny-pack I bought you?"

Magicians do not wear fanny packs.

"You work with what you have available. The New Dead is back where it belongs, and nothing came through."

Porter pointed at the small burn marks on my chest and arms. "Nothing, eh?"

Damn woman is like Arthur Conan Doyle's great-great-grand-daughter.

"Just Hell Fleas. Don't worry, I got 'em all. Besides, they can't survive long in the real world."

"Why do they come after you?"

"The Fleas? They are just looking for tasty flesh to dig into—"

Porter rolled her eyes. "No, you ninny, the dead. Why do they hate you so much?"

I let the shower water roll down my back.

"I don't know, but it's not just me; there are a lot of Magicians the dead hate—"

"Name one," Porter said, crossing her arms.

"Ah. There's—" I shoved my head under the water, washing away the glorious soap-hawk and making it impossible for Porter to understand my nonsensical response.

"Nice try, but there aren't any that you know of because there aren't any other Magicians in this part of the Sunshine State."

She was right again. There'd been a real drop-off in practitioners of the Magickal Arts as of the last decade or so, and Florida was no exception. Most of the great Magicians that had lived in the area were either dead themselves, or getting up there in years and had moved out to Key West where the shuffleboard and Piña Coladas flowed like milk and honey.

"Yeah, well there are a few—just can't put my finger on their names."

I turned off the water and wiped the steam off the shower door.

"Whoa, honey, turn around," Porter said, her face suddenly close to the glass.

"What?"

"Turn around—your back."

"What about it?"

"It's got all these little scratch marks on it," my wife said, now standing in the shower, scant inches from my shoulder blades.

"Oh, I'm sure it's just Hell Fleas—little bastards were everywhere."

"Are you sure, these look like tiny claw marks…"

I pulled the towel off the hanger and dried my hair. "It's nothing. Could have just been me rubbing my back against the seat."

"I guess. Still, someone should put something on all those little scrapes and burns—they could get infected."

I snapped the towel out and wrapped my wife's butt, pulling her against me. "You volunteering?"

"Another night, Magick man. I've got my trainer in the morning—but make sure you put something on those scratches before you go to bed. They look bad."

Porter kissed me on the lips, a staccato-style peck that shut the door on any extracurricular activities, and then shimmied out of my towel and the bathroom all together.

I stole one last look at her butt, then tried to angle my back to see what she was fretting about. The shower door reflection didn't offer much, and in the end I gave up and trudged off to bed—it'd been one hell of a night.

8

DEAD END DRIVING

J sat in the driveway and stared at the check engine light. The Dad Wagon rumbled beneath me, its engine sputtering ever so slightly.

Damn it. What now?

I'd just gotten it checked out by Rob and his crew at *The Qwik Fix* a few weeks ago. Even though the Mazda was getting up there in miles, Robbie rarely charged me for services. A few years back I'd taken care of a small problem he'd had with a Succubus, after which Rob and I had had a long conversation about the girls, or in his case, the sexy demons you can meet on those dating apps.

He'd taken my advice and uninstalled the app altogether. Last I'd heard he'd met a nice girl on the force—might need to see her about some tickets my wife had accumulated. Still, I was looking forward to hearing all about her when I brought the Dad Wagon in today.

She just better not be a Demon.

I honked the horn and my kindergartener piped up from the back seat. "Do it again, Dad!"

With five-year-olds it was always the little things—I honked again.

His cherubic giggle in the back seat put a short-lived smile on my face.

Come on, Cathy, we're going to be late.

I was on child delivery duty this morning, with Porter at the gym getting her flex on, and my teenager wasn't making that easy.

"Do it again!" Kris shouted, hammering his tiny fists against the car seat. A medical alert bracelet bounced up and down with each thrust and looped expertly around that chain was my rambunctious son's Logic Loop.

That's how you get him to wear it? I married a genius.

I had only just placed a hand on the horn when my white-hot ball of teenage angst stormed out the front door and slammed it behind her.

"Good morning, Cathy!" Kris screamed from the back seat as his sister yanked open the car door.

"Morning, midget," Cathy said, but her tone gave every indication there was nothing good about it.

My teenage daughter crammed an overstuffed backpack onto the floor and threw herself into the Dad Wagon's faded passenger seat. She leaned over to slam the door shut, and I noticed just how little she was wearing underneath that sweatshirt she'd wrapped her butt in.

"Cathy..."

"I know, 'Hooters called and they want their shorts back,'" she said, her tone so close to Porter's I had to do a double-take. "Mom said they were fine."

"Did she know you were going to wear them? Or was she thinking they were purely decorative?"

"Dad!"

I contemplated sending her back in to change, but I glanced

at the clock, then hit the garage door button—we were already late.

"Hold on, kiddos," I said, backing down the winding driveway then putting the Mazda into drive. Porter's sleek new Honda rolled around the corner and pulled up alongside the rattling Dad Wagon.

With a smooth hum her window rolled down, and she leaned out to wave at the kids. My wife is beautiful, but with a light sheen of sweat and her hair tucked back in one of those wide fabric bands she could stop traffic.

"Krissy, you gonna have a good day at school?"

"I wish you wouldn't call him that, his name is Kris."

"Yeah!"

Porter smiled, then took a sip of her post-workout coffee.

"You look great, Cathy."

Our daughter was already lost deep in the vapid black hole of social-media photo feeds, likes, and posts—too bad I didn't have a Magickal charm to protect her from that.

"The shorts are a little—"

"They're shorts, Gene. Get over it."

"But…"

Porter blew me a kiss. "You're gonna be late. Don't forget, it's Friday."

My wife let the word hang in the air, where it was kept aloft by my unbridled hopes and the subtle twinkling of her eyes.

Date night.

"Yes, ma'am," I said, giving her the perfunctory man-nod and rolling up the window. The glass only made it halfway before grinding to a halt and shuddering inside the door frame.

Porter didn't notice, she was already up the driveway and rolling into the garage.

"Bye!" Kris shouted.

I didn't have time to deal with a busted window—or a check engine light for that matter. It was after seven, and that meant the Mad Max road race to get your children to school was upon us.

* * *

WE'D MADE good time thus far; the Dad Wagon may not look like much, but looks could be deceiving. We'd already woven our way through a set of semis coming off the highway and deftly avoided two school-bus stops. We were cooking with gas, but so was the radiator.

I rolled to a stop at the light while the needle dipped into the red, not certain I could make it to school as well as *The Qwik Fix* without a minor miracle.

I turned off the AC and rolled down Cathy's window. The sudden change in environmental temperature was enough to bring my daughter out of her social-media zone-of-judgement to throw a little shade on her old man and his car.

"What are you doing?"

"The car's overheating. I can't run the AC while we're stopped."

"Ugh!"

We weren't far from Kris's kindergarten, and Cathy's high school was only a block from there, but if the Dad Wagon overheated, it would be a long walk.

Cathy clicked her phone off and shoved it in the folds of her butt-warming sweatshirt. "Are you really going to make me learn to drive in *this* car?"

I decided against taking the bait and instead followed the movement in the rear-view mirror that had caught my attention.

A middle-aged woman was working her way between the cars asking for change. Her hair was tangled and dirty, and her once-white shirt had long since yellowed with sweat. She circled a few coins in a tall plastic cup for the car behind us; I couldn't see her face yet, but the clunk of more coins being deposited was unmistakable.

Could use a little karma after yesterday's New Dead fiasco...

I reached into my center console to grab some of my toll money, but first I rolled back up Cathy's window—just to be safe.

The woman worked her way from car to car behind us, stopping at a white van to collect a donation, and as she did, I kept one eye on my dash and the fluttering temperature needle embedded in it.

Just hold up...

I couldn't roll my window down all the way—it was still stuck in that highly stylish yet wildly impractical half-down position—but I figured I could toss a few coins in.

The woman reached my window and placed a tanned and dingy hand on the glass. The smell hit me first. It wasn't the odor of the unwashed masses, or even the funk of yours truly after a few hours in the yard. It was the same unmistakable scent I'd practically marinated in last night.

New Dead! Twice in two days is a record, even for me.

"Got any spare—" she started to say, then stopped the instant we made eye contact.

"Magician..." she hissed as the skin around her eyes blackened like the edges of a scorched paper.

"Dad!" Cathy cried, covering her nose with one hand and pointing past me at the New Dead. "What the hell is that!"

The New Dead dropped the plastic cup and shot a hand in through the open window, grabbing hold of my neck.

"I'm going to crush your pencil-dick neck," she growled, her words deep and rumbly in my ear.

The light turned green, but the car in front of me hadn't moved yet. I laid on the horn, making Kris shout from the backseat.

"Do it again, Dad!"

My daughter froze, her mouth open and lost in an expression of complete terror—all of which was perfectly typical for a new Magician, or anyone coming face to face with the supernatural for the first time.

So, we now have two Magicians in the family. I wonder if there's a sympathy card for that...

I pried at the New Dead's wrist, but she held on tight, hard enough to make me wonder just how much force it would take for her to succeed in snapping my pencil-dick neck.

I really need to start working out with Porter.

I laid on the horn. The car in front of us shot off, but not before giving me a single finger salute from the rear-view mirror.

Right back at ya buddy.

I punched the accelerator down and the Dad Wagon roared in full-throated defiance, then stuttered to a halt.

The cars behind us started laying on their own horns and my ever-happy five-year-old shouted along with them.

"More, Dad. More!"

* * *

We'd overheated—it was the only logical explanation—but try telling that to the chorus of car horns and the Hellspawn trying to perform successful DIY surgery on my trachea.

"Cathy!" I shouted, pulling at the possessed's scorched digits. "Glove box!"

My daughter remained frozen, her doe-like eyes unable to pull away from the withering, burnt flesh of the New Dead.

"Cathy!"

The possessed slammed a rotting fist against the glass while the irregular symphony of car horns rattled my brain. My loving son, who thankfully couldn't see me or the enraged panhandler from his car seat, was in heaven.

"More!"

A couple of cars roared up onto the sidewalk and around us, their drivers following the same single finger gesture we'd seen earlier. I'd have loved to return the salute, but was far more concerned with keeping my head attached.

I reached for the glove box, but came up just short. Seeing me leaning for it jarred Cathy from her trance and she popped it open.

A burgeoning stack of papers along with various odds and ends tumbled onto my daughter's overstuffed backpack.

I really need to clean the car out from time to time.

I scanned the floor, looking for anything I could use to complete the Magick.

Crack!

The New Dead's fist slammed against the glass and created a crack in my window—a long and jagged split in the already dirty glass.

"What do I do?" my daughter shouted, digging through the pile of loose items at her feet.

There were a couple packages of wet napkins from Hooters —part of the pre-Porter era—as well as the normal glove box citizens: insurance cards and registration.

"Get the—"

Cathy picked up a tire pressure gauge—it wasn't Magickal, except in that no one else in my family had mastered the simple act of using it.

"—the scraper..."

She dropped the gauge and picked up an ice scraper, holding it up like some alien artifact.

"That's it!" I shouted.

Porter's old window scraper, an object of ridicule in the early years of our marriage, but now exactly what I needed with New Dead and an over-heated engine.

God bless my little Midwestern transplant!

I reached for the scraper, but the New Dead had a different plan. It forced a second hand through the open window and yanked my head back against the glass. I couldn't fight it off and get the Magick going at the same time.

"Press it—" I grunted fighting against the seared fingers. "—against the dash!"

Cathy stared at me dumbfounded. "Huh?"

"Just do it."

My daughter pressed the steely edge of the old scraper against the dashboard and that's when I felt it—Catherine Law had Magick in her blood, and it was right about to blow.

"Think of the winter in Wichita!"

"Dad!"

"Just do it, Cathy!" I shouted, losing my battle with the New Dead's burnt fingers.

"Okay..."

"Now tell it to get cold—in Spanish."

"Dad, I don't—"

"Español, Catalina. Ahora!"

"Hace Frio!" my daughter shouted, squeezing her eyes shut and pushing the scraper hard enough into the dash to leave a mark.

A Midwest winter roared into the engine compartment and all the way to the radiator. Ice crystals raced across the dash and up the window edge. The full tilt red line on our temperature gauge dropped halfway—good enough for me.

Shatter!

The driver-side window exploded under the strain as New Dead's hands clawed at my face. The overwhelming stench of death and decay filled the car.

Cathy screamed again, and Kris—no doubt pushed over the top by the breaking window—chose that moment to burst into tears.

I turned the key and the Dad Wagon roared back to life. The

light had turned yellow, but I didn't care. We shot through it like a jackrabbit: me, my screaming kids, and the frost-covered Mazda.

I stole a glance at the rear-view mirror and found the New Dead staring at me, unwavering, its tar-black eyes and charred flesh full of pure, unadulterated hatred.

Maybe Porter's right—maybe the dead really do hate me.

9

STAY FROSTY

*W*e hadn't gone two blocks before Cathy started dry heaving in the front seat—thankfully my daughter wasn't much for breakfast. Kris was still whimpering, but he'd largely cried himself out at this point.

I slowed the Dad Wagon and pulled us off the highway. "It's okay. You did great, honey."

"I… can't…"

I patted her on the back; she might have been a know-it-all teenager that was more than capable of grappling with the big dogs, but Wild Magick and the first sight of New Dead would get anyone—especially the tough ones.

"Just slow down and take a deep breath. You can do it, count to five. One…"

"Two!" Kris shouted from the backseat.

My daughter ignored us both and continued to gulp down air like it was going out of style.

I pulled off into a gas station parking lot and threw the car into park. We got a few confused looks from the commuter crowd when they caught sight of the Mazda's frosted hood, but it was Florida, so they just shrugged and kept on going—there's a reason most Magicians end up down here.

"Dad…"

"Just breathe, honey. I'll explain everything," I said, keeping a sharp eye on the radiator needle. "One… two… that's it."

Cathy shuddered a few times, and would certainly have booted all over the front seat if she'd eaten anything for breakfast, but after a few minutes she achieved a solid, unbroken breath.

"Good. There you go."

I pushed opened my door and brushed the glass off my pants.

"Dad… I'm shaking."

"That's the shock. Stay here," I left the Dad Wagon running and ran in to the convenience store, returning with the highest-sugar-content soda I could find.

Cathy's fingers were a mess, so I opened the bottle for her. "Drink this."

"Dad, I—"

"Drink, Catherine—now."

Cathy chugged the soda, and I pushed the frosty Dad Wagon back out onto the road.

"It's just the drop off from Wild Magick, you'll be fine—happens to all of us in the beginning. The Magick felt good didn't it?"

What are you doing? Don't say that.

My daughter nodded, drinking more from the can.

I checked on the wee one in the rear-view mirror—his eyes were a little on the red side, but he seemed to be handling everything just fine.

"Listen, sweetheart, there's a lot of stuff you don't know about, and I don't have time to explain it all to you now."

"Wild Magick?"

"Right, unfocused channeling of cosmic power. Especially impressive given the effects of your necklace."

Cathy fingered her necklace.

"Is... it going to come after me?"

"No."

"How can you be so sure?"

Good question.

"I just know, okay?"

Lousy answer.

"But—"

"Drink the soda, and help me get Kris to school, then I'll explain what I can before I drop you off."

"You expect me to go to school after this?!"

"Yes, I said you'll be fine—just do what I tell you."

My daughter nodded and wiped her nose; the kid was tough —maybe she did have more than a little Porter in her after all.

We took the next turn and wedged the melting Mazda into the kindergarten drop-off line. "You have a chemistry test today —which is no end of ironic given what you are drinking—so, just go about your day like nothing happened."

"Nothing happened?!" Cathy shouted, pointing at the frost-covered dash. "You call that nothing? I want to know what that was. Dad, it... it looked..."

"Dead."

"Yeah!"

I inched forward waiting for the Millers to let off their volley-ball-team worth of children—it was like watching a cavalcade of Shriners exit the car bedecked in pink bows and blond braids.

"That's what it was, Cathy."

"Good Morning!" Mrs. Clarke shouted, pulling open the back door—the shock of it nearly cost my daughter another of her nine lives.

"Good Morning, Mrs. Clarke!" Kris said, somehow finding a

way to accentuate the typically silent 'e' and bring a smile to his teacher's face.

Tabitha Clarke and Porter had been friends for years, going all the way back to when Tabby had been a compounding chemist. She'd lost her husband a few years back to cancer, and for a while she'd all but dropped off the face of the earth, but now, that ex-scientist was teaching kindergarten and, according to Porter, loving every minute of it.

Science and Magick have a funny relationship, one even I don't completely understand. But I do know one thing: Tabby, like most scientists, is a human wet-blanket when it comes to Magick.

Just standing near the woman could defuse about all but my best efforts, including the one currently keeping my radiator from overheating.

"Off you go," I said, my eyes drifting to the temperature gauge.

Kris popped up from his car seat and out the door, his troubles all but forgotten.

Oh, to be five.

We pulled back out into traffic and the temperature gauge fluttered upward—as did my daughter's nerves. "Is it going to come after me?"

"Nope."

"How do you know?"

I pointed at the Logic Loop dangling from her neck. "You've got some premium Dad brand going there. It'll keep you safe—provided you keep it on."

Cathy fingered the necklace. "What do you mean?"

I took the next few turns and narrowly avoided a pothole, before rolling to a stop in front of her high school. "I'm going to make this really brief for now. What you saw was Magick. Not the Vegas-style street magicians, but the real deal—the bending of reality to my, well your, will."

"That's…"

"Crazy?" I said, dropping the Dad Wagon into park.

"Yes!"

"Guess what, you're about to be neck deep in it, because it would appear you have the same genes as your old man."

Cathy's eyes widened and she ran her fingers over the defrosting dash. "I… really?"

"Cathy," I said, looking my once-defiant teenager in the eyes. "You've got a lot of questions, and I promise I will answer them, but for right now I need you to do three things for me."

Cathy stared at me, her eyes wavering between determination and abject terror. "What?"

"One. Don't tell anyone."

"They wouldn't believe me if I did."

True.

"Two. Do not, under any circumstances, ever take that necklace off."

Cathy placed a hand on Lenar's Logic Loop and squeezed it until her knuckles turned white.

"And three, go crush your chemistry test."

"But Dad, I—"

"Tonight. I'll explain everything tonight."

"You promise?"

This is going to be worse than the birds and the bees—which I'm still damn glad I had Porter do.

"Yeah, I promise."

Cathy wiped her eyes and climbed out of the Dad Wagon. In mere seconds a tall, spindly boy broke ranks from the rest of the herding young adults and caught up to my daughter.

What did Porter say his name was? Triscuit?

"Hey, Cat. You okay?"

Cat? Who calls her Cat?

"Hey, Tris," Cathy said, throwing her backpack over her shoulder.

Tris... Tristan! That's right, boyfriend of the month.

Bean-pole Tristan leaned down to peek through the open car door. "Hi, Mr. Law."

"Howdy, Triscuit."

"Dad!"

"You forgot your chem lab bag, Cathy," I said, pulling a drawstring bag out of the second seat. I handed the bag to Tristan, but not before a pair of heavy rubber gloves fell out.

"I got it," he said, dusting them off and shoving them back in the bag.

My slightly embarrassed daughter took the bag from Tristan, and together they joined the herd of students headed to first period.

I pulled the Dad Wagon back onto the road, but kept an eye on her from the rear-view mirror. I didn't know if she was ready for this—or, more importantly—if I was.

PART II
NEW PAINS AND OLD MISTAKES

10

QWIK FIX

*J*coasted into *The Qwik Fix* with the needle precariously wavering just under the red line. The Dad Wagon sputtered, but had somehow found the will to surge the remaining hundred feet up and into the lot as the engine heat and Florida sun dripped away the last of my car-saving Midwestern winter.

The Qwik Fix was a squat little building with six car bays and a small front office. Tall stacks of tires huddled around the entrance like giant-sized poker chips pressed together for a big wager. They partially blocked the entrance to the small office, but it wasn't the office that demanded my attention, it was the parking lot.

Rob ran a tight ship, but he and his guys could fix damn near anything, so damn near everything ended up at *The Qwik Fix*. The lot was a labyrinth of vehicular history, from roadsters to minivans, with more than a few motorcycles stuffed like bookmarks between the folds of painted steel.

I squeezed the Dad Wagon between a sixties-era Volkswagen, and a brand-new Caddy—it just felt right—and stepped out into the full brunt of the heat and humidity to look for Rob.

I hadn't even gotten the trunk open before the cotton folds of my shirt began to soak up sweat like a paper towel.

"Morning, Gene—whoa, is that glass?"

Rob Kelly, master mechanic, ex demon lover, and all-around great guy, was a short and remarkably fit young man. He kept his ginger-red hair cut tight to his scalp, which had the effect of making him look like a member of the Leprechaun Marines—however, having dealt with a real Leprechaun during my one summer abroad, I was damn glad Rob wasn't one.

"Yeah, long story," I said, pulling my bag out of the trunk and setting it next to the car.

"What's the problem?"

There might have been a few people ahead of me, but Rob always made room—save someone from a lifeforce-draining Succubus and I'm sure they'd make room for you too.

"Overheating."

Rob shook his head and climbed in to pull the hood release. "Whoa, Gene, your AC going out too? Looks like it frosted up in here."

"Oh—"

"I'll check it, too, but first let me get a look at the engine—oh man!"

"What?"

"I should be asking you that. What the hell? Did you have like a badger in here or something?"

I joined Rob at the front of the car, and together we stared in awe at the shredded innards of the once-proud Dad Wagon's engine compartment. A potpourri of fluids had already begun to pool under the car—the kaleidoscope of colors sure to be as toxic, and as expensive, as it was beautiful.

"It's like every line has been sliced—every single line," Rob said, then got down to eye level with the radiator hose. "Gene, it's a miracle you even made it here."

You don't know the half of it.

"Yeah, sure looks like it."

Rob pulled back some shredded plastic insulation. "Looks like you're gonna need a new battery too. There's some serious terminal corrosion."

"Ah, yeah—*serious* corrosion," I said, without a clue as to what he was pointing at.

I had no doubt Rob knew that I possessed zero car knowledge beyond where the gas goes, but he was the sort of polite mechanic that played along.

Rob dropped the hood back down and guided me away from the Dad Wagon's bleeding corpse.

"Listen, is this like one of those"—the mechanic looked around the tire stacks to make sure none of his guys were close by—"you know, those demon-sucker sort of things?"

Demon sucker... oh, the life-draining Demon sex-kitten.

"No, I honestly don't have a clue what happened to the Dad Wagon, but it wasn't a Succubus. Remember I got her a job at the Hospice? She really was a pretty good one—as infernal Hellspawn go."

The color returned to Rob's face. "Thank the Lord. I've been dating this new girl now, and she's amazing—I was so worried you were here to tell me she was a dragon or something."

Only one dragon I know of, and he should still be sleeping in the Everglades. Pretty sure you're safe.

"Nope, I'm sure she's wonderful... and completely normal."

At least I hope so. This part of Florida is getting too weird, even by Sunshine State standards.

"Thanks, Gene. I'll get the Dad Wagon working. No charge as usual," Rob said, guiding me back around to my bag and the pooling remains of the Mazda's vital fluids.

"No, you've got to let me pay—"

The best mechanic in Florida shook his head. "Nope, like I said, free car repairs for life."

"Rob..."

The young man ran his hand through his hair. "Well there's one thing... but no, look it's nothing. No charge."

I really didn't want to push the issue: I'd been attacked by New Dead twice, Cathy was getting her Magick on, and the Dad Wagon was a murder victim. But Rob Kelly was a good soul, and you took care of good souls.

"What is it?" I asked, holding out the keys to the Mazda.

The mechanic accepted them and leaned in closer. "It's Justine, the girl I'm dating. Her mom passed a few days ago."

"I'm sorry."

Don't ask, please don't ask.

"Yeah, and they weren't really talking. She's all torn up about it and I thought. I was just wondering..."

"You want me to play operator and complete a call to the afterlife?"

Rob nodded. "But, listen, it's a big ask. I know you don't talk about what you do and all, but she's just a wreck, and I can't stand seeing her like this. She just wants to apologize."

"Ah..."

I didn't want to do it. There's a reason why Death Magick had earned the reputation it had—Necromancy was serious Deep Magick. Don't get me wrong, I'd put down New Dead and wrangled a couple of Poltergeists, but mediumship took skill— real talent—and it always drew attention. All of that was exactly the sort of thing I *didn't* want to get known for, but this was Rob, and he didn't ask for anything. Ever.

The ginger-haired mechanic looked away. "Yeah, I thought so. Listen, I haven't told her anything—it's fine."

"I'll do it."

"Wait—what? You will?"

I nodded, then picked up my bag and slung it over shoulder —surprised at just how heavy it felt.

I've got to get back in shape. One class with Cathy and I can't even lift my bag without grunting.

"So, can I get that ride to the office?"

11

69 MALLORY LANE

I spent the car ride with one of Rob's guys thinking about Cathy. A small part of me was happy to have another Magician in the family, especially given recent frustrations with my current apprentice, but a much larger and more rational part understood just how dangerous a daughter exposed to the unadulterated darkness of the supernatural world was.

"Take the next right," I said, guiding my driver toward the office. He seemed to know this part of town pretty well, and as such knew to stay off the main streets and away from the rest of the commuters, but he still missed the turn.

"No problem, I'll get the next one."

It *was* a problem, a rather serious one. I just didn't know how to tell him.

The car turned and hadn't gone more than a hundred feet down that alternate street before it hit me like a wave of dread. Each second we drew closer to it I found the air in my lungs harder to hold on to. My driver whistled along with the radio, completely oblivious to the malevolence he was barreling toward.

It was a simple white house with covered windows and a yard full of overgrown weeds. Paint peeled away from the siding and fell in long strips along its wide front porch. A single faded rocking chair faced out to the street, surrounded by rolls of newspaper stacked like cord-wood, while a bent mailbox stood at the road's edge, leaning toward the pavement as if it wanted to make a break for it, but couldn't get up the courage.

No squirrel dared set foot on that accursed ground, the few nearby going so far as to skitter between the trees to avoid passing near the white house on Mallory Lane, and it wasn't just the mammals that avoided it either. I spotted no lizards sunning themselves on the broken sidewalk, and no dragonflies humming above the bent grass blades. Even the air was empty. Blackbirds were perched on electrical wires along the street, but not a one got near the house on Mallory Lane. They squawked and jockeyed for position, but never along the wires that draped above the white house.

The closer we got to that evil place the stronger its pull became. I found my fingers tracing the car door handle, and I immediately pulled them back. The sense of morbid curiosity and dread fascination was intoxicating. My feet wanted to walk through those tall weeds, and my hands yearned to turn the door knob and step back inside that evil place, but my soul was frosted over in fear—it wanted no part with what dwelled at 69 Mallory Lane.

My driver sped past the tiny white house without paying it the slightest bit of attention—I envied the blessing of normalcy even as I pressed my fingers against the glass.

Was it my imagination, or did something move beyond the thick white curtains?

We took the next turn and left Mallory Lane behind us— gone, but not forgotten.

* * *

WE PULLED into the lot and he dropped me near the front door. Never more happy to see the boring mundanity of the builder's front office, I practically leapt out of the back seat. "Thanks! You know how to get back?"

My driver nodded and gave me a wave before pulling back out onto the street.

I slung my bag over a shoulder and pushed on into the glorious air conditioning.

I'd worked for Kinder Construction, LLC for a few years now—ever since we'd moved to this side of town and I'd run into the owner, John, at a Girl Scouts outing when Cathy was younger. He's a pretty decent boss and a good dad—not perfect, but no one really is.

That weekend had been a harrowing experience with one of the last remaining Dryads in the Sunshine State. In short, the nigh-immortal oak spirit had been quite displeased to learn Mr. Kinder had torn down a few of her hundred-year-old besties. Two days of Girl Scouting, an attempted Magickal transmogrification, and a last-second wild fire, and John had been ready to give me a job on the spot.

We agreed on a sort of mid-level manager position, exactly the kind of thing I'd always said I'd never do, but at the time with Kris so young—and Porter still trying to handle life as a stay-at-home mom—sacrifices had to be made.

In the end, John and I had decided it was best to keep the Magick talk between us—no sense in making him look crazy, or bringing a bunch of suspicion to my doorstep.

"Morning, Gene," said a sweet southern voice from behind the high walls of the reception desk.

Marjorie, our elderly receptionist, was sweet as pie and true Old Florida. She knew this part of the Sunshine State like few others, and as such was a wealth of information—provided you were willing to pay for the coffee.

"Hey, Marge."

"Running a little late today?"

"Car trouble," I said, nodding along with her sigh. "Oh, before I forget. You know a Claudia Wilson?"

"Yeah, sure do—real piece of work, that one."

I glanced at the desk clock. "No time now, but will you be around this afternoon?"

"Sweetheart, I'm here all day."

"Coffee's on me, I've got some questions for you," I said, giving Marge enough time to nod before racing past the grandeur of client reception and straight up the stairs. Kinder Construction had poured more than a few dollars into that receiving area, outfitting it with nice leather couches, a bubbling fountain, and even some beautiful floating water lilies, but none of those niceties made it to the back office.

At the top of the curving stairs I left the beauty of reception behind me and turned off onto a side hallway, razor-focused on the nondescript steel door at the end—it would be better to slip in the side door now that I was sure to be late for the morning meeting.

For just about anyone else, that would be a problem. The side door led through Information Technology—the domain of one Adam Grayson, equal parts caring man-child and crushing viceroy of techno torture. Anyone else daring to request entrance to these hallowed halls would be subjected to a series of complex riddles based on a vexing mixture of mythology, retro-video games, and Buffy the Vampire Slayer, and should that poor soul survive the riddles and find them- selves on the other side, they'd still be neck deep in a mine- field of sarcasm and cringe-worthy references to obscure trivia. All of this meant one thing—Adam didn't get a lot of visitors.

I, however, was immune to all of his chicanery, as I had the one thing he wanted more than kombucha and beard butter —Magick.

I stopped in front of the door and stared at the small dome camera mounted at eye level.

"Hey, Adam."

There was a short pause before the satisfying click of the door's mechanical lock popped open.

I smiled—it was about time something went right for me today.

12

THE FISHBOWL

"*Y*ou're late," said a voice not accustomed to same-species interactions.

Thanks, Adam. You're a paragon of emotional support.

"Yeah, I see that," I said, navigating my way through the complex maze of boxes, wires, and assorted techno garbage that made up 'the fishbowl.' His office was a sort of combination computer room and Grayson retention pond that had long ago expanded to a stomach-churning level. Back in those early days, we did what any sane set of employees would do when they couldn't live with—or without—the guy who knows how to make all their computers work; we pitched in to add blinds to the long glass window that dominated the far side of that narrow room.

In Magick, as in IT, a little mystery is appreciated.

Adam, the firm's Lone Ranger of the digital realm, hadn't moved from his command center. A short in stature but high in prosperity gentleman, Adam was well ensconced behind a wall of computer monitors that kept razor-sharp tabs on the entire organization as well as two or three of the top junk sites that were a bonanza for potential Magickal memorabilia.

Someone walking in off the street and seeing Adam in his element would have thought we made nuclear warheads or split atoms.

Nope, just the occasional commercial office buildings or sensible apartment communities.

Adam slid a pencil deep into the unkempt recesses of his man-bun before taking a long pull from an oversized plastic cup that proclaimed his love for 'The Big Gulp.' "Hey, you should look at this—"

"In a minute," I said, tip-toeing through a sea of old mother-boards, stacks of backup tapes, and flocks of long-discarded phones on my way to the window. I tilted open the blinds just enough to get a look at the main conference room. The meeting was already in full swing—God, I hated walking into a meeting late.

"They have donuts," Adam said, his head appearing under my arm, the man-bun pencil poking at my side.

"How do you know? You never leave the fishbowl."

"Email."

I set my bag down and let the blinds slide closed. "What did I tell you about reading other people's email?"

Adam slithered back to his chair like a dragon returning to their hoard.

"It was in the meeting request," he said, rolling his eyes before taking another slurp from his oversized cup.

I frowned. "I take it you declined?"

The High Priest of the Keyboard gestured to his digital subjects whirring away in their glass and aluminum village. "I'm running a couple of complex searches. I'll drop in for the last few minutes and get the untouched box of glazed that Marjorie always leaves me."

"What was it you wanted to show me?"

Adam perked up and his bearded face took on an almost cherubic grin. "I think I found you something..." My junior apprentice paused for what he certainly assumed was dramatic effect. "Something Magick!"

I'd brought Adam into the Magick fold a few years ago when it became clear to me he had at least a little sparkle in his cholesterol-laden blood. The exact details of which I prefer not to speak of, but it involved an exotic dancer, Goat Yoga, and the most crudely concocted Love Jerky I'd ever seen.

Who even tries to make Love Jerky? My apprentice, that's who.

It'd taken me days and a host of different sigils to get his hairy butt back to normal, plus a whole month to save up enough cash to replace the grass he'd destroyed. As tough as Adam could be as an apprentice, he had been far worse as a goat.

Porter had wanted to send him to a petting zoo—my wife, ever the comedian.

"Well?"

Adam's screens filled with photos from what looked like a yard sale.

"I came across these on a search through old social media photos," he said, pointing at the card tables full of junk in the background, while the same time trying to ignore the buxom young girls that made up the foreground.

"I see, *special* internet search?"

Adam ignored me. "This guy puts on a yard sale during spring break every couple of years, but, that's not the key part—look here." My apprentice pointed to a brown smudge tucked inside the crook of a grinning spring-breaker's arm.

I squinted. "What am I looking at?"

"You really should wear your glasses—"

"Can't you zoom in or something?"

Adam sighed. "This isn't TV, you know. First, I had to find

71

this image, then I had to see if she'd posted a higher-resolution version of it."

"So you had to creep through her entire photo-stream?"

"Yes, and on *two* services."

I chuckled. "My heart bleeds for you…"

Adam waved me off with his hand. "Just taking one for the team. There were a lot of spring break photos to go through, but I'll recover. Look at this."

My apprentice adjusted his screen to reveal a perfectly taken photo of the table, packed to the gills with oddities, but with a single item sticking out in exquisite detail—a broken-up brown log, riddled with pockmarks and termite damage, and a rusted metal spike sticking out of the top of it.

"You see that there, on the spike?"

"I don't know, can you zoom in?" I asked, leaning against Adam's shoulder to get a closer look.

"The image is at a high enough resolution where I believe I can load it in a—"

"Adam!"

"Zooming…"

The spike filled the screens, and etched in the nail head was exactly what I'd hoped to see—a perfectly obscured Magickal symbol.

"John Henry's last spike…" I said, letting the words fall from my mouth with hushed reverence.

"Huh?"

"You don't know who John Henry is?"

"Did he play for the Rays? You know I don't do sports."

"Railroad, steel-driving man, any of this ring a bell?"

Adam tilted his head to one side. "Ah…"

"Damn it, man, you need to read some folklore. So much of Magick is tied up in it."

Adam ignored me and turned back to the picture. "So… what does it have to do with us?"

"John Henry's last spike was part of a Magician's feud going back over a hundred years."

"Really? It's a rusted piece of metal…"

"Correction, it's a rusted piece of metal with the Magickal power to end anything."

"Huh? That thing was part of a feud?"

"Yes. Are you familiar with Henry Plant, you know, railroad baron of West Florida?"

"No…"

"The guy practically built this town, haven't you ever wondered why like half the place is named after him?"

"Oh, right. *That* Henry Plant—why didn't you say so?"

Nice try.

"Yeah, he was embroiled in a feud with Henry Flagler down in South Florida for years. Neither of them was what you'd call the best Magician, but they were both insanely wealthy, and they accumulated Magickal items like the fishbowl here accumulates old hardware."

"Let's skip back to the insanely wealthy part—when are we going to cover turning lead into gold?"

I patted Adam on the back. "Yeah—that's a myth."

"What?"

"Sorry, no lead into gold."

"So how did these railroad guys get rich?"

"The old-fashioned way," I said in a hushed tone.

"Which is?" Adam asked, leaning in, his eyes full of anticipation.

"Inheritance!"

"Gah, Gene, that's a terrible story."

"Whatever. There's Magick in that spike, I know it."

"Really? An old railroad spike?"

"A *Magickal* old spike," I said, correcting him. "Flagler and Plant fought like hell over that spike. Rumor is Flagler sent an assassin to take out his rival and collect the spike. As the story goes, Plant trapped the assassin in the Old Tampa Hotel, but somehow the spike got away. It's been lost for over a hundred years..."

"Until now."

"Right, until now. Where is it? I've got to get my hands on that before it disappears again. All these New Dead can wait—this is more important."

Adam's voice squeaked. "New Dead?"

"Yeah, two in less than twenty-four hours, if you can believe it. I had to open a Hellgate to get rid of one of them, and the other I left on the on-ramp. So, where's the spike? Can you print me the directions?"

"Remember, these pictures were taken last year, but yeah I can send you the location. He's doing another yard sale Saturday, the question is—"

"Will it still be there..." I said, finishing this thought.

"What about the New Dead, Gene?" Adam asked, more than a hint of concern in his voice.

"That's right—find me everything you can on the Brighton 8," I said, picking up my bag and zipping it shut.

Funny, I don't remember opening it.

"I've got to make an appearance in this meeting. Listen, good work—really good work. Maybe we should go out for a drink after I get the spike. You know, to celebrate."

"Really?" The anticipation in Adam's voice was palpable.

"Why not?" I said with a wink as I slung my bag over my shoulder and slipped out the ice box door.

To remove 69 Mallory Lane from the world forever... I'd celebrate that with just about anyone—even New Dead.

All of this excitement must have spurred on some serious adrenaline because my bag felt light as a feather.

13

STICKS AND STONES

*I*t was impossible to sneak into the conference room —John Kinder was a smart designer and he'd made sure of that. I decided to go with an alternate tactic and instead walked in with feigned confidence. Now don't get me wrong, he definitely wasn't going to fire me or anything, but John wasn't a fan of late arrivals to his meetings.

The meeting room held a long oval table surrounded by stiff-backed swivel chairs and most of the Kinder Construction team. There was the foreman, Reggie, a tough-as-nails former concrete hauler that I swear had troll-blood somewhere in his family tree. He was a good guy, but his hands looked like the kind that routinely ground bones to dust for his sack lunch. Charlie was there as well, representing the gaggle of book-keepers and accountants. While his close proximity to the single most mind-numbingly boring activity in the known universe meant he had about as much Magickal energy as drywall, it didn't stop him from looking for all the world like Old Dead. Charlie was tall and unbelievably thin, and when Cathy was little she had been terrified of his pasty-white skin and long skinny fingers. So was I when I first met him, but over the years

I'd grown to appreciate the sheer mundanity of Charlie Wickers. Sometimes it was nice to know there were places with no Magick left in the world—accounting was one of those places.

John had asked a few other members of his management team to join. Our land development guy, Omar, was there. Omar was a master of finding good property and convincing the owners of said property to depart with it for just the right amount of cash. When he'd first arrived I'd been sure we were dealing with someone Magickal, but after a few surveillance lunches I removed the mental flag I had on him—Omar wasn't Magickal, but his eyebrows might be. They were like two perfectly unkempt wooly caterpillars that lounged above sparkling eyes. As the older man talked those furry creatures would wake from their slumber and begin the dance of wooly head fairies.

People rarely said no to Omar and his dancing eyebrows.

Last but not least, John had asked the lawyer to come in. She was a smart cookie, even as lawyers went, and I didn't mind working with her. She was easily the best-dressed member of the team, and with her bright red skirt-suit and tightly managed blond hair, Sharon was an attractive woman, but I felt for any of the field guys that had to meet with her. She was about as warm and fuzzy as the computer servers busy whirring away in the fishbowl.

Then there was me.

I would have liked to say I was the company's best Magician, but since anyone outside of John who knew that might commit me to Shady Acres mental hospital, I went with my more mundane title: Eugene Law, a professional fixer of problems and doer of things that need to be done.

It was my job to keep the business running right by handling the one-off supernatural issues that cropped up from time to time. Ostensibly, this involved making sure we didn't run afoul of any Magickal beasts, upset any ancient Native American burial sites, or dump toxic gypsum into ground water and get the Alligator Men in a tizzy. Lastly, it was my job to keep an eye on the techno-machinations of the Boy Wonder—the email must flow and the spreadsheets must spread.

I took my seat at the table and set my bag on the floor. I'd joined the conversation late, so I tried to figure out the gist of what was going on before I said anything.

Better to stay silent and be thought the fool than to open your mouth and remove all doubt.

"Where are we with the Old Tampa Hotel?" John asked, not to anyone in particular, but Reggie responded immediately.

"That's what I was saying earlier: we've got a problem."

Omar's eyebrows enacted the best yoga-pose I'd ever seen on inanimate forehead-hair. "What sort of problem?"

John tilted his head. "Everything looks clean on the contract, zoning is fine. We've got all the permits lined up."

"It's bad…"

When Reggie said something was bad everyone knew to lean in—the stone-biter almost never classified something as bad—when he'd broken his foot a few years ago he said it was 'a minor setback.'

Only broken in five places—minor setback, no biggie.

"The guys found bones."

If Reggie had chosen that moment to change into a man-eating ogre and start tearing Omar's arms off, I'm not sure it would have broken the stunned silence in the room.

I'd been worried about the Old Tampa Hotel remodel ever since I'd heard we won it from Jeff Masterson—that was the same night both he and his wife had narrowly escaped being murdered by what I believed to be a vengeful spirit. The Old Tampa Hotel had secrets, and they were secrets I didn't want anything do with.

"Excuse me—bones?" Sharon asked, her pen dancing across the legal pad in her lap.

Reggie nodded.

We'd dealt with gopher tortoises and scrub jays before, but never human remains. The former were pretty standard fare in Florida. We'd call in the right environment crew and they'd haul them away with expert precision—provided John wrote a large-enough check—but human remains were a whole different animal.

"Are they old?" Omar asked, his brows bunching up in frustration.

"Huh? I don't know. Do I look like a bone expert?"

Omar pursed his lips. "The estate never gave me any reason to suspect there might be a burial ground there…"

"That's not the worst of it. Ever since they discovered them I've got half the crew out—"

"What do you mean out?" John asked, leaning forward in his chair.

"They say the place is haunted."

My chest tightened and I tried to hide the concern on my face. There'd been problems at the Old Tampa Hotel in the past, and it now seemed they hadn't gone away after all.

Mr. Kinder shook his head, then turned to me. "Right. Listen, Gene, you're the fixer here. Can you fix this?"

"I—"

Sharon jumped in before I got another word out. "We need to call the Florida Department of Law Enforcement. This could be a crime scene."

John sighed and got up from his seat—the man's brain was directly wired to his feet, and he did his best thinking while pacing. "Okay, call in FDLE, but I want you working with Gene on this. Reggie, tell the guys there's nothing to worry about."

"I tried, but—"

"Gene. Fix it."

I nodded with no idea what fixing it meant.

"Good. Reggie, tell them Gene'll get it fixed."

"Okay..." Reggie gave me a skeptical look.

John pushed his chair in. "We've got to get this project started—the delays are killing us."

"Third loan payment is due Monday," Charlie said, his voice a near perfect monotone.

In the next moment the conference room was filled with the chirps, dings, and beeps of phone alerts. I retrieved my own phone from my pocket just as the 'Black Magic Woman' guitar riff was heating up.

YOU HAVE 6,667 NEW MESSAGES.

What the hell?

Judging by the rest of the faces in the room it appeared everyone else was having a similar experience. I opened the email and found hundreds of pictures of gyrating couples in various and unseemly poses.

"What the—Gene, you manage Adam. Go find out what the hell is going on. So help me God if we get a harassment claim out of this he's gone," John Kinder said, slamming his phone against the conference table.

"On it."

I pushed my way out of the conference room door and into the main hallway just in time for the fire alarm to go off.

BAT OUTTA HELL

*a*dam pounded away on the keyboards in front of him, switching from screen to screen like he was neck deep in a game of whack-a-mole. Tiny beads of sweat appeared along his brow—my apprentice was nervous.

"What's going on?" I shouted, slamming the fishbowl door behind me.

"I don't know!"

If Adam didn't know that meant one thing—we were deep in it.

"Can you turn off the fire alarm?"

Adam clicked a few buttons and the wailing fire alarm stopped.

"Oh thank God—did we get hacked?"

Adam wiped the sweat from his face and sucked down as much soda as he could in a single gulp. "It's... No... Well, maybe. It's like all the systems are going haywire. Thousands of lines of code have been changed."

"Changed? Like scrambled?"

"No," Adam said, pointing to the screen. "It's like someone came in and patched things to have the worst possible affect."

"How—"

"Look—right here." Adam highlighted a few lines of undecipherable text on the screen. "There's the fire alarm. It's now been set to go off anytime someone is looking at porn."

"Are you looking at porn?"

"Well, not right this second!"

"So it could be a hacker?"

Adam pointed to the bright red network cable now hanging like a limp noodle on the far wall. "Not unless they found a way to break the WiFi encryption, we are disconnected from the internet."

The Hellgate.

The Dad Wagon.

Adam's Servers.

"I think we have a stowaway."

My apprentice stopped his frantic typing. "What do you mean?"

I held a finger to my lips, then leaned in to whisper in his ear, careful to not touch the edges of his oiled beard. "We need a box, I'm guessing something roughly squirrel-sized. What do you have?"

Adam jumped out of his seat and dug through the cornucopia of junk that lined the wall behind him.

While he hunted for a suitable container, I took a moment to gather my strength. I'd left my bag in the conference room, which meant most of my go-to Magickal items were somewhere entirely unhelpful, but it didn't matter. I had a really good idea of what we were dealing with.

Much of my early Magickal experience had come during my college days, thanks to and at the hands of, one very challenging young woman.

Morgan Crowley.

It had started out simply enough, like most of those things do. She was one of the goth coeds with the black eyeliner and leather corsets who got a huge kick out of some very dark Magick. She'd gone all in on some dangerous conjuring, and since I'd been pretty keen to conjure those corsets off her nubile frame, I'd made a few less-than-stellar life decisions in the process of helping her.

When you spend your first semester skipping prerequisites for a business management degree to learn the complex sigils of dangerous Magick just to see some boobs, you come to realize your decision-making has been delegated to the wrong organ.

That semester had been a blur—the corsets came off as much as they went back on—and I ended up spending far too much time with a very tricky and unpleasant Imp.

And then I go and open a Hellgate and bring one right back, and there wasn't even a corset in play—nice work, Master Magician.

Adam returned with a plexiglass and metal box that had three large spools of plastic filament hanging off one side. He held the box out like an old-fashioned lantern and dangled it in front of me. "This work?"

"What is that?"

He looked at me like a visitor from the distant past. "It's a 3D printer."

"What the hell do we need a 3D printer for?"

Adam shrugged. "If I don't spend all my budget it gets cut."

"Gah! What else have you bought?"

Adam's face fell, and he slipped one of his hands behind his back. "I needed the watch for... monitoring... um... the stuff."

I took the 3D printer from him and navigated my way through the refuse to the server rack. Dozens of dark metal cases, stacked like evil pizza boxes, blinked in seemingly random patterns along the far wall. It was like a terribly tight and compact harvest festival of lights—just the place for an Imp to hide.

Imps live for tight spaces—which is rather fortuitous for them, because as nefarious Hellspawn go they really do dwell solidly at the bottom of the food chain. They cram their rubbery little bodies into all manner of impossibly small spaces to keep from becoming hors d'oeuvres for the bigger, badder, and more ravenous citizens of the unspeakable depths.

Yeah, small places, like the middle of my back.

"Here, hold this open," I said, handing the 3D printer back to Adam. "Be ready to close the box the moment I say to."

My apprentice nodded his man-bun in assent.

"What do you think it is?"

"An Imp…"

Adam's fingers quivered against the box's edge. "Are they… evil?"

"Yes."

"Like scary evil?" he asked, his tone indicating he was rather inclined to believe me.

"Nah, more like obnoxious evil."

"So… like…"

"Like that annoying apprentice who asks a ton of questions while you're trying to focus on a very particular Magick—*that* kind of obnoxious evil."

Adam clamped his mouth shut.

What was it again… All I can picture are corsets… Oh, right!

"Nullus latebras!"

The Magick surged through me like a lasso, and the server rack rattled, sending tiny screws falling to the ground only to be lost in the great junk wasteland of the fishbowl.

"What's happening?" Adam said, backing away from the gesticulating mass of computers.

"Nullus latebras!" I shouted again, inwardly proud of myself at the undergarment reference that just happened to find its way into my Latin.

A bright pink ball of rubbery flesh shot out of the server rack as if it had been fired from a cannon.

"Catch it!" I cried.

Adam tried to line up the case, but he moved like that lethargic kid at tee-ball only there to scope out the snacks. "I got it!"

He didn't.

The Imp slammed into the man-boy's chest, missing the printer box entirely and knocking Adam's prosperous butt to the ground.

I peeled the tiny Demon off my apprentice's hoody and dropped it in the printer case. The Imp was a little dazed from his high-velocity expulsion but still more than capable of spewing a decent amount of salty curses in demonic low-speech.

"Yeah, I feel the same way about your mother too," I said, closing the door on the tiny Demon.

He wasn't much larger than a yard squirrel, with bright pink flesh and a long, crooked nose. His black eyes were set deep in an over-sized skull that perched precariously on a neck far too thin to hold it properly. The Imp's tail whipped back and forth in time with his tiny wings. He banged on the tiny glass and let me have an earful.

"Yeah, yeah. If I had a nickel for every time some Demon cursed my man bits to shrivel and die I'd have a big stack of nickels and two fewer kids—I don't care that you know Asaroth the Defiler on a first-name basis, you aren't getting out of that box."

My phone chirped, and I handed the Imp-box to Adam.

FDLE wants to meet us at the site now. I'll drive. - Sharon

"I've got to run off-site with Sharon."

Adam blanched at the mention of the lawyer's name.

"I need you to keep an eye on this until I get back," I said, tapping the box with my knuckle, further enraging the diminutive beast.

"What?! I don't know... What do I do with it?"

The Imp continued its stream of various curses and unbridled opinions about my genetic lineage.

"You're a Magician's apprentice, right?"

Adam hesitated. "Yeah…"

"You'll think of something."

"But…"

I patted him on the shoulder. "Just ignore his curses and, whatever you do, *don't* name it."

"Why?" Adam asked, holding the box at arm's length.

"Because if you do, he'll be bound to you for all eternity."

"Oh, right. That."

"It's all covered in the book I got you—you did read at least some of it, right?"

"Totally…" Adam stared at the diminutive monster now tearing apart the insides of his 3D printer.

I dismissed Sharon's message and found the link he'd promised me below it. John Henry's spike would have to wait—I had a job to do.

15

JOB SITE SIGILS

*S*haron drove a nice Lincoln town car, the kind with thick leather bench seating and strong air conditioning. She had NPR going and was tuned in to a segment on our American heritage. The reporter was interviewing an elderly woman on her family's rather tawdry history on the wrong side of the Civil War.

The sins of the father...

Aside from the radio we rode in relative silence. Sharon knew nothing of my Magick, and I wasn't much for the law beyond the few simple rules I'd picked up in college. I highly doubted she'd want to discuss the finer precepts of Business Law 101.

The Old Tampa Hotel was a decent drive from the office, so the NPR correspondent had just wrapped up her interview with a surprisingly forgiving elderly woman by the time we pulled off and found a spot behind a forensics van and a couple police cars.

"Let me do the talking," Sharon said, taking her phone and leaving her purse in the car.

"You got it."

I wasn't going to be interacting with the officers any more than I had to—I'd had a few law enforcement entanglements over the years and was more than happy to keep a low profile. When your off-hours profession involves all manner of strange and arcane practices, you tend to end up on the wrong side of the law fairly often. The real trick was getting over to the right side and making sure no one remembered it.

My goal today was simple: figure out what the hell was going on at the Old Tampa Hotel and try not to get killed in the process.

That's a tall order for you nowadays.

Sharon introduced herself to the detectives—two average-height gentlemen with thinning hair and exceptional tans. This wasn't South Beach, but short of some rolled-up sportcoat sleeves we had old men Miami Vice working the scene.

The Old Tampa Hotel was a city landmark, with its Moorish minarets and soaring brick facade. Henry Plant had built it back in the late 1800s, all part of his plan to get more rich people taking his trains down to Tampa. It had worked for a time—at least until the city grew up around it. Now most of it was used by the University of Tampa; however, part of Plant's deal with the university included keeping the southeast wing set aside as future museum.

John Kinder had scored a plum contract to do some remodeling on that museum, one I hadn't been overly keen on winning. I'd spent a decent bit of time dealing with a malevolent spirit in that converted hotel and still had the healthy fear of flying cutlery to prove it.

"Glad you called," the slightly more prosperous of the two gentlemen said, pointing to a taped-off area at the top of the stairs. "I don't think it's a crime scene—looks like your guys stumbled on some sort of walled-up grave. So far they're telling me it's a single body, but they're still trying to put together all the pieces."

I didn't need the officers to fill in the details; I could feel the evil like a normal person picks up the pressure drop before a storm—something bad was buried here and was not keen to see us. At one point as a kid, I'd knocked a massive hornet nest off a tree in the backyard. I must have received a dozen stings as a reminder of that lapse in judgement. Right now, standing at the bottom of these stairs felt for all the world like that day—we'd just poked something very terrible with a wicked sharp stick.

"Wait, pieces? Are you saying it's incomplete?" I asked while trying to avoid Sharon's withering gaze.

"Yeah, it's pretty typical. We'll piece it together, but so far we know we're missing the head."

That's a relief.

In the olden days people understood the significance of dismemberment.

Oh, how far we've fallen.

Someone back when Mr. Evil had been killed had the foresight to separate the head from the body. Was this the assassin sent by Flagler all those years ago? Even I didn't know how much of that old Magician's yarn was true.

What are you hiding?

I slipped past Sharon and the rest of poor-man's Miami Vice, then up the stairs and into the lobby. The Old Tampa Hotel had a large and ornate foyer, with a round bench presided over by a large statue of Henry Plant himself. The bronze giant eyes stared down at me over a wooly mustache.

So was it true? Did Flagler send something terrible after you?

I gave the old Magician's statue a nod before turning down the hall and heading toward the pops and static of police radios.

I considered using Magick, but it had to be small and simple. The air here was thick—not just with humidity, but with a malevolent frustration that I had no interest in drawing the attention of. If Porter was right, and the dead really did hate me, then the last thing I should be doing was shining a flashlight in their empty eye-sockets.

I stopped not far from the taped-off job site crawling with police officers and crouched down next to a few bags of cement mix. It wasn't dirt, but it would do—I just needed something simple to see what we were dealing with. I pulled one of the bags away from the wall and found a thick black glove pressed up against the corner. It was the sort of glove I'd used last summer when I stripped the deck, dense rubber with a bit of tack poured over a white fabric base. The glove itself had already picked up a contingent of concrete dust I had to brush off. Underneath that dirt, and barely visible along the dingy cuff, were the letters "TS" in permanent marker.

I turned the rubber over before tossing it aside. This was an active job site, and anything I found could have been brought in by anyone.

I opened one of the concrete bags and let the fine powder spill out over the wood floor, then dug my finger into the loose aggregate and began drawing the sigil. A few more flashy bits of Magick came readily to mind, but this was far safer—sort of like testing the water with your toe before you jumped in.

I finished the symbol and brushed aside the loose mix, waiting for something to happen. The complex series of interlocking circles and radiating lines had a gothic motif going for it, which made sense given I'd picked up the trick from Morgan. She had been a master at sigils, and her fascination with the designs of a particularly dark Magician had made this one a frequent visual. The girl was convinced the Ten Spins and the other long dead old Magicians had secrets to share with her, and in the end it was that belief that had done her in. It took me a while to come around to that, and I still wasn't keen on seeing, let alone using any of that old Magician's designs, but it was certainly what the task called for today. Ten Spins' Infernal

Bonelight only glowed in the presence of the scariest and most powerful of the dearly departed, Old Dead.

While New Dead were a whirling mess of fiery spiritual energy, Old Dead meant they'd found a way to avoid being kicked off to the netherworld—and had grown powerful in the process. Old Dead had secrets, deep and powerful secrets, and they weren't afraid to use those secrets to keep them here. That's what made them so dangerous—the will to live when coupled Deep Magick was a terrifying one-two-punch.

The key was their bones, and for maximum power they all had to stay together—which is why it was so important they didn't.

The symbols in the concrete dust remained dark.

Thank God. I've got too much on my plate already.

My phone chirped twice in rapid-fire succession, pulling me away from the undead detector.

The first was from Cathy and caused my heart to skip a beat.

Dad, u there?

Yes, you okay?

Y, found magick stuff on internet :D

I ran a frustrated hand through my hair. My daughter was now scouring the internet for Magick with her phone—while at school—and undoubtably finding all manner of nonsensical made-up bullshit. She'd gone from ready to vomit all over the front seat to being an internet Magician.

No! Please don't, just focus on your chemistry test.

:(

I mean it, Catherine Law.

I looked up the necklace. It's a Lenar's Logic Loop, right?

Yes. Keep it on!

Says it will mute my Magick :(

Cathy!

Fine... :/

Technically she was right. The Logic Loop would do exactly

that, keep her Wild Magick outbursts under control, at least until she was strong enough to overpower it—that was a sobering thought.

Are you wearing the necklace?

My daughter sent back a 'nod' emoji along with a string of tiny icons there was no way I'd decipher without my glasses on.

Is that a yes?

While I waited for my daughter to respond I checked the second message. It was from the world's best mechanic.

Gene, got to order a few parts, going to be a couple days. Sorry!

I let Rob know it was okay—I'd had an Imp in the engine compartment and must have sent the little guy into fits when I froze up the radiator—whatever it took to fix that amount of damage was fine.

No problem, Rob. Thanks.

Sure thing. Will let you know on Justine.

Crap, I'd completely forgotten about that promise. Still, Rob was repairing what had to have been many thousands of dollars in Dad Wagon damage for exactly zero dollars. The least I could do was hook up his girlfriend with the spirit of her dead mother—provided the ghost actually *wanted* to talk to her daughter.

My phone chirped again—it was Cathy the sorceress supreme.

I'm wearing it, except when I took it off to try some Magick!

I turned the screen off before my head exploded. At that moment, I was sure if Justine was anything like my daughter, her mother might not be too keen on talking to her regardless.

"Gene, anything else you want to do? You need to burn some incense or do a little dance or something?" Sharon asked, joining me in the hallway.

"Uh, what?"

"John told me all about the 'magic' you used to save him from some tree person a few years ago. I want you to know I think you are a complete sham and a charlatan of the lowest caliber."

"Okay—"

"And if it were up to me I'd be talking to FDLE about you, not some ancient bones tucked into the wall of this museum," Sharon said, her eyes burning holes in my chest. "So, do your dance or whatever, and I'll be waiting at the car—you've got five minutes."

This sort of reaction to my profession wasn't unusual—in fact, it was rather commonplace—but it wasn't something I had been expecting from Sharon.

So much for Magickal foresight.

Right. I'll get my MC Hammer pants on and bust out some of my best moves on this epicenter of evil unrest—the dead hate modern dance.

"No. I've seen what I needed to see. I did notice we might have some wiring issues. We could get dinged for that."

Sharon glared at me.

"But hey, what do I know? I'm just the exorcist."

The lawyer stomped back toward her car and I turned to wipe away the sigil with my foot, then stopped. I'd missed a loop and bent down to fix the mistake.

The instant my finger closed that circle in the dust the seal glowed a bright and angry green. That's when I felt it: the surge of evil Magick, both wild and unpredictable, coupled with the distinct sound of crackling electricity. Kinder Construction was in the process of taking down some walls, which meant they'd have to have turned off the electricity, but I'd have to tell that to the live wire that dropped from the ceiling and snapped to life behind Sharon.

Crap.

16

THAT'S ALL VOLTS

*W*hile I wasn't the biggest fan of Sharon the lawyer, I wasn't about to watch her get murdered by Old Dead—not on my watch.

"Sharon!" I shouted, trying to get the attorney's attention.

"Save it for someone who cares, Gene," she said, continuing to stomp her way back to the lobby, completely oblivious to the spark-spitting utility-grade death-viper stalking her like a nature documentary predator.

Damn it—why is it always the skeptics that need saving?

There wasn't enough time to catch up to Sharon, and I wasn't equipped to tangle with however many watts that wire was carrying. I was a Magician—what little I knew about electricity I'd picked up from the home improvement store.

Don't touch the black wire, Mr. Law.

The sparking copper head poked up only a few feet from Sharon and her flashy sportcoat.

Shit!

I traced the wire back to a utility box just past the police tape and ripped it open, then yanked out the cut-off and tossed the black plastic breaker to the ground. I spun around, expecting to see an impatient Sharon and an incapacitated black wire—no such luck. Then it hit me: our wire snake wasn't channeling his power from the grid. The Old Dead bones were funneling a few thousand watts of evil juice straight through the wall—more than enough to leave us with a crispy critter instead of our lead counsel.

"Hey, what are you doing over there?" one of the police officers assigned to the scene shouted to me. She was a young woman—mid-twenties maybe—with her short hair pulled back tight and serious expression on her face. She'd already stepped right through my sigil and was now eyeing me with more than a healthy dose of suspicion.

The glove!

"I need that glove," I said, alternating between the young officer and the killing coil of copper.

"That what?" she said, approaching slowly in that nonchalant-yet-puma-taunt manner that good cops pull off with ease. "What glove?"

I pointed to the wire snake now scant inches from sending untold watts of heart-stopping power into Sharon and her skirt-suit, then to the dust-coated-neoprene glove not far from her boot. "Glove, now!"

"Oh, shit." The officer finally made the connection and tossed the dirty rubber glove to me.

To anyone watching this was just a solid piece of situational awareness. Rubber is an excellent insulator, and jamming it in between these arcing poles should stop the conga-line of electrons rolling down the wire.

Yeah, that's what it *looked* like, but that wasn't what it *was.*

These weren't normal electrons, this was Magick—evil, Old Dead Magick running up from a wall that was saturated in it. The only way to break that flow was with Magick's mortal enemy—science.

I jammed that dirty piece of chemistry between the poles, stuffing it into position and hoping to hell it worked. Sharon and I might not see eye to eye, but she was doing her best to protect her client, and I could respect that—no sense in her getting fried for it.

The surge of evil Magick flickered but still found a way to roll through the expertly crammed neoprene. The live wire reared back for the strike, sparks dripping from its coppery teeth.

I don't get it, the rubber... it's covered with dust, you idiot!

I pulled the glove back out and rubbed the concrete dust off on my shirt before stuffing it back in the control box. I now had a nicely stained white dress shirt, but there was enough science making contact to put a damper on the flow of Magick.

Just like in-laws during the holidays.

The wire snake clattered to the ground, its black body vanishing amid the construction debris. The sound of it falling must have gotten Sharon's attention, because she swung around and motioned to me to get moving.

No, no thanks necessary, all part of my job as the company's resident exorcist.

"Wow, that was close," the young police woman said, admiring my rubber-glove-stuffing skill. "How did you think of that?"

I shrugged. "School, I guess."

The police woman's eyes traced the wires, then she stopped, tilting her head to one side. "Hey, the wires are disconnected, how..."

I didn't turn around to respond, but instead beat a path for Sharon's car. There was no time to explain the physics of Magick—I had a job to do, a pissed-off lawyer to deal with, and now Old Dead in my town.

Life just keeps getting more interesting.

* * *

WE DROVE BACK to the office in silence, and frankly I appreciated it. I had more than enough mental ground to cover all by myself. Somehow in less than twenty-four hours I'd managed to turn my life completely sideways.

I had a daughter who was now starting to experiment with internet Magick; I'd narrowly avoided being murdered by New Dead twice; my apprentice had an Imp I'd accidentally brought back from Hell trapped in a 3D printer I was sure we didn't need; and, to make matters worse, there was a partial Old Dead skeleton being exhumed from the property we were responsible for.

Sharon parked her town car in one of the reserved spaces and we parted ways with little in the way of words spoken. Like a separated couple we'd keep it civil in front of the other employees, but there'd now be a constant undercurrent of frustration.

Just another thing to add to the list—the lawyer didn't like me. I swung by the vending machine on the way to my office, my stomach reminding me I'd missed lunch. I fed the few dollars I had in my wallet in and received a package of salt-coated peanut butter crackers for my efforts.

I opened the door to my office and tossed the opened package on my desk. John might have given me a great opportunity, but he hadn't really set me up with much in the way of a space to work in.

'This used to be the mail room, Gene. Sorry, was the best we could do on short notice.'

This was my fourth year in that office. So much for short notice.

It wasn't that bad—it had a wall covered with tiny wooden cupboards, each one a numbered mailstop for inter-office messages that had long ago been replaced by emails and texts. I'd re-purposed them as a holding place for details on Magickal items, derelict spirits, demonic sightings, and even the occasional coupons for Porter's favorite clothing store. That wall had become a physical representation of my hopes and fears—thank God it had enough boxes to keep up.

I took a seat in the taped-up green chair behind my desk. The desk was an old utility door with a few 4x4s drilled in for legs. I didn't complain. It was solid wood, and I figured in the event of a doomsday scenario—Magickal or otherwise—I'd be safe hiding underneath it.

The chair was another story.

At first I'd accepted it because it was the polite thing to do, and even then I was certain given its age and terrible wear that it had to be Magickal. Perhaps my butt would join the butts of other great men and women in that wondrous green-duct-taped chair of destiny.

Yeah... no.

It was just a swivel chair with a few busted springs. No Magick, no padding, and no way I could sit on it without getting a sharp spring in the backside.

I hated that chair.

This was the time I would have loved to look out a window and take in the majestic Florida afternoon—perhaps admire some sand hill cranes as they grazed in the short grass, or watch the clouds roll in for the afternoon rains, but that would mean I had a window with a view of that. I didn't.

My office offered an exquisite vista of the back parking lot: broken pavement, a towering stack of pallets, and blocking most of that amazing view—a concrete post.

I sighed and returned to the tall stack of papers sitting on my desk.

When I wasn't handling the rare Magickal issue, I'd become

Kinder's only Human Resources representative. These daily missives from the rank and file formed the bulk of my job.

OFFICIAL COMPLAINT - Lunch taken from the fridge. I placed a nice pastrami on rye with...

I picked up my phone and pressed zero. "Marge, let's get that coffee."

17

CREAM, SUGAR, AND CREEPY

*M*arge and I didn't go far. We liked to use the client-entertaining conference room on the first floor. When John Kinder wanted to impress the big bucks, he brought them to that room, so logic would hold that that was where the best coffee would be too.

"Um, Donut Hut, or the good stuff?" Marge asked, spinning the tiny display of plastic single-serve coffee packs.

"Marge…"

"Right," she said, pulling out the secret stash of name-brand pods from inside one of the myriad of cabinets below the counter. "Why did I even ask?"

"Damned if I know," I said, kicking back in one of the plush leather conference room chairs.

Not a single butt-offending spring. Is this how the other half lives?

"What's on your mind, Gene? You look like hell."

Funny you should say that, I opened a portal there last night. Hell is hellish this time of year.

There were a lot of things I wanted to say, but Marge was about as Magickal as dryer lint, so I had to keep this talk well within the realm of the mundane.

"I went to one of Cathy's martial arts classes last night—still feeling it today."

Marjorie smiled—one of those whole-face, room-warming smiles that reminded me how much I enjoyed talking to her. She may not have a lick of Magick in her, but she had mastered the art of friendship, and I was lucky to have her in my life.

"That's a really sweet thing for you to do. That girl is lucky to have a dad like you. I bet she's getting big. Oh, it's been forever since she came in the office. How's she doing in school?"

"She's got a boyfriend," I said, using fancy air-quotes that fit perfectly when talking about Cathy's suitors.

Marge's smile shifted right into a laugh—one of those good-natured kinds that you can't help but join along with.

"Ha! I'm guessing you aren't too keen on that? Still, she's getting older. Why, when I was her age I'd already had multiple boyfriends. One of them talked about us getting married after high school but—"

"Gah! No more!"

"I was going to say that was a different time. Kids these days get to go to college, and from the looks of it, Cathy's more than smart enough to get into just about any school she wants to."

"College? Marge, you're killing me. I just need her to learn how to drive without smashing a mailbox or rolling through someone's garden first. Let's save the college talk for a few years down the road."

"Oh, Gene. It'll be here before you know it. One day you'll wake up and look in the mirror and wonder where all the days went. Trust me."

"Already there," I said, pointing to the gray streaks above my ears. "My family is draining my lifeforce from me."

Marge chuckled and adjusted her mug. "You look dashing, Gene, you always have. I bet Cathy's boyfriend is just the same —tell me all about him."

"I'm still in the information-gathering phase, but I'll let you know as soon as I find out more. I just try not to think about it."

I've got more than enough things to think about right now as it is.

"I get it, but she's growing up. You better look alive before these moments pass you by."

"Way ahead of you. I'm thinking I'll just lock her in the house until college."

Marge took a minute to refresh our mugs. "How's Kris and Porter?"

"Kris is Kris—still loving life, still a ball of energy, and I'm still not positive we're related."

"Oh, I don't know. You aren't one to sit idle."

"Yeah, and neither is Porter..."

"You didn't call me for coffee to shoot the shit about your kids, you want to know about Claudia Wilson."

"Guilty as charged."

"So what do you want to know?"

Is she an evil Magician hell bent on raising an army of New Dead to drive people to her newly remodeled movie theater?

"She's re-opening the Brighton 8 over by Cathy's martial arts school."

Marge rolled her eyes. "So she bought the theater? Doesn't she know that place never makes it? How many times has that thing changed hands? Four? Five?"

"Yeah..."

The receptionist shook her head slowly. "You'd think she'd be smarter with her money..."

"How so?"

"Her husband died a few years ago. Claudia was devastated, but it turned out he'd been hiding a considerable fortune from her, which she ended up with after the funeral."

"Why pour it into an old movie theater?"

"Who knows? Claudia's an odd duck. Then again, she practically went into hiding after Walt died, so it's good to see her out and about again. Still, why do you ask, Gene?"

"Nothing in particular. Like I said, I ran into her yesterday evening after Cathy's class. They did a decent job on the remodel, and I wanted to get some contact details, in case we need a sub-contractor for anything—like you said though, she's an odd duck."

"She just thinks you're out for her money. I wouldn't pay much attention to it."

"True," I said, swirling the last of the coffee in my mug.

"Now," Marge said, leaning forward in her chair. "I want to see some recent pictures of Cathy and Kris—you've been holding out on me."

Like any good dad, I pulled out my phone and swiped through pictures of Porter and the kids. Marge and I shared more than a couple of laughs at how big they'd gotten in just a few short years.

"Wow. Before you know it Kris'll be bigger than Adam."

"He's certainly more active—"

My apprentice!

I'd left him with an extra-dimensional hell beast for—I glanced at my phone—over four hours!

"Sorry, Marge, I've gotta run. I completely forgot about something I was having Adam check on—"

"No problem. I'm just glad someone keeps an eye on that kid."

I crammed my phone back in my pocket and made a mental note to find a little more on Claudia Wilson's dearly departed husband, but first I had to make sure Adam hadn't made any soul-trading deals with the monster currently living in Kinder Construction's only budget-saving 3D printer.

"Gene, wait," Marge said, leaning forward in her chair.

"Yeah?"

The receptionist's voice changed, it shifted an octave,

twisting into something altogether different. She placed a wrinkled hand on mine. "Why didn't you drop by on your way in today? You drove right past without stopping."

"What are you talking about, I didn't drive by—"

The House!

I'd kept 69 Mallory Lane out of my life for so long, yet here it was, right back like it'd never left and inhabiting the body of a dear friend.

"That's the first I've seen you in a long while—almost thought you were avoiding me. You never call, you don't write. What am I to do?"

"Get out of her," I said, placing my hand firmly on top of Marge's.

"I missed this—maybe we should get together more often? What do normal people do today? Whatever, I'll stay in touch. We've got business, you and I…"

"That's not gonna happen."

"What's not gonna happen?" Marge asked, her voice back to its cheerful self.

18

DOOM

he House...

I'd been so careful to avoid it, to stay out of its view, but now all my efforts were out the window. It had found me again.

Marge wouldn't remember anything—the House wouldn't let her—but I knew it wouldn't let me off so easy.

I ran through the empty lobby—most of the staff had already left for the day by the time I'd remembered our Imp problem. No light peeked out from behind the fishbowl's blinds, which only worried me more.

What could he have done?

There were a lot of things Adam could have done, and my hyperactive brain was more than happy to play them out for me. The Imp might have found a way to communicate with him and perhaps offered him the services of a much more powerful entity in exchange for a small trifle—some part of his childhood, maybe? Or his first hoodie? Or perhaps the memory of the first girl he'd kissed, provided such a thing existed—to be honest I wasn't sure.

Imps liked to start small, but then move the stakes quickly

and ramp right up like a fancy casino. The more memories you surrender, the more of your soul you lose. Cast aside too much and you stop being the person you were and start becoming something *different*.

Light flashed through the seams of the darkened blinds followed by the telltale guttural laughter of a demonic entity.

"Adam!" I shouted, banging on the window. "Don't do it, don't give in!"

The Imp's voice grew louder behind the glass; whatever was happening in there it couldn't be good.

The fishbowl's door stayed unlocked during the work day while Adam was inside, but after hours the door locked automatically. I turned the knob only to find the bolt had already engaged.

He wouldn't have left the Imp in the office alone, would he?

I twisted the knob again and banged on the door. "Adam! Let me in."

I received no response for my efforts.

I took a step back and brought up the words of my favorite unlocking spell, then stopped. Imps were exceptional at screwing with Magick—it was part of what made them both dangerous and useful. If that little bastard had wanted to, he could have put all manner of deadly traps on the door just waiting for me to trip them.

"Damn it, Adam! If you are in there let me in! Imps are dangerous."

Still no response.

I grabbed my phone and hammered out a text, hoping to God the Boy Wonder was safe and sound on the other side and cursing myself for leaving a defenseless man-child with a nefarious creature from the fiery lakes of Hell.

Adam, where are you?! Are you safe? Where is the Imp?

I stared at the phone screen, half-ready to throw it across the room. Where could he be? The kid lived at home still—he had plenty of school loans and more than half his take-home cash was driven back into video games—but his mom didn't seem to mind. She let him live in a spare room over the garage rent-free; I think she just liked knowing there was someone else nearby.

More flashing whites and reds lit up the seams between the blinds, followed by the unmistakable gravelly and malevolent laughter of an Imp.

I checked the phone again—no response.

That's it, I'm coming in—Magickal Demon or not.

I placed a hand on the knob and summoned up my best unlocking spell.

"Mihi—"

The phone chirped in my hand, shattering my concentration.

In the office—u still here? I'll unlock the door.

The electronic bolt slid home and I burst into the room with my hands and head ready for anything—well, anything *except* what I walked into.

Adam was seated at his command station wearing an over-sized set of headphones. He had a large assortment of vending machine fare laid out across his desk and all four monitors wired together to display one enormous digital Hellscape. A Cheeto-laden video game controller rested in his orange-tipped fingers—which complemented the cheesy dust on his beard perfectly.

On any other early evening none of this would seem out of the norm, but not this evening. This evening my apprentice had an Imp perched on his head.

The Minor Demon also held a controller in his tiny fingers and was going ballistic on the keys. Periodically he'd smash his pointed tail onto one of the buttons and a series of explosions would flash across the screen.

"Adam!"

My apprentice pushed his headphones back, careful to not disrupt the Imp's game.

"Hey, Gene, what's up?"

"What the hell are you doing?" I'd gone from happy he was safe to ready to throw the kid into oncoming traffic all in the span of about three seconds.

"What do you mean?"

What do I mean!?! You have a denizen of the lower Hells on your head—What do you think I mean!

At that very moment words failed to properly capture the frothing sea of emotions surging below my skin. "Gah!"

"Oh, you mean mister—"

"Stop," I cried, my eyes trying to burn holes in his head, but to no avail.

"What?"

"Do not give him a name."

"It's just a nickname—well, more of a gamertag really. He's like a damn monster on the first-person shooters, bro."

"He *is* a monster!"

"I know, right?"

"Adam, did you name the Imp?"

"No, I know you said not to talk to him and stuff, but we both got *really* bored. Did you know he'd started eating the plastic filament from the printer?"

"You didn't feed him did you?"

"No, he just ate the filament."

"Well, he's an Imp."

"Yeah, but plastic filament? Still, I figured if he was gonna eat the box anyway I might as well take him out."

My hands opened and closed involuntarily, and I was certain my face was turning beet red. "Adam…"

"Whoa, Gene—chill. All I did was fire up a few video games. He wasn't really keen on anything until I turned on Hellfire."

The Imp used his wings as fingers to hit a combination of

buttons and launch fiery digital missiles into the pixilated denizens of video game Hell.

"Just look at him—he's a natural!"

The Imp rattled off a string of insults at his computer-generated opponents—seemed the tiny demon had a few thousand years of pent-up aggression to get out.

"Didn't I tell you…"

"Right, I totally did not try to negotiate with him—heck I don't even know what he's saying—but holy crap, man, can this guy play. I'm thinking I need to get him in a tournament. You know, I bet we could totally clean up."

"Adam—"

"—I'd split the cash with you ninety-ten. I mean, I did teach him how to play, and technically he's using my account which is semi-pro status and has—"

"Adam!"

The Imp completed this level, filling Adam's monitors with an explosion of semi-realistic digital gore, then pumping his tiny fists in the air.

"Way to go—"

"Do not name the Imp!"

"Imp," Adam said, his excitement muted.

"Honestly, what were you thinking?"

My apprentice tilted his head. "Huh?"

"You want it attached to you for life?"

Adam shrugged. "I don't get it—it's just a name, Gene."

"Names have power."

"Yeah, I don't know—"

"How'd it feel when kids called you names in school?" I asked, emphasizing the words perhaps a little harsher than I should have.

Adam's back stiffened. "That's not—"

"The same? Like Hell it isn't. Names change people, and not always for the better."

Adam's face softened. "Sorry."

"You didn't name him, right?"

"Right."

"Good," I said, scooping up the 3D printer box on the floor near Adam's desk—he wasn't kidding, the Imp did appear to have eaten the filament right off the rolls.

You name it, it's yours... for life.

I placed the box on Adam's desk and slid the remaining snack wrappers out of the way.

"Wow, look at the time," I said, pointing to the clock on his screen. "Sure is getting LATE."

"No, it's not, it's like six o'clock. How early do you go to—"

"It's LATE isn't it, Adam?" I said again, this time letting my eyes convey the severity of the message, and for the second time today my apprentice whiffed—hard.

"Gene, I routinely stay up well past—"

"Somnum..." I whispered, running my hand over the Imp's bald head.

He yawned, and stretched, then curled into a ball on Adam's scalp.

"Oh, shit." Adam said, his hands reaching for the diminutive Demon.

"Don't even think about it." I picked up the printer case. "He's coming with me until I can get what I need to send him back to Hell. Get your keys, you're giving us a ride home."

Adam nodded and started digging through his desk for his car keys.

I took one last look at the sleeping demon.

Porter's gonna love this.

19

LAW ESTATE

I had my second silent car ride today, but this time it was a sullen apprentice and not a self-righteous attorney. The end result was still the same though, it gave me time to think.

My most immediate problem was the Imp riding in the back seat. Sure, he was asleep now, but he wouldn't stay that way forever. I needed to get some banishment supplies and try to hunt down the proper sigil—my last Imp banishment had been in college, which was in no way recent.

Then there was the Old Dead. It couldn't have been a coincidence that it should be discovered right around the same time New Dead were popping up like stink on a dead rabbit. I believe in Magick, but draw the line at coincidences.

A Magician's life is never dull.

My apprentice avoided Mallory Lane, but not because he knew it; I'd long ago enchanted his mother's car to avoid the street. It was a side road that few people would have driven on anyway, but our present ride would miss it completely—I'd made certain of that.

I let my mind wander to John Henry's spike, and the yard

sale tomorrow. Magickal items and their yard sales were not for the faint of heart, nor were they easy to find. Adam may not have much in the way of casting power yet, but he was decent with Magickal items, and had a knack for combining his technology skills with an innate Magickal talent. He didn't hack all those computers before I met him through sheer technical skill —he'd used a little Wild Magick. The best part was he hadn't even known it.

Still, there was no way I was bringing him with me to the yard sale; it would be early, and it would be dangerous—the former far more important than the latter.

Sufficient unto the day is the evil thereof.

St. Matthew was one heck of a Magician, but I bet he had wanted to bop a few apprentices in the nose once in a while.

We took another turn, and I checked on the Imp box. We'd found an old hoodie in the back seat and used that to cover the case; like a songbird he'd stayed quiet in the artificial darkness of the smothered printer cage.

I'd have loved to pull over right there and send that Minor Demon back to Hell, but that was how I'd gotten in trouble in the first place. Porter had been right, opening a gate like that was a reckless—albeit impressive—move. The Hell Fleas alone would have been bad enough, had it not been for the destroyed Dad Wagon and the pink monster-in-a-box.

There's an Imp in the back seat, but at least he didn't name it.

Somewhere I knew the cosmos was laughing at me.

Adam pulled up to the house, but didn't turn into the driveway; instead he rolled up against the swale.

"Careful," I said, keeping a sharp eye on the plastic pink flamingo flock that dotted my lawn. "Don't hit the yard art."

The Law Family estate was a simple remodeled bungalow with a sprawling front porch complete with slow spinning ceiling fans. Porter and I had purchased the house not long after I took the job with Kinder. The original owners had been a little difficult to exorcise, but that can happen when your house was built in the early nineteen hundreds—we'd long since cleaned up all the ectoplasm and made it our own. Its mint green exterior and wide front porch gave it a distinct 'Old Florida' feel, and the flock of pink yard ornaments didn't hurt either. A few years ago, we'd swapped the old car port out for a small garage, and I couldn't have been happier. It was great to have a place to keep the car, but it was equally important to have a space for Dad's less-than-savory Magickal problems, such as the Imp currently sleeping in the back seat.

Soft orange light shone out the front windows, spilling out over the porch and its unused rocking chairs, and affording us the perfect silhouette of one Cathy Law, practically plastered to the glass. My daughter's long hair was pulled back in a pony tail, and while I couldn't see her eyes, it was easy to imagine them filled with giddy anticipation. What I didn't have to imagine was the overgrown weeds in front of the porch. Porter had been on me to take care of them for a while, and I'd been all set to get started, but the new pump sprayer was currently in the belly of a disassembled Dad Wagon.

I'd hear about that this evening, but only if I could get a moment's peace. Cathy wouldn't have forgotten our conversation from earlier. I just hoped I'd get enough time to hide the Imp in the garage, since there was no way that thing was coming into the house.

"I'm going to give you a call tomorrow," I said, unclipping my seat belt.

"Oh, wait, Gene, I almost forgot. I did a little digging on the Brighton 8."

"And…"

"There's a record of multiple hauntings at the theater," Adam said, counting them off on his fingers.

"Someone die there?"

"If they did, it never made the official record—I haven't found anything."

"What about the hauntings?"

"They've all appeared in theater eight—same story each time. Whispered sounds, disembodied hands, you know, the standard fare."

"Sounds like a great movie-going experience."

"I know, right? Do you think it's a Thinning?"

"We don't have enough details yet, but it could be. Four hauntings in one place does have me wondering... perhaps the veil between the worlds just needs a little touch-up there—just like nine tenths of the state—nice work, though."

"Thanks, listen I'm sorry about the Imp, I just—"

I waved it away with my hand. "You didn't mistakenly give him a name and officially bind him to you, right?"

"I didn't, I promise."

"Good, cause then I'd have to banish both of you." I gave him a wink then pulled the Demon box out of the back seat. "Oh, and I'm keeping the hoodie."

"But it's one of my favorites—"

"Good night, Adam."

* * *

I HADN'T MADE it halfway up the driveway with the sleeping Imp before the garage door started opening. Heels, curve-hugging dress, arms crossed, beautiful head cocked to one side—my brunette bombshell had remembered date night even if I hadn't. "You're late. Oh, and where's your car?"

That is becoming my anthem.

"I had to leave the car with Rob, and I had a *thing* at the office," I said, holding up the hoodie-covered box.

"What is that?"

"Remember those scratches the other night?"

"Yeah…"

"Well I figured out what they were from."

My wife frowned. "I don't want to know, do I."

"No, I don't think you do."

"Do we need to cancel?" Porter tucked her clutch under her arm and pulled a stray hair away from her face. This had the immediate effect of making my heart race just a touch faster. We'd been together for over ten years and that woman could still get my motor running.

"No!"

"Well what are you going to do with… it?"

That was a really good question. One I hadn't figured out the answer to yet.

"I'm going to leave it in the garage," I said, beating a path to my workbench. It wasn't one of those crafty-dad sort of workbenches with their custom files and precision hand tools laid out in pristine harmony, so much as it was the place my family liked to shove things they didn't know what to do with.

I pushed a few broken toys in dire need of gluing out of the way, along with the microwave Cathy had busted last year when she forgot to take the foil off her lunch burrito, and found a spot for the Imp box.

"Who's babysitting?" I asked, tightening up any loose hoodie edges.

"Cathy."

At the sound of her name our daughter burst in from the house. "You're home!"

That was the first excited greeting I'd gotten from her since she was Kris's age—you'd almost think she wanted something from me. That's right, she did.

"She's been like this all afternoon," Porter said, then pulled the car keys out of her clutch. "I'm gonna back the car out."

"Hello, Catherine," I said, watching Porter's stunning legs climb into the car.

"Dad, it's so great to see you. How was your—wow, what's under the blanket? Is it something Magickal? Is it for me?"

"No."

"No, it's not Magickal? Or no it's not for me?"

I tightened the hoodie—she was right, though, it did appear large enough to be a blanket.

"Cathy, please don't touch this," I said, knowing full well I'd basically just put a neon 'please, touch this' sign on the Minor Demon box.

"I won't."

Sure you won't.

"Good, because the last person that did had all their hair fall out."

My daughter giggled. "Sure, very funny, Dad."

I pursed my lips and picked up my work bag.

"You're kidding, right?"

I let my fingers pantomime hair falling out as I handed her the bag.

"Dad? You're kidding?"

Just keep a straight face...

"Dad?"

Porter beeped the horn.

"Keep an eye on your brother. We'll be home in a few hours."

Porter and I backed out of the driveway as the garage door closed, with our daughter on the other side giving the Imp box a wide berth and checking her ponytail.

20

COFFEE TALK

A small jazz band played in the corner of the dimly lit bistro, filling the room with the wailing notes of a trumpet and a sultry young crooner's baritone pipes.

The sparse crowd did little to fill the restaurant's limited seating, but we weren't surprised; once we'd had kids we'd quickly joined the early bird set. Still, even after two curtain-crawlers and a few gray hairs, 'Date Night' was high holiday, and all but mandatory.

Our college-aged waitress ran down the specials as I sipped at a glass of chardonnay. We knew what we were going to order, but that was no reason to have the young girl skip her prepared speech.

"—in a crushed-pepper cream sauce."

Porter nodded. "We'll just get the salmon."

"Certainly," she said with a hint of disappointment.

I waited for the waitress to move on, then practically squealed with excitement. "We found it."

"You found what?"

"The spike."

"What spike?"

116

I unrolled my napkin and laid it across my lap. "Honey, we found John Henry's final rail-road spike—the last one, the Magickal one Plant and Flagler fought over."

I waited for my words to sink in, but judging by my wife's face, they were more in danger of floating away than sinking.

"I don't understand."

"Mallory Lane."

My wife's face darkened, and she squeezed her fingers around the stem of her wine glass. "Gene, you said you weren't ever going back there—it's too dangerous."

"It *is* too dangerous, but that's why I have to go back. It has to end."

Porter frowned and curled up her lip on one side; it was clear she wasn't convinced. "Don't you think you're taking on a bit much?"

"How so?"

My wife shook her head and let her hair caress those strong shoulders. "Well, let's see. You've been attacked by New Dead once—"

"—twice, actually."

Porter glared at me. "Twice? When did that happen, and when were you going to get around to telling me?"

"This morning."

My wife slammed her glass down. "With the kids in the car!"

"They were fine, I'm fine. The car needs some work, but none of that matters—the spike is here, in Tampa, and I'm going to get it."

My wife's fingers tightened against her glass. "Are you listening to yourself? You've become obsessed."

"But you don't understand—"

"I *do* understand," Porter said, her voice raising ever so slightly. "You're losing perspective. You're missing what's really important here. You're aware your daughter is coming into her Magick, right?"

How did she know that?

My wife could undoubtably see my surprise and continued before I had a chance to respond. "You don't have to be a Magician to check your daughter's phone—she's used the same passcode since forever. What I want to know is why you thought you should hide that from me?"

"I…"

I didn't want you to worry.

"How's everything tonight?" Our waitress said, returning at the exact inopportune moment.

"Fine," we said in near perfect unison—at least we were on the same page with one thing.

"We're supposed to be a team here, Gene."

She's right, you idiot.

"I know—"

"Well then act like it. I don't want to be left in the dark on these things anymore. Cathy's my daughter too, and I want to know when I'll have to start worrying even more about both of you."

A busboy swung by the table and deposited a small wire frame basket of bread. My wife stabbed a petite loaf out of it with viper-like accuracy.

"I'm sorry."

Porter chewed on the bread before responding.

"Good. Let's start again. How was your day, dear?"

I took a long sip of wine before answering.

"What have I told you about Old Dead and Minor Demons?"

* * *

PORTER and I were finishing up the last of our salmon when the waitress came back to see if we wanted coffee.

"Yes, I think so," my wife said, in a much more relaxed tone of voice.

We'd spent the past hour going over the entire day, and while she'd started out more than a little concerned, we'd been game-planning for a while now and had a decent set of options.

"And for you, sir?"

"Sure."

Our waitress left us to walk through the plan one more time while she procured the coffee. By now the restaurant was filling up with young couples, forcing the band to compete with the ambient crowd noise.

"What about the New Dead?"

I folded up my napkin and tossed it on the table. "That's got me stumped. I'm convinced there's something going on at the renovated theater, but I haven't figured out what. So far, though, it's been minor."

"I don't know. We've never had an issue like this before."

I slid my plate over to make it easy for our waitress to collect it. "Maybe, but we did have that poltergeist at the Old Tampa Hotel, remember? During that charity event?"

Porter nodded. "That's not the same. This is different."

I wasn't going to argue with her, because technically she *was* right—a lone poltergeist wasn't the same as what certainly appeared to be a targeted effort.

"So far it hasn't gone beyond individual events, and I've been fine."

My wife pounded her hand on the table. "Fine! Like opening a gate to Hell *fine*? Like narrowly avoiding having your throat ripped out on the highway *fine*?"

"All things we can handle."

My wife tossed her napkin on the table next to mine. "You keep saying that, but at some point you're going to be wrong. At some point it's going to be too much for you, and then what? What happens to the kids, Gene? What happens to me?"

"You're protected."

Porter yanked her ring off her finger and slammed it on the

table. "Protected? Damn it, Gene, you don't understand. I'm worried about *you*! I don't want to see my kids growing up in a world without their dad, as frustrating as he can be sometimes."

"Porter, please put the ring back on…"

Our waitress chose that moment to return with the coffee; she set mine down, and then leaned over to give my wife hers. Those hands hadn't traveled a few inches before someone bumped the young woman from behind and the scalding-hot coffee splashed on to Porter's silky dress. "Ah!"

The young girl grabbed a napkin and tried to dab at Porter's chest. "Oh my God, are you all right? I'm so sorry."

"It was an accident. I—wow that hurts. I'll be right back."

The waitress rushed off to replace the spilled coffee cup while my wife pushed upstream toward the ladies room against a young and increasingly raucous crowd.

She had just disappeared into the darkened hallway past the bar when the telltale stench of New Dead hit me square in the face.

That was the moment I realized Porter's best and only line of defense lay sparkling on the table in front of me.

21

UNMADE

*I*t happened fast.

The pleasant smell of exotic Tapas had been replaced with a burning rot that practically leaked from the walls—it radiated from everywhere, making it next to impossible to narrow down an exact source. To make matters worse, the band switched to a more high-octane set, and the lights dimmed for the younger and decidedly more hip crowd around the bar.

I scooped up my wife's ring. Its Deep Magick hummed in my fingers. Porter might be pretty tough, and downright terrifying with a softball bat in her hands, but against the New Dead she was a lamb to the slaughter.

Shit.

A growing crowd of millennials mixing in front of the bar blocked my way to the restrooms. I pulled my phone out and fired off a quick text.

New Dead. I'm coming.

I hit send and climbed out of the booth, only to hear the clutch she'd left on the seat buzz. I picked it up only to finding an image of my smiling face and the warning text shining up at me.

Shit!

That stupid purse tucked in my hand, I pushed my way toward the bathrooms. The smell of New Dead was overwhelming, hitting me in waves, but still impossible to place. It seemed to be coming from everywhere at once, but in the dark and the mass of bodies I couldn't find a single set of ashen limbs or blackened eyes.

Like the fish we'd just consumed, I found myself swimming upstream against a powerful current of youth and vitality. The formerly subdued band now hit the power chords and rocked their audience with high-intensity sound. This only got the crowd going harder; young men and women blocked my path and danced to the rolling beat. For a brief instant my wife's silken mane appeared in the space between the bump and grind.

"Porter!"

She turned to face me, and for a narrow moment her eyes stared back at me, ringed with fear and uncertainty. I lost those eyes for a just a second behind the crowd, but when I caught them again, my heart froze—black pools of a near infinite hatred greeted me from beyond the crowd.

A dress that just moments ago exposed hints of beautiful skin now gave me an eyeful of newly ruined flesh—smoldering and falling away like cigarette ash on a windy day.

New Dead possessed the love of my life.

"Porter!"

The dead thing riding shotgun smiled, showing me charred teeth and cracking gums, then headed for the door.

It has Porter...

I tried to shake off that thought, but it beat on my skull like a bass drum—I had to break the possession before she got away. I scooped the salt shaker off the nearest table and pushed my way after her. In hindsight that's when I should have noticed it. The

New Dead are often lone wolves, but can work together if properly motivated. A pack of them is a scary thought, and I had now firmly planted myself in exactly that—a pack.

I wasn't ready for the first punch, it caught me off guard and blasted into that soft spot just below my ear. The restaurant spun sideways. I lost the purse, and my balance, falling over only to be caught by the hands of our young waitress—her burning, ash-covered hands.

The she-dead slammed a bare knee into my man parts and ejected what little air there was still left in my lungs. I crumpled onto the hard tile, gasping for breath with one hand on the salt and the other on my wife's ring.

That's when the kicking started.

Dress shoes, heels, boots—my attackers landed blow after blow with wild fury. I scrambled for the table, but our waitress-turned-demon-child slammed a tray across my hands and broke the top off the salt shaker. I tossed the salt at her feet, my blood mixing the fine white granules into a pinkish powerhouse of dispelling Magick.

"Relinquo," I said through bloodied lips, letting the Magick flow from my bruised fingers.

The circle wasn't perfect, but it didn't have to be. The New Dead roared out of our waitress and up into the air, no doubt headed for a new host. The young woman crumpled like a spent balloon and I dragged her with me beneath the table.

I still held the ring in my hand, squeezing it tight between my fingers and letting the Deep Magick I'd invested in it wash over me. It was useless, the enchantment had been designed for Porter—it wouldn't help me any more than her dress would have fit my ill-inspired frame.

The New Dead were everywhere—too many to count. There wasn't enough salt in the bar to contain them, and I didn't have the strength for a gate to Hell big enough to haul them away. Mercifully the booth table was bolted down, but that didn't stop the hands from clawing at us, nor did it stop the kicks and stomps.

The waitress's eyes fluttered. "Eugene…"

Her voice wasn't the voice I remembered telling us the specials; this was a soft voice, barely audible over the screams of the New Dead—this was the House.

"Not now," I said, tearing a burnt hand off my wrist.

"I don't suppose you want to hear the specials?"

Large arms shot in under the table, followed by an equally massive body that wielded those arms like steel tongs to wrap my neck and squeeze.

"No—" I said, using what little air I had left.

The waitress frowned and brushed her hair out of her face. One of the New Dead grabbed her arm to pull her free from under the table, but she crushed its bones like I'd crumple a beer can.

The strangling New Dead pushed its way under the table and on top of me, pinning me down with tremendous force. The waitress adjusted her apron and lay down beside me, the bruises on her face healing beautifully. "So, is this fun or what?"

"Not… what… I—"

"All this excitement. New Dead! In Tampa! I knew if I was just patient it would all work out, I just knew it—and here we are again, Gene. It's like old times. Now, are you sure you don't want to hear the specials?"

I pounded on the undead hands crushing my neck, but they didn't budge, instead pinning me to the ground like rebar.

"Ah—"

"Excellent! First, we have the seared and sundered Magician, it's a house specialty. It comes with a side of possessed wife and pureed child souls. We're running a double side for free on that one. I won't say it's a favorite of mine, but who knows, it might be *your* favorite."

My vision dimmed, the edges fading away like burning

paper. One by one those distorted faces melted until all that was left were the hands crushing my throat and the waitress's smiling face.

"Stay with me, big guy—you haven't heard the second special," the waitress said, slapping a hand against my numb cheek. "It's a power-packed breakfast. Yeah, yeah, breakfast for dinner is hip to the point of lame I know, but you look like a guy who could use a nice pick me up. So what do you say? You ready to break bread with me?"

"No…"

I gave up clawing, I gave up fighting, I let the darkness slip over me like a warm blanket. Porter's ring bit into my palm, but I didn't care, I squeezed until my knuckles turned white.

"Here I am, offering to make you whatever you want, and all you can say is 'no.' How about a little gratitude, huh?"

Make… Made—that's it, the ring!

My blood mixed with the cheap plated gold of Porter's ring and the hum of Deep Magick shook my body.

"What are you doing, Eugene? That's not on the menu."

It is now.

There was only one option left that kept me and my head attached, and not a slave to 69 Mallory Lane—the ring had to be unmade.

22

PARKING LOT LOVER

I squeezed the ring deeper into the meaty flesh of my palm and tried to find the strength to undo its power. Blood trickled over the tiny diamond setting and down my arm.

"Now, now. Let's not get crazy here," the waitress said, her voice softer now. "Even if you survive an unmaking, what happens to Porter? What about that loving wife of yours, unprotected out in the world? You wouldn't risk your sweetheart, would you?"

Deep in my oxygen-depleted gray matter I knew the House was right—unmaking was nothing short of insanity, and without Lenar's Logic Loop, Porter would be exposed to all the evils of the supernatural world. Still, I had to try.

The waitress placed her soft hands on my face. "Oh, for the love of all things unholy. You are such a pain in the ass, you know that?"

Funny, that's practically the exact same thing Mom used to say.

A surge of energy flooded my body and caught me completely off guard. It hit me like that first cup of coffee in the morning—times a thousand. I ripped the New Dead arms off my neck like snapping dry branches, innocent bones crushing under the newfound power humming in my hands. The pain vanished, and an inhuman strength swelled in its place. Technically I hadn't agreed to anything, but the power felt so good, so right, it was next to impossible not to scream out for more.

"Feels damn good, doesn't it?" the waitress said, her whispered words tickling my ear. "And that's just a taste, wait till you get the full course. So what do you say, Master Magician? You ready to wear the big-boy pants?"

I wanted to say it sounded horrible, but when the next punch slammed into my head I lost my words, and almost lost my way.

"You..."

"Yes?"

"You can go to Hell," I said, kicking back at the mass of New Dead clawing for me under the table.

"You're impossible—but I'm totally down for impossible causes. We'll be together. You are exactly what I need..."

"I said, go to Hell!" I shouted, turning my head to find the waitress unconscious on the tile floor.

The House was gone, but it had left me with enough to survive an unmaking.

I hope.

There was no way to safely unmake a Magickal item—it simply didn't work that way. My memories were bound up in that ring, tight as a drum and powering the Magick that had kept Porter safe. To unmake it now meant sacrificing those memories and willfully setting fire to each one, then letting it burn away to be lost forever. After that, even if you got all that right, you had to be ready for the blowback; you'd be releasing a lot of Wild Magick—which had a fifty-fifty chance of searing your face off.

So, who wants to be a Magician? Anybody?

I squeezed the ring in my fingers and kicked away at the

clawing New Dead. The memory of our first date queued up in my mind—pizza at Leonard's by the Slice just off campus. We'd been kids ourselves, not much older than Cathy. Still, I knew then what I knew now; I didn't want to let this one go.

A young Porter's smile burned away at the checker-cloth table in my mind.

I squeezed the ring tighter and let its Magick flood my hand and race up my arm—a warm and tingly feeling that quickly shifted from oddly unpleasant to nigh unbearable.

"Irritum Facit!"

The ring melted away in my fingers, freeing the memory I'd sacrificed and with it the Magick bound up in the cheap jewelry. One by one the still frames of that night turned to ash in the fire of my mind: her hair, the smell of her skin, and at last the heart-stopping twinkle of her eyes in the dark. "Argh!"

The resulting surge was far beyond the House's gift—this was love, and love meant sacrifice.

An explosion of blinding white light erupted from my body. I was a one-man pyrotechnic show. Wild Magick roared through me like a live wire and flooded the room with tremendous force. Glass shattered and tables overturned. The booth we'd huddled under tore free of its mooring and crashed into the bar, taking several of the New Dead with it.

I couldn't control it, I couldn't direct it, and I couldn't contain it. This was Wild Magick, and like a river that jumped its banks, it was without bounds. It surged over the New Dead caught in its tide and dragged them under waves of pure energy, their scorched flesh fading like dust in the wind. My hand throbbed, and I tried to drop the ring, but those fingers remained closed—the uncontrolled fury of Wild Magick kept them shut and the torrent coming.

It wanted more—more memories, more soul, more me. The Wild Magick wanted out—it was tired of being trapped in my body—and sensing the outlet it blew out a sidewall: flirting with

Porter in history, her short-shorts and wry smile calling me to action—burned away in a flash of Wild Magick, racing across campus on an old rusty bike, hoping to catch her before her last class of the week—melted away in a surge of Wild Magick.

No! Stop!

But it didn't stop. The fiery waves of cosmic power wouldn't cease, not unless I found the strength to end it. Glasses exploded and bottles shattered; the bistro had become a mini-cyclone of debris. Innocent people had to have been injured in this onslaught.

What have I become? Was the House right?

I pounded my hand against the floor, raining down my fist and praying for the strength to make it stop. My fingers loosened, bloody and bruised; they still held the last vestiges of the ring and weren't yet ready to give it up. One last memory flooded my mind. This time it wasn't Porter—it was the girl who'd come before her. The one I'd left for greener pastures, the one that had taken me down a dark and twisted path, the one that had showed me just how terrifying Magick could be.

Morgan's tears burned away in the searing fire of Wild Magick as the melted remains of a once-great Logic Loop dripped onto the cracked tile floor. The Wild Magick vanished, and with it went the New Dead.

I willed myself up and limped for the door, hoping to God that Porter was still close, and in one piece.

* * *

I HADN'T HIT the street before I found her.

My wife had her blackened tongue deep in the valet's mouth. With a hand down his loose pants and the other pushing his head into hers, she rubbed her body against him. Together they gyrated on the curb like the opening scene from some cheap porno.

The stench of New Dead was overwhelming, and I knew this wasn't Porter, but seeing your wife with another man was just too much to take. Still riding the high of surviving an unmaking I lashed out with my Magick and sent a pen from the valet stand rocketing into the young kid's thigh. His muffled scream was lost in Porter's gaping mouth as he clutched at the pen jutting out of his leg.

What are you doing? He's just a kid!

The unmaking made it hard to think straight and that coupled with the New Dead riding my wife, meant I wasn't firing on all cylinders.

Porter tossed her parking lot lover aside and turned to smile at me, her bloody tongue licking cracked lips. "I told you I'd be back."

"Get out of her now!"

I reached for my wife, but she backed up toward the street, her heels now only feet away from traffic.

"Not so fast," the New Dead said, grabbing my wife's breasts and squeezing them. "So good... Come on, let's you and me have some fun. I bet this body rocks like a metal concert."

"Hurt my wife and I'll destroy you."

"Those are strong words coming from a man in khakis. How did you even get a girl this smoking hot? She damaged in the head? I bet she's some nut-case right? Doesn't know what a real man looks like?"

Anger surged, and I reached for my Magick, but found it waning. The unmaking had taken too much, and I'd just used what little I did have to stab an innocent kid—the tank was coming up empty, and going too much farther might be my undoing.

"Porter! You've got to fight it. I know you're in there somewhere. This isn't you. Push that thing aside and take the wheel."

My wife's blackened eyes stared back at me—cold and soulless. I found nothing of the woman I loved in them.

"Sorry, Charlie, she can't hear you. I got her down deep, on her knees and giving it to me right." The New Dead pushed my wife's broken lips into a tight 'o.' "Yeah, she knows how to suck —you musta taught her right. I bet you've sucked a few in your day too."

"Let her go!"

My possessed wife flung her hair back. "That's exactly what I'm gonna do. Don't get me wrong, she feels good—all silky smooth—but I've got a job to do, working for the man and all..."

"Who? Who are you working for?"

The New Dead didn't answer me; instead, it kicked off the curb and threw Porter's body into oncoming traffic.

23

DON'T FORGET ME

*M*ovies love to show time slowing down when something really terrible happens. That's a load of crap. If anything it ramps up to warp speed.

Porter's body hit the street hard, her head snapping against the concrete like a rag doll. With cars coming fast I didn't stop to think. I threw myself onto the road behind her, scraping my knees on the pavement and flailing my hands in a desperate attempt to break her fall.

The spirit was willing, but the flesh—especially my flesh—was weak.

The New Dead vaulted out of Porter like a teenager springing from the pool. He tossed his translucent frame up and on to the still-warm pavement without giving me a second glance.

I made a half-hearted grasp for his leg, but came up short. My bigger concern was Porter, and while I would have loved to know who was running this New Dead circus, I wasn't going to risk my wife for it.

I considered Magick, but had barely enough left in the tank to hold up my pants let alone grab on to New Dead. Unattached I knew he couldn't go far—the New Dead can't do much without a host—but he didn't have to, he had a ride waiting. A large white van shot by, going the opposite direction. He latched on to a hand hanging out that van's open window and shimmied in as the vehicle roared past.

Taillights whipped by, and if I'd been thinking clearly I might have remembered to get the license plate, but my brain was on tilt.

Porter!

I scooped her into my arms and tried to drag her back toward the curb. Limp in my hands, she flopped like a wet noodle. Bright lights of an oncoming car flooded my vision, and like a deer on the highway I froze. Somewhere deep in the dark crevasses of my mind a scared voice screamed out for help.

I'll make the deal! Whatever you want, just save my wife!

But there was no response—we were alone.

The headlights bore down on us, and I knew there wasn't enough time to get back to the relative safety of the curb. With my Magickal reserves all but spent, there would be no fantastical escapes, no grand portals to safety, no brilliant displays of cosmic power. We'd die tonight beneath the grill of that steel beast, our bodies crushed by tires and our children lost to a series of foster homes. My mind played through a thousand scenarios in the span of seconds, showing me the tapestry of possibilities my poor kids could face.

I squeezed Porter tight against my chest and let go of our future. We'd never grow old together.

Old!

I'd said before, but Magick is about belief, and sometimes you don't need much to make those beliefs come true—especially if they're damn plausible.

I wrapped one arm around my unconscious wife and extended the other toward the oncoming car.

"Obliviscatur," I said, willing the last scrapes of Magick left in me toward the driver seconds away from crushing us.

Forget...

The car's brakes squealed on the smooth pavement. Its front end dipped, pulling down as the car tires tried desperately to cling to the road. I closed my eyes, certain that this was the end, and tried to shield my wife from the worst of it.

I held my breath—nothing.

I peeked out to find the car's front bumper bobbing gently in front us, mere inches from Porter's bloodied face. I exhaled, clutching my wife with shaking arms as the adrenaline wrecked my nerves.

Thank you...

The driver door opened and a pair of pristine white loafers stepped into view. A brilliant and confusing pair of wild-print argyle socks rose up from those loafers, then vanished under the cuffs of some of the most elaborate plaid pants I'd seen since my days working at the golf course.

"I'm telling you, Irma Lee, it's right here. This is the place."

Another voice, from the sound of it a member of the same generation, bellowed from the passenger seat. "Damn it, Omar, you can't just stop the car in the middle of the road. Get your butt back in the seat and pull us into the parking lot."

Horns blared and more cars ground to a halt behind Omar's Lincoln.

"I'll have you know this is a perfectly fine place to stop."

It sure is.

"They're honking at you, you idiot. Get back in the car."

The white loafers moved back toward the car, then stopped and resumed a rather defiant pose. "I will not."

Before our unlikely savior could change his mind, or the adrenaline left me entirely, I scooped up my unconscious wife and carried her to the curb.

"Get out of the damn road, you ninny! You're going to get us killed," the passenger shouted.

Omar stood his ground. "I will not, you are allowed to park on the curb, and that's exactly what I'm doing."

The driver door slammed shut in time with the faint hum of a window rolling down.

Irma Lee continued to berate her husband as I carried Porter past them and into the parking lot.

I whispered a silent prayer, thanking them for forgetting at just the right moment. Magick was funny that way, sometimes the best results were the ones that you'd never guess were Magick in the first place.

Porter's head leaned against my chest, my shirt wicking up the blood rolling down her temple. Her chest moved softly against mine—I knew she was alive, but I had no clue just how much damage she'd sustained.

I found our car keys on the abandoned valet stand. With Porter's car unlocked, I laid my wife gently in the back seat.

We pulled out of the far side of the lot to avoid the backup Omar and my impromptu Magick had created. Traffic was light, making it easy to merge onto the street and then onto the highway. I pushed the pedal down and sped off toward the emergency room, unable to stop checking on Porter in the rear-view mirror every few seconds.

Magick has one singular truth—it demands sacrifice, and it doesn't give a damn who from.

Come on, honey—stay with me.

24

STITCHES AND FIXES

I didn't get more than a few feet inside the automatic doors before the nurses had my wife and started peppering me with questions. One of them must have noticed my cuts, which had already begun to diminish thanks to the gift from an unwanted benefactor, and pulled me into a separate room to get them stitched up.

"Is she going to be okay?" I asked, rolling up my sleeves.

"We'll do our best."

That was fair—not what anyone wants to hear, but fair. There was no way to know what sort of injuries my wife had sustained. I knew she'd taken the pavement hard, but there was no telling what else the New Dead had subjected her to before that.

"Do you have someone you should call?"

Oh my, God—Cathy!

I let my nurse get her tools together and pulled out my phone. My loving daughter had already sent me a text.

Hey Dad, can I have the last of the ice cream?

It's funny how the things that seem important one minute pale in the next.

I punched up her number and let it ring; this was not something you text.

"Hey, Dad—before you ask I left you some cookies and cream."

"Cathy."

I didn't know what to say. How do you tell your daughter that her mother was just possessed by a spirit of the damned, ridden like a plow horse, and tossed into the street?

"Yeah? How's the date night?"

If she was really coming into her Magick, then my daughter was going to have to know about all these things: the Imp in our garage, Old and New Dead, and even 69 Mallory Lane.

I wasn't ready for any of that.

I took a deep breath. "It's fine. I need you to do something for me."

"Sure."

"Is the house locked?"

"Ah…" Cathy let her response draw out while she went from door to door.

Click. Click.

"Yup. All locked up."

"What about the garage," I asked, seeing the nurse glance at her watch. "Is the garage door locked?"

"No. Do you want me to lock it?"

"Yes."

"Dad, what's wrong?"

"Just do it, Cathy."

Click.

"Done. Is Mom there?"

The nurse loaded a small syringe.

"I have to run, Cathy. Just, I need to know, do you have your necklace on?"

"Yeah, but I was going to ask you if I could—"

"Is your brother's bracelet on?"

"I think…"

The nurse injected a small amount of local anesthetic in my cheek.

"Damn it." I switched the phone to my other side.

"Dad, what's wrong? You're scaring me."

"Good, you should be scared. This isn't something to go texting about while you're at school. This is serious, deadly serious, and I need you to focus. You're going to become a target, Catherine, and I know for a fact you aren't ready for what that entails."

"Where's Mom, is she okay?"

The fear was rampant in my daughter's voice, and I knew I'd gone too far.

"She'll be fine," I said, trying to turn my face so the nurse could get her needle through the skin. "She just took a bad fall, and we stopped at the ER to get her looked at."

"What?!"

"Listen, whatever you do, don't take off those charms, either you or your brother, and do not go in the garage until I get home. Do you understand me?"

"Yes…"

My headstrong daughter's voice had never sounded so small, or so weak before.

Magick has a price.

"Good, I've got to go. We'll be home when we can. Do not open the door for anyone."

"Yes, Dad."

"Cathy, I love you."

"I love you too, Dad, I'm sorry about the texts, I'll forget all about Magick."

"No, you won't—your mother and brother need you. We'll talk about it later, sweetheart."

"Okay."

I hung up and let the nurse finish her stitches. I knew they'd fall out on their own by tomorrow. Magick does strange things to the body, and even without the gift from Mallory Lane I knew I'd heal up faster than a normal person.

I thought long and hard about that while I waited for word on Porter—she had no such power, and her ring was now unmade, meaning I might as well be ringing the dinner bell for the dark things that prowl just beyond the shadows hungry for innocent flesh.

I'd spent my entire marriage keeping my wife—and later my children—safe, and all of that hard work had spiraled out of control in the last forty-eight hours: Cathy was finding her Magick, what I thought had been a few stray spirits appeared to be a well-organized hunting party of New Dead with the Law family in their crosshairs, and now my beautiful wife lay unconscious in the emergency room. All of this on top the Minor Demon in our garage, Old Dead being unearthed, and John Kinder's attorney wanting me out on the street.

Maybe Porter was right. Maybe I'd taken on way too much—maybe I'd gotten too sure of myself and lost sight of what was really important.

The nurse wrapped up and placed a bandage over her stitch work, then ducked out the door, letting me know she'd go check on my wife.

The dark phone screen reflected my bruised and bandaged face.

You can't do it all, Gene. It's only a matter of time before you won't be there to save them.

I tugged at the edges of the bandage and peeled up enough to see the gash reflected in my phone.

I can't put Cathy through this—but can I really stop it from coming?

There was nothing I could do. Cathy and Magick were on a collision course, and once they reached critical mass we'd have even worse things banging down our door. I couldn't stick my head in the sand and hope that it all passed, nor could I lay enchanted baubles on my family and hope they stay safe from the darkness that thrived in my world.

Cathy needed to be trained, and we'd start tomorrow—we had an Imp to deal with, after all.

"Mr. Law? Your wife is conscious, and she's asking for you."

25

SEAL OF ARIADNE

*P*orter didn't remember anything after the coffee spill. This was both a blessing and a curse; she couldn't tell me anything about the New Dead that had possessed her, but any reminder of the possession would have been crippling for my wife, and she'd find a way to blame herself.

The doctor explained concussion protocols to us, but to be honest I was only half-listening. The other half of me was too busy trying to determine where we'd go from here. We had more than a few problems to contend with, but after tonight the New Dead had rocketed to number one on that list.

We drove home in silence, my wife staring absently out the window, her knuckles white against the dark and torn folds of her dress. We pulled into the garage, and I shot around to the passenger side to help her out of the car. Porter leaned on me, her body cold and fragile in the humid evening air. Together we slipped past a sleeping Cathy and into the master bedroom.

"Honey, are you—"

She brushed me off. Porter didn't want to talk, she only

wanted to lie down. I helped her peel out of her dress and into pajamas. She shoved the wad of silky fabric into my hands.

"Burn it," she whispered, then crawled into bed.

Lying there under the sheets she looked so small and fragile —the tough-as-nails woman I married was like an exposed raw nerve that hurt to touch.

I woke Cathy up and helped her to her room. She was too tired to ask questions, but I knew they would be there tomorrow—too many to count.

With the rest of the family asleep I checked all the doors. True to her word my daughter had made sure they were locked. Those locks would keep the burglars and robbers at bay, but more than that they'd keep the supernatural solidly on the other side of the door. There were rules when it came to homes, and I used them all to make sure mine was well fortified.

Satisfied the Law Family estate was on lockdown I crawled into bed beside my wife and shut my eyes. Sleep was elusive. An hour dragged by as I listened to the quiet of the house, my restless mind studying the problem from every angle.

This wasn't a random or uncoordinated spiritual mob—this was a direct assault.

You're in no position for projection. Wait until morning.

The logical half of my brain was right, but after an hour spent listening to that wet blanket, along with Porter's labored breathing, I gave up. I slipped out of bed and into the living room.

Kris's toys consumed the shaggy rug that dominated our family room. Quiet as a church mouse I removed the bright plastic cars one at a time. Careful to remember the ones with batteries and blaring noise-makers, I turned them off first, then lined everything up against the wall. We used to have a coffee table, but after Cathy was born and we watched her tumble head-first into one of the corners, that devil-desk ended up at the end of the driveway for the garbage men. Now the rug was easier to get to, but I still hadn't touched the Magic underneath it in years—the Gloom was serious business, and more than a little dangerous—yet I needed to get past Claudia Wilson, and that dark place was my best option.

I peeled back the edge of the rug slowly, letting the ragged end curl up on itself, and create a man-sized cigar roll of dust and dander next to the cars along the wall. I blew off the stray cheerios and flecks of glitter to reveal, in exquisite detail, the only sigil I considered myself any good at making, the Seal of Ariadne. I crawled into the center of the swirling lines and symbols, planted my tired butt and exhaled.

You dummy, you're too spent to do this.

Porter mumbled something in her sleep from our bedroom, and while I couldn't understand the words, the pain was evident in her addled voice even down the hall.

No. I'm doing this.

Ariadne—the girl and her string. History hadn't been kind to that young Greek woman, but she had left us one heck of a useful Magickal sigil. Ariadne's ball of string had been instrumental in keeping Theseus from being lost forever in the Minotaur's maze—having met a Minotaur once while vacationing in Crete, I would have been a lot nicer to Ariadne. Still, whether she was real or not, the seal was ascribed to her, and was the fastest way to travel light.

I let the seal's Magick wash over me like the gulf at low tide —a soft lapping wave, it soothed my wounds and pulled the tension from my muscles. I took a deep breath, and placed my hands one inside the other, then let my lungs swell with Ariadne's Magick.

There was a gentle pop, and then the sensation of flight. I opened my eyes to find myself staring down at my quietly seated body. I was happy to see my hair wasn't thinning on top —you don't normally get to see these kinds of things—which was a short-lived but welcome relief. Streaming down from my translucent form to my body lay a softly billowing silver cord. I was free from my mortal coil, but like an astronaut on a mission in deep space I was tethered to the physical me which was still seated and breathing quietly in the Seal of Ariadne. Much like the Greek girl's string, this silver thread was the only way to make it home again. Without it I'd be lost to the Gloom, a revenant buffeted by the winds of darkness. Who was I kidding, though? Before that happened I was sure to be eaten by something with a taste for modestly aged Magician soul—the Gloom was full of just that kind of hungry.

I floated into Cathy's room, passing through the wall with ease and stopping only momentarily to admire the complex mess that was my daughter's closet. Cathy lay quietly sleeping beneath the sheets, her soft face turned away from me in the dark of the room.

You see things differently detached from the Gloom. With the masks of flesh and bone gone, the true souls of things are laid bare. My daughter's Magick swirled like a bubbling brook just beneath her skin, rich colors shining through in vibrant purples and blues. Cathy would be a force to be reckoned with one day—I just prayed I'd taught her enough to make sure she played for the right team.

I drifted into Kris's room to watch the smallest member of the family sleep. His bed was like a puppy mound of stuffed animals, making it difficult to locate the littlest Law. Thankfully, he rolled over and knocked an overstuffed Akita to the floor, giving me a chance to see his sleepy smile. I brushed a translucent hand over it and would have tousled his hair had I substance to tousle with.

Satisfied the children were safe, I pushed through the wall and left them to restful sleep, descending instead into the master bedroom. The sadness was suffocating—thin stabs of moonlight sliced through the blinds and fell across my wife's tortured form. Her soul was caught in a fitful and restless slumber. Slender glowing fingers would clutch at the sheets, then release them again in unceasing frustration. In a fit of desperation her spirit cried out and sat up—eyes looking without seeing, locked in a thousand-yard stare of unreconciled pain.

I placed a translucent hand on hers and held it, willing what tranquility I could to still her fearful soul. She turned over, dark hair covering her face, and her soul lay back with her.

I let go of her hand and hovered there for a moment, gathering my strength. I needed all I could get where I was headed. I closed my eyes and painted the picture in my mind, holding tight to Ariadne's thread—it was time to pay a second visit to the Brighton 8.

Let's all go to the lobby...

26

AFTER MIDNIGHT SHOWING

$\mathcal{N}$arrow spotlights of orange cast from humming street lamps cut through the damp parking lot in the pre-dawn hours. I willed my translucent form down to the street level and coasted gently between the spaces. There were no cars in the lot, but given the time of day that wasn't unexpected. The jiu-jitsu school didn't do much business at two AM, and neither did the Yarn Barn—both of which appeared relatively normal even in the Gloom. This was a welcome relief, as there was no way to tell what dwelled in either place in this dark and twisted half-world.

The Brighton 8 was another story entirely. Claudia's crews had put in a serious effort, raising a fifties-era art déco sign above the box office windows, complete with chaser bulbs and a considerable amount of neon. At least that's how all of it would have looked if it were on, and if I weren't floating in the Gloom holding on to Ariadne's thread like a life-preserver.

Here in this world, it was on fire.

Broken chaser bulbs dripped sparks from blackened bases, and flames licked at the edges of the melted sign. Smoke billowed from the box office windows, rolling out in thick clouds of noxious black. Soot covered the glass doors to the lobby, and even the metal frames bent under the heat. The building itself was bent and warped, pulling away from the foundations like melted wax. In fact, the Gloom version of the Brighton 8 appeared to have received the brunt of a blow torch. I floated closer, keeping Ariadne's thread safely behind me and out of harm's way—I had no desire to risk losing my way home.

The lobby doors bowed out as if struggling to contain the roaring heat behind them. I placed a translucent hand against the hazy glass and pulled it back quickly, shaking off the searing heat.

Here goes nothing.

I pushed my way through the warped doors and right into the fires of Hell.

* * *

I'D BEEN inside the theater before, but here in the Gloom it was a far different place. Flames licked the walls, dancing in conga lines of whipping orange and red. The carpet itself more resembled molten rock than the movie-star red of the real world.

Would have made it easy to play 'The Floor is Lava' when Cathy was little. Except falling in would likely burn away your immortal soul—yeah, no good.

The pictures that had been propped against the wall were melted and broken. Their frames were crumpled and the oily canvases beneath them wadded and scorched. I whipped a few loops of Ariadne's thread around my hand and let the silvery cord float gently behind me. The lifeline might have had an infinite length, but something told me to keep it close.

I floated past Claudia's office. A small bonfire roared on the desk; papers and books burned in equal measure in that cramped office and sent thick plumes of noxious smoke into the air.

I pushed my way farther into the theater, and the deeper I went the higher the heat became. I knew at home my poor body must have been sweating like crazy, and soon the temperature would become too much, but I wasn't about to turn around yet —not with my wife's tortured face filling my mind. I floated past the open caskets and burned-out display, which had no doubt been arranged as part of a promotional pitch for the upcoming film. The lid of one of them was open, but at this angle I couldn't see much beyond the burnt edges of the lining —not without getting closer.

"Hey, Gene," said a light and airy voice, intermixed with spurts of coughing. "Wow, you just find all the best places, don't you?"

The burned body of Claudia Wilson sat up in the coffin. Her face was charred and ashen, with streaks of skin like bubbled wax. Something formless shifted behind the old woman's parchment skin, something I knew very well.

The House.

"Whoa, man, would you just look at this place?" Claudia took a deep breath and coughed again, this time dislodging bits of her nose. "Huh, they just don't make manifestations like they used to."

"I don't have time for this."

Claudia nodded, her neck bones crackling. "You're always short on time. Sort of comes with the whole mortality thing, eh?"

I floated past Claudia, ignoring her uncoordinated attempt to climb out of the casket.

"Should have thought this through a little better," the malignant manifestation said before tumbling to the ground and propping herself up on creaky joints. "Yeah, next time I'm going with something more coordinated. Your imagination leaves a lot to be desired."

The concession stand was a smoldering wreck. The popcorn

machine's painted sides were browned and bubbled, and the scrollwork edges had been burned beyond recognition. I pushed deeper into the theater. "What are you doing here?"

"Gauging my investment," Claudia said, somehow now holding a bag of mostly burned popcorn.

"I'm not your investment."

The broken manifestation shuffled along behind me, her bones popping with each step. "Well, actually, you kinda are. I mean, who took care of you in the fiery dark of the library? Who checked on your ruined hands in—"

"Don't—"

"That would be *me*. Who has been there for you through it all, Eugene Law?"

I willed myself forward, past the theater doors and deeper down the fiery tunnel. Claudia's voice echoed in the narrowing hall behind me, intermixed with the snapping of burnt tendons. "Me again!"

I tried to ignore her, and instead focused my attention on the individual theaters. Each door was dark—except for one.

Lucky number eight.

Flames flickered along the door seam, and the metal push plate glowed a bright red.

"*Demon High...* They did a remake?" Claudia rolled her partially detached eyes. "Couldn't just leave well enough alone. The original was a classic—inspirational story-telling."

"Demons and cheerleaders?"

Claudia nodded, her boney jaw popping on the burnt corn kernels. "Yep, *inspirational*."

"I'm going in."

"Actually, I think it's time you headed back, Gene. Ariadne's thread's getting a little crispy around the edges and all."

"No." I floated closer to the door. "I'm not leaving until I find out what's on the other side."

"You read the story about the cat, right?"

The Claudia-shaped house was right, Ariadne's thread *did* look a little worse for wear, but I hadn't come this far to turn back now. I had to know what lay on the other side of that door.

I pushed my translucent form through the flame-kissed wood, holding tight to the silvery cord while wondering if I was ready for what lay on the other side.

27

INNOCENCE, IT'S WHAT'S FOR DINNER

A gob-smacking Claudia leaned against the wall on the other side of the door. "Would have been nice of you to open it for me, you know, chivalry and all—"

"You aren't human."

"Ah, I see. So politeness doesn't extend to—"

"No, it doesn't extend to things like you," I said, floating past the mostly burned woman and down the narrow hall toward the seats.

The projector's flickering beam cut through the smoke and ash of the theater, covering the silver screen with what I could only guess was *Demon High*.

"I know we're from different worlds, but why won't you go to Prom with me?" said a forlorn high school boy, his face tinged purple and his head sporting a pair of curving horns.

"What the—"

Claudia pushed her way past me. "I remember this part... 'We aren't from different worlds—we're from different planes of existence. It'll never work, Trevor,'" the manifestation said, quoting the cheerleader who appeared just off frame.

"This is a thing?"

Claudia nodded. "Yeah—we're human too, you know."

"No, you aren't."

"Right, but we do have feelings."

"Murderous feelings?"

"They count."

It was my turn to roll my eyes, then investigate the theater itself. The seats were empty, but a decent number of seat bottoms were flipped down, as if someone was sitting in them.

I willed myself higher, passing through the projector's beam while the film continued to play.

"But Cindy—"

"No, Trevor, I'm going with Bryan. He's captain of the football team, and his skin won't clash with my dress."

Looking down from the highest point gave me an excellent view of the seating—but more than that, this view made it easy to see the pattern.

"It's a sigil…"

"What?" Claudia said from below. "A sigil? Of course Cindy's wearing a sigil on her shirt, Trevor made it for her."

"The chairs…"

The seats were raised and lowered like placards at a stadium, and at this position it was easy to see the symbol they spelled out.

"It's a conjuring circle," I said, hovering above the design. But it wasn't just any circle. The sigil's complex whorls and curving lines brought with it memories of my college days, of mistakes, and of dark power my old girlfriend had given her life for a taste of—Ten Spins Infernal Constructs.

Much like all of the ancient Magician's works, the sigil was a masterclass of precise design. Whoever had drawn it though, had gone ever further. They'd used the seats themselves in a complex pattern of crooks and turns, and combined with the master Magician's seal, the overall result was a perfectly designed pattern for calling and trapping a very powerful being.

The half-melted Claudia shuffled over to examine the circle. "Wow, now that's one hell of a conjuring circle—Magician's got talent."

As much as I hated to admit it, the House was right. Conjuring circles were all about confusion and mental gymnastics. Honestly, that's why some of the best conjurers in the world were just a hair shy of bat-shit crazy—or actually psychotic.

"But what are they conjuring?"

Claudia placed brittle digits against what remained of her chin. "You mean who... Hmm, you know, I think—and I'm just spitballing here—I think they're trying to get in touch with Asaroth."

"Wait, Asaroth... *The Defiler?*"

Claudia rolled her undead eyes. "Okay, let's set something straight. It's not a nickname if you give it to yourself. You do know he *gave* himself that name, right? Just up and said 'call me The Defiler.' I told him that's crap, that no one gets to go around giving themselves nicknames."

"Yet here we are, calling him The Defiler..."

"Well, you are. Don't lump me in with your stupid," Claudia said, crossing her boney arms.

"Why would someone summon The Defiler?"

Claudia shrugged her shoulders. "Why do some kids pull the wings off butterflies when they could just burn ants with a magnifying glass?"

I floated closer to examine the sigil.

"Don't get too close. It was built to summon and hold The Defiler—damn it, now you have me calling him that—it'll hold you just the same."

"But I don't get it... why the New Dead?"

"Asaroth has been hoarding New Dead for centuries—built

his own personal army. Not my style, of course, but it suits him just the same," Claudia said, placing a hand on my silver cord like a kid with a Eugene-shaped circus balloon. "Hey... what's this?"

I felt it too—something soft, loving, and innocent at the end of Ariadne's thread.

Cathy.

"Oh, man. Do you feel that?" Claudia said, rubbing the silver cord against her decaying face. "That's some serious innocence."

She pushed the thread against her nose hole. "The bouquet. I'm getting hints of willful righteousness, a dusting of fiery compassion, and—oh, this is too much—virginity!"

"Stop, don't even—"

Claudia placed a burnt and spindly leg on one of the seats of the sigil. "I know this is going to be hard for you, Gene, but I think it's time we see other people—"

"No, you stay away from—"

"Don't get all uppity about it. I've given you countless opportunities, and just like Cindy the Cheerleader you've kicked me in short hairs. Well, I know when I'm not wanted, and I also know tasty potential when I smell it."

I scrambled down the thread. "Don't you dare—"

"Goodbye, Magician," Claudia said, pressing down on the seat bottom and closing the sigil's pattern.

Demon High vanished, and in its place the screen filled with an uncountable mass of black and twisted tentacles.

"So that's what he's going like these days. Odd," Claudia said, taking a seat in the newly turned down chair and guiding my floating body toward the screen. "Tell The Defiler—damn it, I did it again—I said hey."

Evil, pure and unfiltered, oozed from the undulating mass of slimy flesh, but it didn't stay on the screen. The snake-like arms reached out, testing the air, and looking for me.

I tried to will myself away from the reaching tentacles of Asaroth, but Claudia had the thread, and kept guiding me back.

"He's over here… Come on, Gene. Maybe Asaroth just wants to take you to the Prom?"

A tentacle passed close to my face, sending a cold shock of pain through my overheated translucent body.

"There you go, now you've said hello. I'm sure he'd love to give you a nice hug."

More tentacles broke free of the silver screen and reached for me. I tried to scramble down the thread, but Claudia kept giving me more line.

"Where are you going, Gene? He's right there! Don't be like Cindy."

I willed myself along the thread, but The Defiler was unrelenting, and quickly filled the air with glistening black feelers.

"Stop fighting and just let it go—aargh!" Claudia snapped her fingers off the thread. "What the… that daughter of yours has some talent," the woman said, blowing on her fingers.

I didn't have time to respond. A sharp tug on Ariadne's thread and I was whisked off, pulled past the reaching barbs of the Defiler, and over the head of one very displeased Claudia-shaped house.

"Tell Cathy I'll see her soon!" the undead manifestation shouted, just before my world went white.

* * *

I OPENED my eyes to find my daughter, still in her pajamas, holding my hands. "Dad?"

"Cathy?" I said, my voice rough around the edges. "How did you—"

"How did I what?"

"How did you pull me back?" I said, blinking the sweat out of my eyes—my body was soaked in it. If I'd taken a dip in the Gulf with my clothes on I'd have likely been less wet than I was right now.

"Um, I don't know."

I let go of her hand and stood, my knees popping like packing bubbles. "You had to have done something."

"I got up to get some water and saw you on the floor. You were breathing really strange, and I tried to get you to wake up. I grabbed your hand and—"

"And what?"

"And that's it."

Wild Magick.

"That was dangerous."

"What were you doing, Dad?"

How do I tell her? How do I tell my daughter that the House has developed a taste for her?

"I'll explain it later—you need to get some sleep. Your training starts tomorrow."

Cathy turned back toward her room, her tired feet shuffling on the bare wood.

"Wait, honey—"

"Yeah?"

"Thank you."

My daughter smiled before disappearing in the darkness of her bedroom.

What have I gotten myself into?

I located my phone and fired off a quick text to Adam.

Are you awake?

I waited patiently for the three dots to appear that told me my apprentice was burning the midnight oil.

Yeah wots up?

Would it kill you to use whole words?

U txt lyk my mom

My knuckles whitened against the phone, but I resisted the urge to hurl it across the room.

The theater is one massive Thinning. If Claudia Wilson is a dead end, find out what you can on any employees.

Wow wot hapnd?

That one I didn't need mental gymnastics to translate, and I hoped he'd understand my response.

Evil. A whole lot of it.

2 8

BIG TRUCK BELVIN

*S*and hill cranes, oversized brownish-gray birds with red feathered crests, strutted across my front yard, while behind them a watercolor-pink sunrise hinted at the day to come. Occasionally, one of those prehistoric beasts would needle their sharp beaks into my unkempt grass and come back with a bright green lizard, only to toss it into the air and gobble it down.

Red sky at morning; lizards take warning...

I slipped Porter's car quietly out of the garage and on to the street. Sure, I hadn't slept, not after the night I'd had, but the spike was too close to pass up—with any luck I'd be at the yard sale and back before anyone noticed.

I'd stuffed a decent bit of cash in my wallet, but that was to pick up a few last-minute breakfast items for the kids before I got home. This was a Magick yard sale—cash wasn't going to do me any good there.

Yard sales were a competitive sport in Florida—Magickal or otherwise. The trick was to arrive at least an hour *before* the established start. If the flyer said six in the morning, you'd best be there by five. It had gotten so bad that a few years ago people started showing up the day before to try to talk the owner out of the best items early. Based on the printout I knew better than to try such a stunt—the little people don't take kindly to cheaters.

I turned Porter's car onto the yard sale street, and my heart sank. It might have been only just now five minutes to five, but there were already a few cars idling along the side of the road.

So much for getting there early.

I pulled up behind the last car and waited, letting the engine rumble and the air conditioning hum. The sun hadn't come up completely yet, but the humidity was already climbing.

I found the house exactly as marked on the photos Adam had sent me. It was a small yellow bungalow, with a car port on one side, and a luxurious green lawn on the other. The driveway wasn't paved, just simple bleached-white shells with two narrow tire grooves. Large accordion-like awnings sat propped up above each window—old-time hurricane protection that more often than not ended up as hornet homes most of the year.

There was nothing outside to indicate a yard sale, which wasn't surprising given what this was, and who was putting it on.

Magickal yard sales worked a bit differently than the regular kind. First, there would be no items on display until the seller decided to make it visible. No sense in scouting out from the street, since there would be nothing to see—nothing that is, except for my competition.

Most of the cars I didn't know, but the vehicle right in front of me was all too familiar. That monster-sized pickup gobbled up our lane, and a little of the one next to it, and that was with three of its six tires in the swale.

Horatia.

I didn't know her last name—not only because I didn't care to, but because I was pretty sure Belvins didn't have last names.

Horatia wasn't one of those sweet fairies that pranced under the full moon, she was the real deal, a fully retired house sprite from upstate New York.

A fat, ruddy, and long-nosed Belvin, Horatia was mean and cantankerous down to the core, but damn good at one thing—making a deal. She'd been at more than half the yard sales I'd hit ever since she'd moved into town, and somehow that Belvin always had what the proprietors traded in—she was flush with it.

Memories.

That was a currency for Magickal yard sales: memories, either yours, or someone else's you'd come about through some less-than-savory means. It was easy to see why, if you stopped to think about it. Cash was too cheap and easily lost, and gold was a proper twist of Magick or alchemist's trick away, but memories were irreplaceable.

It'd been said that no one can really trade away their soul; instead, what they are really doing is trading away their memories. In the end, our memories are who we are—you lose enough of them and you stop being you, and become someone else entirely.

At that point haven't you really lost your soul anyway?

Horatia's scraggly hair jutted out in random directions from behind the driver seat. Belvins were an intractable lot, fickle and hard to follow. I'd never owned a house with one, and I most likely wouldn't. You didn't find them often in Florida, as the heat and humidity really got to them, and there just weren't enough old houses. Too much of the state was brand new construction, and Belvins hated new construction. More than that, the little buggers live to clean, and most new houses had so many cleaning gadgets and amenities it became next to impossible to keep them busy.

Want an angry house sprite? Take away their work.

Horatia leaned a stubby arm out her window and flicked ash from a smoldering cigar.

What's she here for?

I couldn't imagine any reason why John Henry's last spike would be on her list, but she was a Belvin, so she might just have been here to screw with the other buyers.

That's a Belvin for you.

If she did have her beady little eyes on my prize, I'd have to hustle if I wanted to outbid that cranky old house sprite.

Are we here for the same thing?

The digital clock in the dash of Porter's car switched to five AM, and what had been a barren shell-stone driveway was now a hoarder's paradise: stacks of boxes burgeoning with oddities; long card tables covered in trinkets, figurines, and knickknacks; and more than a couple hanging racks of clothing—none of which I paid any attention to.

My eyes never left the small table by the register where an old rotten block of wood sat with a perfectly bent railroad spike that practically beamed at me.

I wasn't even out of the car before Horatia waddled into view, heading toward the register, and my spike.

29

DEAL AND DASH

*T*he yard sale was impressive, even by Magickal standards. Our host had pulled out all the stops in providing quite an array of the mystical and the mundane—none of which I stopped to admire. On any other day I'd be lost for an hour exploring the table of yard art alone, but this wasn't any other day. There was a spike by the register that had my name on it, and I wasn't losing it to anyone, especially a cranky upstate house sprite.

"Morning," our host said, appearing almost magically behind the register. A small and youngish looking man with fair skin and short hair, he sat perched on a high stool, letting his sandaled feet dangle casually. He may have appeared harmless, but I knew better than to mistake his pleasant demeanor for weakness.

Leprechauns were just as inscrutable as Belvins, but also far more Magickal. If they wanted to ruin your day, week, month, or year, they could without so much as breaking a sweat. For the most part they kept to themselves, and like most Sunshine State transplants, they enjoyed the warm weather and ample bar scene.

Now, regardless of how you cut it up, the fact that our host was a Leprechaun was actually quite fortunate for me. Hundreds of years of blood-feuds between Belvins and Leprechauns had resulted in a rather strained truce, one that gave me a perfect opening.

That you Porter for insisting on that trip to Ireland.

"What can I do for you?" our cherubic host asked, rubbing the sleep from his eyes.

"I'd like to purchase that old log with the rusty nail," Horatia said, her voice oddly high-pitched when compared to her dumpy frame.

"I see. Well, that's not a small-ticket item. What do you have to offer?"

The Belvin's stubby fingers dug into a dusty fanny-pack around her ample waist. "What do you fancy? I've got weddings, funerals, first loves… and first lovings," she said with a wink.

"I most certainly do not want your first loving—you'd have to pay me to take such a thing."

"It's not mine, you idiot. I only deal in premium memories."

Old feuds rarely stay buried.

"I will not be insulted on my property, Madam. If you would please take your—"

"I'm sorry, did I forget to mention I only deal in premium *rich people* memories?"

Shit. If there's one thing Leprechauns love it's laughing at the expense of the rich and famous.

"You did," our host said, leaning forward ever so slightly. "So, intrigue me; tell me something that will change my mind."

Horatia removed a glass bead from her fanny pack and placed it on the table. A small swirl of color twisted inside like a cheap toy marble. "How's this?"

The Leprechaun picked up the marble and turned it over in his hand. "Unfaithful idiots—not interested."

Horatia's face fell, but she immediately dug back into her bag. It was my turn to make a pitch.

"I'd like to make a bid for the spike."

This drew a stink-eye from the hooked-nose Belvin.

"Great! Now we're talking. So tell me, Magician, what memories do you have to trade?"

"I have—"

"You don't want his dirty Magician memories, they'll give you the gout as sure as the sun rises."

The Leprechaun tilted his head to one side. "Is that true?"

Horatia butted in before I could respond. "It sure is—"

"Not true," I said, scrambling to get a few words in around the intractable sprite. "How long has it been since you were back in the mother country? I've got memories of a glorious trip through the lush hills and verdant pastures—"

"Pass," the Leprechaun said, dismissing me with his hand. "I've seen enough pastures and hills for a lifetime…"

Horatia saw an opening, and she went for it. "Yes, no one wants your boring Magician memories, not when they could have this choice specimen," she said, placing a large red marble on the table.

The Leprechaun picked it up and gave it a strong sniff. "Do I smell… burnt oil? Oh my, is that ashen remains of a favorite vehicle destroyed by sheer stupidity?"

"You have an excellent nose. It is indeed—someone placed a brick on the gas pedal of their favorite Porsche to run the engine and charge up a dead battery."

The Leprechaun smiled, his perfect white teeth gleaming in the few rays of morning sun that peeked between the roof tops. "Now that has potential—it's a decent starting point. What else you got?"

Horatia clearly wasn't prepared for that response. She must have gone to the deep end of the well too early.

Where will she go from here?

"It is a choice memory—can't you feel the agony and self-flagellation?"

The Leprechaun nodded and set the red marble down. "I can, and it's a very nice start. A man, his Porsche, and a brick—but I'm going to need more if you want the spike."

Our host placed a hand on the crooked metal spike and turned to me. "What about you, Magician? Do you have a counter?"

My brain was on tilt. My best plan had been the memories of the green isle; if that wasn't going to work, what did that leave me? "Uh, yes, of course. I have the memories of my first failed Magick as a teenager. I'd—"

The little man closed his eyes. "Tempting, but it would have been much better had the girls' tops actually fallen off at the pool and not the old man's bottoms."

"Terrible," Horatia said. "Why settle for low-brow Magician memories when you can have what I'm offering."

"Which is?"

The stout Belvin rustled through her fanny pack as I looked on, helpless. This wasn't going the way I'd imagined. I hadn't expected the seller would want humorous memories—I didn't know what to offer.

"Ah ha! Here it is. This is a fine memory to go with the one I've already offered. Think of this as a two-for."

The Leprechaun accepted the sparkly glass bead and held it up to the light. He squinted his eyes and stared at the swirling interior of the glass.

Don't like it, don't like it...

Our host burst into a fit of giggles. "This is perfect."

The Belvin rubbed her tiny fists in glee and reached for John Henry's spike. "So we have a deal?"

"We do indeed."

I couldn't believe my eyes. I'd come here ready to trade and had been snookered by a creepy and cantankerous house sprite. "Wait, I... I'll offer—"

"Give it up, Magician," Horatia said, putting her grubby hands on the spike. "You've lost, I've won. You aren't the only one with something important to end, you know."

The Belvin turned around and started walking her prize back to the truck.

"Wait!" I shouted, chasing after her. "I'll trade you the memory of my son's birth!"

Horatia stopped cold. "Go on."

Our host was still chuckling at himself as the next buyer arrived at his table. They were halfway through their transaction when he stopped them to share this latest memory. "So these two guys get in a ball pit: you know, like they have for kids. Then they dump a python in there. It bites his arm—twice! I mean, who does that!"

The Belvin kept a sharp eye on our host and his latest buyer. "Hurry up, Magician. You've got two kids, ain't ya?"

"Yes..."

"I want both their births," Horatia said, clutching the spike to her chest and continuing to steal glances back at the Leprechaun.

"I..."

It was too much—I couldn't give up both memories. Heck, I couldn't really give up one. I was formed by those moments, and even the end of Mallory Lane wasn't worth that price.

The Leprechaun wrapped up with his latest customer and finished the story with a smile, and then, without skipping a beat, the buyer responded, "Yeah, that *Idiots* show was so funny. It's amazing what those morons would do on television."

Television? You can't trade television memories, they're worthless— Horatia just cheated a Leprechaun on his home turf.

Our host froze in place and stared daggers past his customer. "Television?"

"Yeah, it's an old show from back in the day. Everybody's seen it, I'm surprised you—"

Horatia pushed past me and made a break for her still-idling truck.

Even I know better than to do that. You don't cheat a Leprechaun and live to talk about it.

30

DONE DEAL

*H*oratia tossed her cigar to the ground and swung her jiggling body up and into the monster truck. She gunned the throttle and swerved hard off the swale, taking a good chunk of sod with her.

This is not going to end well.

Belvins and Leprechauns didn't get along—they hadn't for hundreds of years—making this a beat down that had been a century in the making. The sprite's truck hadn't gone ten yards before the engine stalled and rolled to a stop. Horatia fought with the ignition, trying desperately to turn the engine over, while in front of her the hood shook, the metal buckling from some force beneath it.

"You might want to cover your ears," the Leprechaun said, crushing the fake memory bead with his fingers.

The pickup's steel peeled back like an overripe banana. A wailing screech of metal on metal shattered the relative calm of an early Florida morning.

Whump.

The frantic fairy spilled out of the truck and on to the pavement. The impact broke an already crooked nose and sent a stream of blood trickling down her face. Breathing hard, Horatia rolled over and scrambled for something in her fanny pack.

I took a few steps back; a Magickal fairy battle was not what I'd signed up for this morning.

Screech!

Fan-blade fingers cut deep gouges in the engine mount, their razor-sharp digits tracing up thick cables and rubber hoses that formed the graceful arms of a feminine shape. A pinched and bird-like head rose above the engine's broken remains, spark plugs sprouting like a glittering mohawk from its metallic scalp.

Banshee...

Sparks rained on the wet pavement from the Banshee's spark plug hair, and pistons roared in the steel woman's chest. Her curving metal lips wailed in tandem with them, the sound violent and otherworldly. With eyes wide, the Belvin crawled backward, trying to keep space between herself and the Banshee. Horatia shouted something and tossed another glass bead, but the metal woman's scream was simply too loud. The glass bauble shattered, along with the rest of the monster truck's windows.

Horatia shouted at the Leprechaun, "You can have it back! You stupid fool, take it and be done with you."

Our host said nothing. He simply stared, his eyes a mixture of amusement and loathing.

The steel woman wrapped those fan-blade fingers around Horatia's neck and pulled her up. Dangling above the asphalt, the Belvin looked pathetic and helpless. Like a petulant child, the sprite swung tiny balled-up fists at the steel beast, but never made contact. The banshee tossed her in the bed of the truck like a sack of last week's garbage.

"I'll—" Horatia's words were cut short by the monster's wail. It returned to the engine mount, and standing like the captain of a ship, let loose another scream before driving the pickup into the morning mist.

The Belvin was gone—and so was John Henry's spike.

For a few moments, no one said anything. Not a single patron moved from their spot, instead preferring to remain rooted in position, not wanting to upset the already disagreeable Leprechaun.

Our host walked down to the street edge to examine the deep tire grooves Horatia's truck had cut out of his grass. He shook his head and collected what sod he could from the street, then laid it back down gently where it had been. "I just put that sod down—stupid Belvin."

The Leprechaun passed me on his way back to the tiny register. "So, you want to make a deal or not?"

"But the spike is—"

He waved me off with his thin fingers. "You think I keep the real one here? That was just a railroad spike, no more, and no less."

"But the..."

"The real one gets delivered after I know your memories aren't fakes."

"Delivered?"

The Leprechaun nodded. "You'll have to sign for it. Now tell me, what do you have to offer."

I decided to change tactics. "What is it that you want?"

The thin fairy chuckled and took a seat on his stool. "That's a question I don't get asked a whole lot. What do I want?" He rubbed his fingers over a baby smooth chin. "You know something?" he said, leaning against the narrow card table. "I've never been married."

"Okay..."

"You married, Magician?"

After seeing what happened to the last person to lie or cheat the Leprechaun, I had no interest in doing either. "Yes."

"How long?"

"Sixteen years," I said, the shock of it hitting me. Had Porter and I really been married sixteen years?

Tempus Fugit.

"Sixteen years, eh? Has it been a good marriage?"

"Excuse me?"

The Leprechaun tapped his fingers on the table. "Seems to me that's a pretty easy question. Has it been a good marriage? You guys love each other, or do you live in separate houses? I'm not interested if that's the case." Our host brushed away imaginary dust with his fingers. "I'm interested in the real deal. Are you happy, Magician?"

"Yes," I said without further hesitation.

Yes, we have our problems, but tell me a marriage that doesn't. Does she make me happy? Yes, without question.

"Excellent!" he said, rubbing his tiny hands together. "You want the spike? I'd like those sixteen years of marriage."

I had plenty of memories I was willing to give up, some gladly—memories of being bullied in school, of bad first dates, and of a thousand different inane injuries over the years—but the Leprechaun wasn't interested in any of those. He'd gone right for the good stuff.

The fairy tilted his head forward, anticipating my response. "I'd say it's a fair deal."

"Maybe, maybe not—but it's too rich for my blood," I said, trying to hide the disappointment on my face. "No deal."

The Leprechaun produced a new metal spike from his pocket and placed it on the card table. "The power to end anything," he said, running a slender finger over the weathered steel. "*Anything...* Surely sixteen years is a paltry price to pay for that kind of power?"

I shook my head and turned away, walking toward the car. "You can keep it. Without those years I might as well willingly submit to the House."

The Leprechaun hopped down from his stool and chased after me. "Wait, what house? You don't mean 'the House,' do you?"

I kept walking, trying to keep up my downbeat demeanor just a little longer. "Depends. How many beings do you know double as property in South Tampa?"

"Son," he said, following me down the coquina driveway, the white shells popping and crackling under his feet. "You didn't tell me you were in a deal with... it."

"There's nothing to tell," I said, unlocking the door to Porter's car. "Good luck with your sale."

"Wait," the tiny vendor said, placing a hand on my door. "One year."

It wasn't as good as I'd hoped, but beggars can't be choosers.

"One year..." I said, turning the words over in my mouth. "I don't know..."

"What's one year out of sixteen? It's *nothing* in the grand scheme of your lives together."

"How do I know you aren't going to cherry pick a year's worth of good memories from the last sixteen?"

The Leprechaun's face fell, and I knew right there that was *exactly* what he had been planning on doing.

"Fine, one contiguous year of marriage—but I get to decide on the year." The diminutive fairy insisted.

Don't do it, Gene. Get back in the car and go home. It's too much to ask. You'll find another way.

"I'll do it, but..." I said, my heart pounding in my chest.

"But what?"

"But only for the next year."

The Leprechaun waved me off with his hand. "Bah, you want me to trade for a year that hasn't happened yet? How do I know you'll even still be together? You could die tomorrow, you know. You did hear the Banshee's wail..."

He's right. Stop now, get in your car, and go home.

"That's my offer," I said, then closed my eyes and replayed the best parts of my marriage for the hard-driving fairy. Images of our honeymoon in the Black Hills of Montana, of camping beneath the twinkling stars, of laughing at our infant daughter tooting bubbles in the bath, and of our wedding night holding each other on a windswept balcony above the crashing waves.

I opened my eyes to find the Leprechaun practically salivating. "Fine. We have a deal. I get the coming year, and in exchange you will receive John Henry's spike."

He extended his tiny hand to shake. "It'll be delivered soon, and you *will* have to sign for it."

31

MAGICIAN'S PANCAKES

I parked Porter's car in the garage and stumbled into the kitchen.

Coffee...

A few seconds fiddling with the coffee maker resulted in tar that didn't want to give back the spoon. I checked the clock and dumped the coffee to start over—Kris would be up soon, but Cathy could sleep until the end of the world if I didn't wake her.

I pulled a bowl from the shelf and set to work preparing something that resembled breakfast for the kids. Sometimes a simple, mundane task like making pancakes was great for clearing the mind and helping me compartmentalize. Successful parenting was all about being able to compartmentalize—in this moment, I was Dad, and that meant breakfast.

It also meant finding a way to get Kris free and clear while I worked with Cathy. The last thing I needed was distraction or a mis-fired bit of Magicking.

I had the griddle hot and was whisking the batter when my son climbed into his chair. That boy could talk a dog off a milk truck, and he was firing on all cylinders this morning.

"Dad, I want ten pancakes."

"How about two?" I said, pouring the cold batter onto the griddle and sending the warm aroma of Magician's Pancakes into the air.

"Okay, then I'll get two more."

"And how many will that be?"

My son's face contorted, his little mental processor churning through the basic addition. Somewhere along the way it got bored, and he settled on playing with a tiny truck he'd left on the table.

"Kris?"

"What?"

I removed the pancakes from the griddle. "How many will that be?"

"Some!"

"Close enough. Here you go," I said, placing a steaming stack of coaster-sized pancakes on the plate in front of my little Isaac Newton.

That's it!

While Kris stuffed pancakes in his mouth, I grabbed my phone and punched out a text to his teacher.

Tabby, it's Gene. Porter

I stopped—I wasn't sure how much to tell her about the events of last night. In the end, I went with the least amount of detail necessary.

Porter took a hard fall last night, she's fine, but I was wondering if you could watch Kris today, I have a daddy daughter day planned.

I hit send on the text and looked up to find that, true to his word, my kindergartener had completed both pancakes.

"More!"

I waited.

"Please!" he added.

"You got it, kiddo. But first you need to wake up your sister."

The tiny tornado shot past me and down the hall, his feet slapping on the wood floors.

Kris loved his sister, and he loved waking her up even more. Besides, better him than me.

My phone chirped, and a message from Tabby splashed across the screen.

Oh my, is she okay? I can watch him, no problem. I have a few old chemist friends coming over from my past life, but one of them has a daughter his age. Is that okay?

I smiled and wrote her back—it was more than okay. The more 'science weenies' we had there the better.

It's perfect. Thanks!

I clicked off the phone and flipped the pancakes I'd just poured. After last night I knew we were dealing with a dedicated Magician. There was someone out there with more than a smattering of Magickal talent—smart, powerful, but also crazy enough to try and summon Asaroth the Defiler.

As such, the Magician—no matter how sane—would still be subject to the laws I was. In essence, steer clear of the science. That meant sending Kris to Tabby's would let me take one more piece off the board and out of play.

My son bounded back around the corner just in time to vacuum up the two pancakes I'd just made, then vanish into the family room. Cathy lumbered in past him and poured herself into her chair.

"Coffee?" I asked, holding off on pancakes for my still-zombified daughter.

Cathy raised her fist and popped out a thumb—that was a lot of communication for my daughter before noon.

I placed the coffee beside her; it was still strong enough to stand on its own without the cup, but Cathy pumped it full of so much milk and sugar I figured she'd be fine—if a step closer to diabetes.

"Today's the day," I said, waiting for a response.

Cathy didn't budge, her head still solidly wedged in her arms.

I left her at the table and slipped into my bedroom. Porter was soundly asleep—the noises of the morning hadn't gotten past her little white-noise fan—and in the still-darkened room I navigated my way to the closet. I located my suits and let my hands slide down the wool fabric to the floor. Before they reached the bottom, they brushed across a bright red duffle bag cleverly hidden behind my most ill-fitting formal wear. I patted the bag gently, eliciting a faint squawk from its contents.

"Not today, Gertrude."

I moved on from the bag and brought my hands across the top of a rough chest tucked in the corner of our closet. I laid one hand on the wooden lid and traced a pattern in the dust with the other. An audible pop sounded, and the chest's lock released. I gently lifted the lid and let what little light there was in the room illuminate my personal library of grimoires.

The collection had started in college.

It had been back in those dorm-living and patchy-facial-hair days that I'd laid my hands on the first real book of Magick. Those original volumes hadn't been mine of course, but I'd ended up with them just the same.

College had been where my Magickal journey began in earnest, and from there the collection grew, until it took a very dark turn. I let my fingers play across the bindings, but stopped before they touched a certain mottled gray-green spine.

It should have been called *E. Evilson's Guide to Evil and Other Dark and Nefarious Stupidity*. My eyes traced the Magickal symbol inked into that drab gray skin—yes, that was actual skin. Yes, I tried not to dwell on that stomach-churning fact.

Ten Spins Infernal Constructs.

I gave the book a wide berth. It held Magick, but it also held memories of a dark and scary time in my life, a time I had no interest in returning to. The book provided details, far too many details, on the blackest of evil Magick. Armed with the knowledge tucked inside those covers, even a junior Magician could bring about terrible destruction. In the end that was why I kept it: it was safer here than anywhere else.

I ran my fingers over the rest of the covers until I found Flaterhaus's beginner tome. There was still a bookmark sticking out of the top; I opened it to the page and chuckled to myself —*How to catch an Imp, and what to do if you succeed.*

"Dad, is that Magick?!" an overly excited teenager whispered behind my back, effectively taking away at least three of my nine lives in the process.

"Holy crap, Cathy," I said, checking to make sure my heart was still inside my chest before tucking the book under my arm and gently closing the chest's lid.

"Is that where you keep the Magick books? Can I see them?"

"Yes... and no." I guided my daughter out through the bedroom door and past the sleeping Porter.

"The books in there are way too advanced for you. Heck, a few of them are even too advanced for me, but this one is a great starter."

I held up the book so Cathy could get a look at the cover. "Now listen. We don't do Magick without your old man around, it's just too dangerous right now. Second, we don't do Magick without your old man around, and third—"

"We don't do Magick without my old man around?"

I shook my head.

"We don't skip breakfast—get back in the kitchen."

Cathy danced about like she'd gotten a second Christmas— she'd all but forgotten about her mom's 'fall' with the excitement of real Magick so close. Truth be told, I'd gotten a little excited too. It was going to be fun to have another Magician in the house—once she got past the awkward phase—and Cathy would be learning from me, and not some old guy who made her clean his toilets and cut limes for his tequila.

And who turned out to be a less-than-perfect role model...

If I'd been paying attention, I would have made sure to go

back and lock the chest, but at the time I was too caught up in the excitement of it all. I'd forgotten the first rule of my chosen profession. Magick demands sacrifice, and as such, is more than happy to gobble up your children—just like lizards in the tall grass.

32

IMPERATIVE

abitha dropped by around noon, and Kris was more than happy to take a ride in her car. I was a little surprised, but I should have known better. The kid had his mom's adventurous spirit and didn't hesitate to try new things. After all the worrying I'd done lately, perhaps I could stand to take a page out of my son's playbook.

Porter stirred briefly and came out long enough to scare the crap out of Cathy. "What is she doing with that book?!"

I ushered our daughter into the den before guiding Porter back to the bedroom.

"Gene, I can't take more Magick in my house!"

"I know, I know, but her Magick isn't going to stop. In fact it's only going to get more powerful—that's just how this works."

My wife stopped to stare at her bandage in the mirror. As I'd predicted, my stitches had already dissolved by morning, but Porter wasn't Magickal, and her stitches were going to be there a while.

"It'll heal up, and before you know it you'll be in great shape. I happen to have a tiny amount of Pixie dander in the office.

Funny thing, Pixie dust is actually Pixie dander. Most people don't know that but wow, do Pixies have scalp problems. Anyway, a little Pixie dander and any scar will just fade away—Magician's honor."

Porter looked up at me with tears in her eyes. "Gene, I hate this—all of it. I feel so helpless. Everything is changing. Cathy is getting sucked up in your world and I'm so afraid of what'll happen to her."

I wiped the tears away and stood behind her in the mirror. "We can't stop it—she's going to be a Magician, but I'm going to make sure she has the power to keep you and Kris safe, even if I'm..."

I tried to stop in time, but the unspoken words were still there, hovering like vultures in the dim light of the bedroom.

Gone.

"Where's Krissy?"

"He's at Tabby's."

"What! Is he safe, I—"

I wrapped my hands around Porter. "He's safe. Tabby's old chemist friends are visiting today. The kid'll be steeped in science sauce, and he's wearing his Logic Loop. He'll be fine."

My wife pushed my hands down and pulled her body away. This wasn't just frustration, there was something more.

"I remember it, Gene..." she said, her voice barely a whisper.

"I don't understand..."

"I can close my eyes and still feel him, every inch of his grotesque—whatever the hell it was—forcing me to... to—"

"Stop, honey, don't relive it."

"How the hell am I supposed to do that? Every time I close my eyes, every time I look in the mirror I see it, the burning skin, the black tongue, *my* black tongue. Gene, I feel his hands—my hands—I..."

I didn't know what to say. The average person never remembers a possession. I didn't know why my wife would remember it now.

"Porter, I don't know what to say. That almost never happens…"

"Does it? You said it yourself those things were everywhere last night. How many more lives are they going to ruin? How many more are they going to…" my wife's words broke up on her quivering lips.

"I don't—"

"And you, why haven't you found a way to stop this? Why haven't you fought back?"

"I've been trying to keep my family safe," I said, reaching for her hands.

My wife slammed those fists on the dresser. "You call this 'safe?'" She pointed at the bandage on her face. "Maybe Magick is different, but here in the real world safe doesn't mean stitches."

"If I teach—"

"Teach? Yeah, that's just what I need, more Magick in my house, more people to worry about, more monsters at my door. Gene, you haven't taught your damn apprentice how to do much more than get a free parking space in downtown, yet you're going to teach Cathy?"

"I'm starting today—"

"I see, so that was after you ducked out in the morning for an hour and left us all alone."

Porter's words pulled the air out of my lungs. "The spike, it's important and I—"

My wife whirled around and put her face inches from mine. "It *is* important. More important than your family, more important than your children, and clearly more important than me."

"The House was there last night, it wants me—"

"Sometimes I wish you'd just said yes, maybe *it* could solve our problems."

My stomach bottomed out. "You don't mean that."

Porter turned away and covered her face. "Just go. Do what you *have* to do, but I want no part of it. I can't stand to look at myself, let alone you right now." She wiped her eyes and crawled back into bed.

"I…"

"Just go, Gene."

I backed out the bedroom door and let it close gently behind me.

* * *

SHE'S RIGHT. *She's completely right. You've spent this entire time thinking about yourself. That stops now.*

"Cathy, where's my bag?"

My daughter popped out from the den. "Last I saw it was on the couch, why?"

"We've got some work to do."

Cathy's ears perked up. "Magick work?"

I found my bag and beat a path to the garage to see what I had on hand, and like a stray puppy my daughter followed.

I set the bag on the work bench and started pulling out supplies.

"Hey, a Demon's trying to get some sleep here," the hoodie-covered 3D printer box grumbled, forcing Cathy to jump back.

"Dad, what's—"

"He's an Imp—Minor Demon, and we're going to banish him shortly."

"Who you calling minor?"

Cathy stared at the hoodie-draped box. "What's he saying?"

"He's telling me that I'm an amazing Magician and that he only wishes to be set free so he can bask in my greatness."

"Gah!" the Imp shouted, banging his tiny fists against the

case hard enough to slide the blanket-sized hoodie onto the floor.

"Holy shit," Cathy said, her voice jumping a few octaves at the sight of a bright-pink and rubbery Minor Demon on my workbench.

The Imp smiled and threw his tiny wings wide. "Wow, how did you get a daughter that hot? I mean, you aren't exactly a perfect specimen of man-flesh or anything? She's adopted, right? You're adopted, right, sweet-lips?"

"No," I said, trying to ignore the chattering Demon.

"Hm, I know! You did it with a Succubus didn't you? You dog, I love it. I should have known—"

"She's not a Succubus!"

The Imp frowned. "Half-Succubus?"

"No."

Cathy leaned in closer to stare at the Imp's bulbous features. "So, what's his name?"

"We don't name the Imp, Cathy."

"Why not?"

The Minor Demon folded its fingers and gave me its best doe eyes. "Yes, why not, dearest father?"

"Because, giving something a name makes it far more difficult to get rid of it. Think of it like this. Remember when your grandma had that chicken."

"Yeah…"

"And you named it Mr. Cluckers?"

Cathy nodded.

"How hard was it to eat Mr. Cluckers?"

My daughter's jaw dropped. "We aren't going to eat it?! Right?"

"No!" the Imp and I said in unison.

The color returned to my daughter's face.

"But," I said, placing a hand on her shoulder. "If I name it, then I've bound it, and once bound to me it takes a lot of Magick to unbind it."

"I get it. Sort of."

"Now, let's go over some of my standard items for handling what we in the business call 'New Dead.'"

"New Dead? Does that mean there's an Old Dead?"

"Yes, but they're way the hell out of your league and even mine. So let's stick to the simple stuff, okay?"

Cathy nodded.

"Salt," I said, slamming a container of Morton's Iodized Salt on the workbench.

"What's that for?" Cathy asked, getting closer, but still giving the Demon a wide berth.

"Spirits of the dead cannot cross a salt line," I said, pouring some of Morton's finest out on the workbench. "Also, it really annoys Minor Demons if you trap them in—"

"Hey! Don't go getting your grubby salt on me."

"What's he saying, Dad?"

"It's best to ignore the Imp, Catherine."

I removed a thin cloth sack from inside my work bag. The sack jingled in my hand, and I counted out a few oversized coins.

"What are those?" Cathy asked, craning her neck to get a look at them.

The Imp brushed off my bag of old coins. "Fifty-cent pieces, really? For the boat man on the River Styx? You should know that Charon retired a few eons ago—everyone uses a multi-pass now."

"These are Walking Liberty half-dollars, made in 1916. Each one contains a little silver, and a lot of Magick."

"Wow—what do they do?"

The Imp shrugged. "Well they don't get you a ride on the River Styx."

"You can trap an unfettered soul by 'buying' it off with a

Walking Liberty. You can't hold it for long, but once you've got it, you can exorcise it."

My daughter picked up one of the coins and turned it over in her fingers. "Amazing..."

The rubbery Demon dismissed me with a wave of his hand. "Whatever, half a soul? That's kid's stuff. Why I could—"

"Cathy, run in the house and get me the bottle of bourbon from the liquor cabinet."

"Uh..." My daughter tilted her head.

"Grandma Jude's favorite drink—the orange-looking stuff."

"Oh, be right back."

Cathy shot out of the door.

"You let her have access to the liquor cabinet?" the Imp asked, scratching at his chin. "I take back some of the things I said about you... I think I could really do well here."

"Not gonna happen."

"Got it!" she yelled, racing back into the garage with a half-empty bottle of premium liquor.

"Whoa, Grandma Jude likes the good stuff!" the Imp shouted, perking his head up upon seeing the label.

"Dad, did he just say Jude?"

She's starting to understand him—her Magick is getting stronger.

I shrugged and placed the bottle on the table next to the salt and coins. "It's best to not listen to Imps."

"What's the bourbon do?"

The Imp rubbed his hands together. "Gets us all good and drunk—plus I'm sure it makes your dad one hell of a dancer."

I frowned at the Imp, then poured the bottle's contents into a small metal flask. "It's for raising up the spirits of the dead."

"Wait, I thought you wanted to get rid of the dead?"

"He does," the Imp said, rolling his beady eyes. "The bourbon's there to bribe the idiots on the other side to do the heavy lifting for him."

"I do, but—"

My phone chirped, and I scooped it up. It was Rob from *The Qwik Fix.*

Hey, Gene... Any chance you could come by and talk to Justine? I know it's a big ask, but she's really torn up.

I wanted to tell him no. I wanted to say I didn't have the time for this, but then I caught sight of Cathy, staring at the Imp and my various Magickal tools. She needed some hands-on experience if she was going to help keep her brother and mother safe, but she also needed to know that Magick wasn't always about monsters, evil, and death—although they did make up the lion's share. Sometimes it was about making people whole.

I should bring her along. It would be good for her to see something genuine.

I punched out a response to Rob.

Yes, will come over now. Send me her address.

Thanks, Gene...

"Cathy, get some shoes on, you're coming with me. I've got an errand to run and I think you should be there."

"A Magick errand?"

"Gah! Yes, just get your dang shoes on!"

33

MEDIUM TO WELL DONE

*I*ce-cold AC from Porter's sweet new ride washed over all three of us. Cathy, the Imp, and I sat quietly in the car and waited for the light to change. It had been the longest stretch of silence we'd had since leaving the house and, like most good things, it didn't last.

The Imp had wanted to get out of the box, which wasn't going to happen. I wanted to put him in the trunk, but my daughter, the ever-sensitive creature, thought it would be better to strap the whole box into Kris's car seat.

The Minor Demon didn't seem to mind; it gave him a great view of this part of Florida, which while it wasn't much more than block-and-stucco homes with an occasional car wash or 7-11, thrilled him to no end.

"Wow, you can almost *feel* the domestic tension. Oh, that house, see that one there with the badly trimmed tree? Yeah..." The Imp took a deep breath as if savoring the air. "... Oh yeah, his wife isn't speaking to him, and... there's a hint of something else..." Our backseat bloodhound sniffed the air again. "Yep, we got some emotional infidelity—the choicest kind. Somebody's been on the Facebook talking to an old flame."

"Dad, what's he saying?"

I glanced at the almost giddy pink Demon in the back seat. "Honestly, honey, you don't want to know."

"How do you understand him?"

The Imp turned his attention to me. "You know something, Magician? For a goody two-shoes you sure know your way around the mother tongue... Who taught you?"

"Would anyone like to listen to the radio?"

"No," both my passengers said in unison.

I pretended to focus on the road for a few minutes, but before long I could tell that neither my daughter nor the Imp were giving up on their request. They were like dogs on the trail of fresh treats.

"Ah, there was this time in college. Let's say I made some less-than-good choices, and I ended up needing to banish an Imp."

"Oh, wow, you've been doing Magick since college?" Cathy said, perhaps seeing her old man in a new light. "Didn't you meet Mom in college?"

"I did, but not at this tim—"

"Banished!" the Imp shouted, banging his little fists on the glass. "Does that mean you brought him here? So lemme guess, you found some hot dish that you needed to sample, and by sample I mean—"

"Watch it, back there. I've banished one Imp, I can do it again."

The Minor Demon's tiny mouth clamped shut.

We pulled into a small apartment complex just off the main drag. It wasn't the sort of place you wrote home about, but clean enough that I didn't feel nervous having Cathy with me. The main building was stodgy and block-like, with smooth stucco and simple nondescript stairs. Each apartment had a balcony with a plain aluminum railing. I found Rob leaning against one of those railings and waving to us.

"Who's that?" Cathy asked, waving back to the stocky, ginger-haired mechanic.

"That's Rob, he fixes the Dad Wagon. Now, today I just want you to watch; don't touch anything and please keep your necklace on. Are you following me?"

Cathy nodded and pointed to the Imp in the back seat. "What about him?"

"He stays in the car."

"Great... sounds like fun," said our less-than-pleased Imp before folding his tiny wings over his face. "Wake me when you're back from your chat with the afterlife—provided you survive."

"What's he saying, Dad?"

"Just keep the necklace on. Please."

* * *

"THANKS AGAIN FOR COMING OUT, GENE," Rob said, meeting Cathy and me in the hallway outside his girlfriend's apartment. "We really appreciate it."

"Sure thing. Rob, this is my daughter Cathy, I'm not sure you two have met before."

The world's best mechanic extended his hand and a warm smile. "Nice to meet you, Cathy. Your dad's a special person—he's saved my bacon at least once before."

Cathy shook his hand and returned the smile.

"Justine's inside. Listen, Gene, she's really shook up about her mom."

I nodded. "What do I need to know?"

"They were really close. Both of them were on the force. Mom was a dispatcher and Justine is working her way up to detective. It was always her mom that did the worrying—no one saw the aneurysm coming."

"They never do."

It was Rob's turn to nod, then he guided us over the threshold and into a small efficiency apartment. A strong and compact young woman met us just inside the door. She wasn't much taller than Cathy, but her toned arms and powerful stance gave off a resounding policewoman vibe, as did the 'POLICE' t-shirt she was wearing.

"Justine, this is Gene Law. He's the guy I told you about, remember? The one that helped me with that issue before we met..."

Getting your groove on with a Succubus is certainly an issue—that's one way to put it, Rob.

Justine afforded me the healthy skepticism I expected. It's not often a Magician enters your life and offers to put you in touch with your deceased mother—if it were me, I'd be just as hesitant.

"Hey, I know you..." Justine said, giving me a completely unemotional once over. "Yeah, we met at the Old Tampa Hotel. You saved that woman's life."

"Dad?"

"Another time, Cathy."

If this is what counts for being shook up, my family must be total basket cases.

"Please, call me Gene."

"Okay, Gene. I'll be honest, I really don't know what it is you're going to do. My mom died without warning. A blood vessel burst in her brain. One day she was here, and the next she wasn't. Do you know what it's like to lose someone like that?"

I do not—most of my losses come after protracted periods of intense pain.

"No."

"It's gut wrenching. Your world is completely blown apart. One minute you're busy preparing for the detective exam, and the next you're preparing for a funeral."

"I'm sorry. That's terrible. Is there a place where we could sit down?"

Justine pointed to a small breakfast table pushed against the wall. It was empty save for a crossword puzzle dictionary.

"Mom loved crosswords—I picked up a damn newspaper every day just because of her," Justine said, her words breaking enough to give me a glimpse of her personality beyond that icy demeanor.

"I understand. Please take a seat," I said, pointing to the opposite chair. The table was cheap Formica, and the chairs had that distinct modern look to them, but neither of those details were important—it was all about the book.

"Can you give me some details on your mom?"

"I'd rather not."

"Justine!" Rob said, a slight edge to his tone.

"No, it's okay, Rob. She doesn't believe in any of this, and I don't blame her. I wouldn't either if I were in her shoes. You don't want to tell me anything because you think I'll use whatever you say to make up a story about your mom. Does that sound right?"

Justine nodded, crossing her arms over her chest.

"And the only reason I'm still here is because you trust Rob, and saw me shove a black rubber glove into the electrical box. Heck, you're even wondering now if telling me your mom liked crosswords was a good idea."

Justine looked away.

"Don't worry. I'm not angry, and I don't need any details if you don't want to give them. Think of me like a paranormal detective," I said, hoping to coax Justine out of her shell.

The young policewoman looked up from the table and I was overwhelmed by the sadness in her eyes.

"Let's do this," I said, placing both hands on the crossword dictionary. "Are you ready?"

"Yes."

I closed my eyes and tried to focus, which was immensely difficult given the events of the last twenty-four hours—but I'd promised Rob, and good people are always worth keeping your promises.

Mediums, spiritualists, and those that purport to talk to the dead are rarely Magickal. Most of them work really hard at faking it by doing tremendous research on the deceased and concocting something beautiful to say at just the right time. Very early on in my Magickal career I'd debunked a few of those cranks, and while I'd really reveled in it in my youth, now I looked back and shook my head. They hadn't been all bad. The ones that didn't charge anything were only trying to give the dearly departed's friends and family a little closure, yet there I was riding in on my white horse to stomp all that out.

Now, there were true Mediums, but they made four-leaf clovers look abundant. I'd met only one in my life: a rather prosperous Indian woman who downright hated her calling, but damn was she good at it. Whereas a Magician like me needed all sorts of mental preparation, items the deceased cherished, and more than a little luck, Pari could do it without any of those.

One evening over cheesecake she'd told me her secret. "Gene, most of the dead are long gone, but the ones that hang around—they just want someone to talk to. It's lonely waiting. Be a good listener. Be someone *you'd* want to talk to, and most of all, be open to hearing what they have to say—but don't be surprised if they talk your darn ear off all day and night."

I checked off Pari's list of steps and waited, holding tight to the crossword puzzle dictionary, but nothing happened.

I was just about to apologize and tell them there was nothing I could do, when a wave of bone-chilling cold washed over me, and Cathy's voice shattered the silence in the room.

"Baby-boo! Oh my God, I never meant for this to happen. I'm so sorry."

The stone-walled Justine crumbled in her chair.

34

NECROMANCY ON TAP

*C*athy casually crossed the narrow kitchen and crouched in front of Justine, taking the young policewoman's hands into her own. "Oh, sweetheart. I've missed you so much."

Wild Magick was the only answer. My daughter hadn't learned the complex intricacies of Mediumship skimming a few pages of Flaterhaus, she'd just *done* it—and with, I'd imagine, very little understanding as to how.

Cathy had a flair for Necromancy—this was equal parts exciting and downright terrifying. Now, just because you can handle Death Magick, that doesn't make you a bad person by default, but it does mean you need to be extra careful, lest you find yourself wearing the wrong team's colors.

My daughter clutched Justine's hands in hers. Cathy's Magick was wild; it had an unbridled and carefree nature that was hard to pin down. Her power twirled and hummed in an altogether chaotic state, but she was young and with experience she'd get better at controlling it. For now it was my job to keep Cathy's channel to the hereafter open and make sure nothing else decided to come through—there were far too many things on *this* side that needed protecting.

"Mom!" Justine sobbed, squeezing my daughter's hands. "I didn't mean it. What I said before, you know I didn't—"

"I know, dear. I know."

The two women embraced like they'd known each other all their lives.

Rob stayed quiet, but one look at him told me what I needed to know—my daughter had brought closure to a young woman he cared about who desperately needed it.

"Mom, I miss you so much," Justine said, wiping her eyes with her hands.

"I miss you too. This young woman was nice enough to let me come see you, but I can't stay long—it's not safe."

The concern in my daughter's voice was enough to snap me back to the present. "What do you mean it's not safe?"

"I'm not alone. There are more... things here, terrible things."

"Mom, are you okay?"

"I'll be fine, honey, I just stay below the radar. They don't come after me if I stay hidden, but when you called I couldn't say no. I couldn't leave things the way we did."

Cathy was doing an amazing job channeling Justine's mom, so much so that it made me wonder how she was getting around Lenar's Logic Loop. That was the exact moment I noticed the necklace was no longer around her neck.

That's how her Magick is so strong. This damn kid is going to be the death of me.

"We need to wrap this up soon—real soon."

"Sweetheart," Cathy said, brushing a loose hair out of her daughter's face. "He's right. I can't stay here much longer. They'll find me."

"Who? Who's going to find you, Mom?" Justine's voice shifted hard from distraught daughter to aspiring-detective.

"They're coming," Cathy said, her voice dropping to a whisper. She clutched at her daughter. "I can't stop them."

A passing cloud dimmed the room, and Cathy's shadow flickered, then changed. It grew, stretching beyond her tiny frame like spilled midnight until it consumed the floors and clawed up the walls. Small red spots, like spent candles drifted in pairs within the growing shade. The burning eyes of angry and vengeful dead had come, drawn by the dinner bell of a young and innocent Magician.

Oh no you don't!

"Time's up, ladies!"

"What's going on, Gene?" Rob said, his voice faltering.

"Just getting a little crowded in here, and I need everyone to go back to where they came from."

"Please," Cathy said, pleading with tears in her eyes. "Just let me say goodbye."

I gripped the dictionary tighter and willed a little more Magick into the connection. "Just a few seconds, then we have to hang up."

My daughter placed a hand on Justine's face. "Sweetheart, he's right. There's more of them coming—too many. It wouldn't be safe for you if I stayed. Please know that I love you, and will always love you. Words can't change that." She turned her attention to me. "There's something terrifying here that wants a piece of you, Magician. Do you understand what I'm saying?"

The Old Dead...

"I do."

"Good. Justine—"

"Mom! Wait, I... Rob has asked me if..."

"Oh sweetheart, yes, a hundred times yes. Marry that man, he's one of the good ones."

The twisting shadows expanded, consuming the walls and reaching for Justine. The cabinet doors in her tiny kitchen flapped like paddle boards, and the overhead lights blared red, bathing the room in a bloody glow.

Something old and powerful was coming.

"Gene!" Rob shouted, closing the distance between him and his wife-to-be.

"Time to go, ladies!"

I let go of the dictionary, and in doing so tried to break our connection to Justine's mother, except the book didn't fall. It remained stuck fast to my fingers.

Shit.

"It's coming!" Cathy cried, letting go of Justine and taking a few steps back. "Dad, there's something coming—it's too powerful. I'm cold... so cold. You have to make it stop, please!"

"I'm trying," I cried, slamming the book and my hand against the table. "I can't let go of the book."

"Dad!" Cathy screamed, falling to one knee. "Help me, I can't stop it!"

"Put the necklace on!" I shouted, ramming the book against the table in a futile attempt to jar it free. "Put it on now!"

Cathy dug into her pocket and retrieved the necklace. The thin gold chain bounced in her shaking hands. "It wants me. I can feel it. Dad, it's so strong—"

"Put it on, Cathy!"

My daughter's fingers didn't budge. "I... can't..."

Even with my own hands still affixed to Webster's Crossword Puzzle opus I lunged for my daughter, but as fast as I was, Justine was faster.

The soon-to-be detective launched herself out of her chair and into my young Magician. With the powerful grace of a jungle cat, she pounced on Cathy and knocked her to the ground. Justine ripped the Logic Loop necklace out of Cathy's hands and pulled it over my daughter's neck.

The shining gold charm sparkled against her skin, its intricate design vibrating in the lifting darkness.

No, don't do it.

The Logic Loop popped off its chain, falling to the ground and melting away on Justine's kitchen floor.

Something had just destroyed my daughter's only protection from the Magickal world, and it did it with the same effort I'd have used to pop a balloon.

Crap.

35

NECRO-WHAT?

*W*e idled, waiting for the light to change. Neither of us had said much since we'd left Justine's apartment. For my part I was all manner of conflicted. On the one hand, my daughter had a decent amount of Magickal talent, arguably far more than I'd had at her age, but she was also willing to take terrible risks—risks that could get her or the rest of us killed.

"I can't believe you took it off—again!"

My daughter stared out the window and traced her finger along the glass. "I know... but her mom was there, right there in the room, and I couldn't stand to think she'd have to leave without talking to her daughter."

"But what were you thinking? That was insanely dangerous."

My daughter turned to face me. "Thinking? I was thinking that's what my dad would have done—insanely dangerous stuff for the people he loves."

My phone chirped, and I reached for it, but Cathy grabbed it before I could. "No texting and driving—family rules."

There's a Minor Demon in the back seat, you almost flooded

Justine's cramped kitchenette with a horde of evil, and you're worried about me texting in the car?

"The text is from Adam. He says 'The theater's got one employee. I'm sending you their address. Am I meeting you there, and are we dealing with a Necromancer?'"

"What's a Necromancer?" Cathy said, scrolling up through my past messages to Adam.

The Imp jumped to attention in the back seat. "She wants to be a Necromancer? I'm an excellent teacher, you know. I've trained the best dead wranglers from here to the fiery pits of the Orgothi Wastes. Listen, if this beautiful woman needs some help learning how to raise herself an army of undead admirers you've come to the right place."

I did my best to ignore the Minor Demon in the back seat and focus on Cathy—and the road.

"It's a Magician who deals in semi-dead, mostly dead, and completely dead things. Frankly, exactly the sort of things you just did at Justine's."

My phone chirped again. "Dad, why—"

"Please, Catherine, I'm trying to explain something."

"But—"

"People are going to tell you Necromancy is bad. It's not. First, you need to get out of your head that Magick is inherently good or bad."

"Okay, Dad, but—"

"Is a hammer good or bad?"

"It depends, but wait there's—"

"Exactly," I said, changing lanes. "A hammer is a tool. You can take that tool to a broken-down house and frame up some walls, but does that make it a good hammer?"

"No," my daughter said, her shoulders slumping.

I nodded. "Right. You could also take that hammer and bash someone's head in. Would that make it a bad hammer?"

"That would make it a murder weapon."

"Don't be cheeky, honey. Do you understand?"

"Yeah, Dad. I understand. Magick is a hammer."

"Good."

"Dad. Why did Adam send you Tristan's address?"

* * *

"THERE'S no way I'm taking you there," I said, pulling on to our street.

"But Dad, he's my boyfriend—"

"I don't care."

Cathy crossed and uncrossed her arms—her resemblance to Porter was unmistakable. "How do you even know Adam's right?"

"Nothing is one hundred percent, but my apprentice is good at tracking and—"

"Yeah, he can track a jelly roll right into his belly, but that doesn't mean he's found the Magician you're looking for, or that that Magician is Tristan."

"No one said that—in fact all we have is an address."

"Dad, he's an 'A' student, and he plays soccer."

"I know that word!" the Imp shouted from the back seat. "It's descended from a Hell game where they kick a sinner's head around, right?"

"Cathy, have you ever noticed anything odd about Tristan?"

Odd, like maybe he's been digging up old bones at a certain construction site?

"No! Dad, he's like the most normal guy I know. He's even more normal than Mom."

"How long have you known him?"

"Almost a year!"

"Does he have any brothers or sisters?"

"No, he doesn't."

"You sure?"

"I'm sure. Listen, Dad. This has to be a mistake, maybe Adam is giving you bad information. Tristan's a really good guy... I like him."

"Which is all the more reason you *shouldn't* be coming—"

"But Dad—"

"Catherine," I said, pulling the car into the driveway and hitting the garage door button. "I'm not going to argue with you. You are getting out of the car, now."

My daughter placed a hand on the door handle and hesitated, then, in a fit of frustration, slammed her shoulder against it and barreled her way out of the car.

"Well, that went well—" the Imp said, his words cut off by the slamming car door.

* * *

I WAITED until the garage door had closed, with Cathy safely on the other side of it, to pull out of the driveway. Just to be on the safe side I circled the block once, but the Law Estate looked no different on that second pass.

It took me a little longer than I cared to admit to locate Tristan's house. It was in a part of South Tampa I wasn't familiar with—the part where people with money lived.

I checked the address again, and my phone's navigation system, then pulled off into a small neighborhood with an ornate sign that proclaimed that area to be 'Sherwood Estates,' a deed-restricted community.

The Imp and I rolled past large, beautiful homes with elaborate landscapes and expensive cars. This wasn't the cheap-seats, this was where the well-to-do lived— you know, the ones that don't have an Imp in their son's car seat.

That's the house...

I pulled up to a two-story home with practically zero lot line. The house's design clashed with the typical Floridian-

Spanish decor—no tile roof, no stucco walls, just bricks, and unlike the song, they don't build them like that in the Sunshine State. Brick was expensive down here, which made Tristan's family all the more interesting.

I slowed down to take in the curved driveway and get the lay of the land, but my heart skipped a beat when I discovered Cathy hopping out of a car in the driveway.

What the hell!

The blue compact pulled out of the curved driveway and as it passed, I spotted that telltale markings of a local ride-sharing outfit.

So, one decade of grounding... or two?

I stopped and pulled Porter's car into the driveway, but not before Cathy caught the attention of a well-dressed woman stepping out of an Escalade parked closer to the house.

"What is she doing?"

The Imp leaned forward against the 3D printer glass. "I'd say she's going to get you killed. Just a hunch. Speaking of which—you picking up on that vibration?" He placed his tiny fingers on the glass. "Yeah, hm, I don't like this."

I could feel it too. It was like a guitar string stretched taut, to the point of near collapse, then plucked.

Old Dead.

"Boss, this is Old Dead. Let's drink the bourbon and keep driving—now!"

What I assumed was Tristan's mom returned Cathy's wave, albeit a bit half-heartedly, her fingers positively dripping with gold.

The Imp caught sight of the older woman. "Oh my! Now that's a nice piece of—"

I tossed a towel over him.

"Hey, I was watching that!"

Cathy must have heard me, because she turned around

briefly before greeting Tristan's mom. "Hi, Mrs. Shelldeck, is Tristan home?"

I unzipped my bag and freed a Walking Liberty from the pouch along with a canister of Morton Salt.

"What's the plan, boss?" the Imp asked, hearing me shuffle around him.

"Keeping you out of the wrong hands—and making sure we have a way out of here," I said, pouring a salt circle around Kris's car seat.

"Hey—that better not be salt…"

"Ah, nope, definitely not."

"Damn it, least you could do is leave me the bourbon to drown my boredom."

"Yeah, no, but here, take this," I said, finding one of my daughter's textbooks on the floor and shoving it in his box.

The Imp frowned at the book. "This isn't bourbon."

"It's English, the bourbon of languages."

"Jerk."

36

SHELLDECK ESTATE

*O*nce outside the car I used up the rest of the salt to surround the vehicle while Cathy kept Tristan's mom busy.

The tall blond woman slung a large and dappled-leather purse over her shoulder and smiled at Cathy. "Sorry, sweetheart. Tris is out with other... friends right now."

"Oh."

"Was he expecting you?"

"Ah, no. I just... no, I—"

I threw the salt canister in the car and closed the door before my daughter could make this anymore awkward.

"Hi, I'm Eugene Law, Cathy's father," I said, extending my hand.

"Jessica Shelldeck, nice to meet you."

Tristan's mother could be best described as a former blond bombshell. She might have been past her prime, but that wouldn't have stopped you from thinking she had a beauty pageant to attend later in the day. Her nails sparkled and her hair fell in soft, golden waves. She wore tight leggings and a sleeveless top which let people know she did more than keep up appearances at the gym.

Jessica Shelldeck was certainly a looker, but there seemed to be more to her than superficial appearances.

Tristan's mother extended a soft and supple hand to shake, which I accepted. I didn't detect anything Magickal, but it might take a little more than a handshake to know for sure.

"What can I do for you two?"

We have reason to believe your son is a budding Magician and is controlling a small team of New Dead hellbent on destroying my family. Oh, and he might be hoarding a skull—an unbelievably powerful Old Dead skull—that should never be rejoined with its body.

"I just wanted to get to know the parents of the boy my daughter is dating. You know—pop in and say hi."

"Dating? These kids with their terms. I never know what Tris is doing one week to the next," Jessica said, her lips falling open ever so slightly and letting me know she was more than a little unsure, and wasn't certain what to make of this impromptu visit. "Well, I guess I can invite you two inside... the maid was here Wednesday, but it's not too bad yet."

We'll slum it.

Adam's car cruised up the driveway, but seeing me out and talking to Jessica, he stopped, then put his car in reverse.

"Friend of yours?" Jessica asked, directing her attention to Adam and his meticulously primped man-bun.

I shook my head. "Nope, must be turning around."

My apprentice tilted his head in obvious confusion before turning back around and driving up the block.

Jessica fished a set of keys out of her purse and pressed the lock button.

Honk, honk.

"Come in, I'm thinking Kelly might be out back," Jessica said, guiding us toward the door. "It's Mr. Law, right?"

"Please, call me Gene."

Jessica unlocked the front door and ushered us inside.

Solid threshold, but nothing Magickal. Certainly nothing that screams 'stay away, we do the evil here.'

Jessica led us into a stunning grand foyer. Dual staircases curved like twisting snakes to a second-floor landing above us. Large gothic columns sprouted from expert-cut travertine-like Roman oaks and kept that second floor from crashing down on our heads. Somewhere in the distance, faint classical music played, and while it clashed with the violins of malignant terror in my head, it still sounded damn good.

So this is what it's like to be rich?

"Beautiful home, Mrs. Shelldeck—"

"Please, call me Jessica."

Our gracious host led us past the stairs and between the columns.

"Enjoy yourself, this is the last time you'll see the light of day for ten years," I whispered to Cathy, trying to keep my voice low in the booming echo chamber that was the Shelldeck Estate.

Cathy hung her head. "Sorry, I—"

"Completely blew it? Ignored your father? Put yourself in potential danger—yeah, you sure did."

"How long have you been in Florida, Gene?" Jessica asked, her heels striking a jarring rhythm against the stone floor.

"I was born here, went to college here. Hell, I'm sure they'll bury me here."

Jessica paused at the next door, placing her hand on the rich oak before turning to face me. "Really? A native. My sister went to college here, but she transferred in from out of state."

"Yep, some of us are just crazy natives. Which school?"

"Florida, but like I said, she didn't last."

Jessica smiled at me. In another other place that would have seemed normal, if not downright pleasant, but against the backdrop of tension in the house it was almost predatory.

"I think she wishes she'd stuck it out, though."

The Imp was right. Something's not quite kosher here, but where is it coming from?

Jessica guided us into the kitchen. You could have fit three full Law Family kitchens in that ocean of granite and mahogany. Two full-size ovens with ranges, two refrigerators, and a glass wall of wine and assorted adult beverages rounded out the room. The Shelldeck larder was stocked for a zombie apocalypse, but judging by Jessica's perfectly manicured nails, if zombies had roamed the street, the Shelldecks would be stuck making reservations.

Well, maybe she'd raise a champagne glass—unless she has a person for that too.

"I'm sorry the kitchen is such a mess. Like I said we typically give the staff time off on the weekends."

"No problem, I understand. I typically give my wife time off on the weekends too."

Jessica furrowed her brow.

Stop screwing around Gene, and figure out where these New Dead are coming from.

"It's a joke."

"Ah," said the woman, who clearly didn't appreciate my sense of humor. "I was right, Kelly is out back by the pool. Let me introduce you."

Jessica led us through the kitchen and over to a wide set of impressively carved french doors, their spiraling wood reliefs exquisitely cut and pressed over panes of perfectly clear glass.

The cleaning staff must work like a NASCAR pit crew to keep the house this impressive.

"Kelly? Gene Law is here, he's Catherine's father."

"Who?"

As much as Mrs. Shelldeck would have given Porter fits, Mr. Shelldeck brought me right back to my awkward days in high school gym class. Kelly's muscles had muscles, plus they were corded, toned, and rippled when he spoke. He might have been lying on a chaise lounge, but somehow his manly physique still looked ready for action.

How does he do that?

It took everything I had to not suck in my gut.

"Catherine, dear. Remember? The girl Tristan is... dating."

That's an odd place for a pause. I wonder if Cathy noticed...

My daughter was too busy staring at the young woman rising up out of the pool, and I was ashamed to admit it, as soon as I noticed her I was staring too—long brown hair and sparkling eyes that matched a bathing suit far too revealing for any sane father's approval. The skin we could see—and that was a considerable amount—was pale almost to the point of alabaster, a milky white that only made her eyes all the more captivating.

"Oh, and I almost forgot, this is my niece Lucina. She's staying with us while my sister is in town on business."

If I lived in a horror movie—and there were times I wasn't sure I didn't—this would have been the exact moment when the violins reached their climax. Tattooed in perfect detail on the curving edge of her ample chest and poking out from the skin-tight seam of a very skimpy bathing suit was an expertly inked sigil I never expected to see again. The curving lines, the complex whirls, all of it was the product of a single frightening mind—Ten Spins.

Just like the theater...

37

SQUIRRELS IN PARADISE

*L*ucina let the water roll off her well-endowed frame with the precision of a girl who knew exactly how to get people looking where she wanted. With a casual grace no member of the Law family possessed, she sauntered past Cathy and selected a tightly rolled towel from the Shelldecks' towel cart. Lucina patted the water from her face, but made zero effort to cover an inch of her marble-white skin.

Even half-obscured, Ten Spins' twisting sigil, with its complex lines and collapsing design, was impossible to miss. I'd only ever known one other Magician obsessed with the dark power tied up in that evil Magick.

Morgan.

The memories came back in a rush. Her bright green hair, her sparkling eyes, and the fiery doors of the ancient library. It had taken me years to get over that moment, and I wasn't about to bring them back now.

Focus on the present...

Ten Spins Infernal Lock was just the sort of body art that branded this young woman a dangerous Magician with a flare for summoning up creatures of the darkest persuasion. The skill itself was a dying art, but not because there weren't things to draw out of the inky depths. Lord no. If anything, the supernatural world was overflowing with terrible and devilish creatures ready to pop in for a visit and some nice soul rending.

I mean, there's an Imp in Kris's car seat and I wasn't even trying— that's how overcrowded it is out there...

Still, summoning powerful entities was hard on the body. Just like New Dead, most of the other unspeakable spirits of the great beyond wanted to hitch a ride on a nice piece of human trim.

Lucina would be impossible to resist, thus the reason for the Infernal Lock.

The design was elegant and powerful; it would keep the spirits out, but it was never something I would have tattooed on myself or any member of my family. The Infernal Lock was meant to keep *all* spirits out—even your own.

Magick has a price.

"Hello," she said, extending a thin hand with well-manicured nails to rival Jessica's toward my daughter. "What was your name again?"

Cathy remained frozen in a perfect catfish-like stare.

"Cathy!" I whispered, giving her a nudge.

"Hi, I'm Cathy," my daughter said, breaking free of her envious trance.

"Cathy," Lucina said, repeating her name like it had come from some foreign land. "And you are dating Tris?"

"I... yeah, I—"

"Odd." Lucina finished dabbing the water from her face and set the towel aside, content to let the rest of the Shelldecks' pool water roll down her ample bosom. "Tris hasn't mentioned you... and we talk about *everything.*"

Cathy struggled to respond—that green-eyed vixen had my young grappling master twisted up far worse than any opponent.

"So, Gene, what can I do for you?" Kelly asked, getting up from his lounge chair and making sure I noticed just how much more impressive a specimen he was standing. He didn't quite tower over me, but he certainly was tall enough to give me just the slightest look down. Unlike my daughter, I was used to dealing with people that looked down on me—I'd spent years around Porter's family.

Is it her? Is she the one summoning the New Dead and trying to bring the Defiler into this world? You won't know unless you ask her, and for that you're going to need to clear the room...

"Oh, I didn't mean to intrude. Cathy and I were just in the area and I thought we'd drop by. You know, do the good parent thing."

Kelly paused as if his brain had broken down processing the words 'good' and 'parent' in combination with my less-than-impressive physique.

I've dealt with guys like you before, Adonis—never as powerful as you think you are.

"I see. Well, in that case, welcome to my home. It's a pleasure to meet you," the big man said, slapping a perfectly tanned hand on my shoulder just hard enough that I had to fight the urge to wince. "Can I get you a beer or something?"

"No, I don't—"

My phone chirped in my pocket and I fished it out. It was a text from Adam.

Out front, what do u want me to do? The Imp is in here?!

Ignore him, don't break the salt circle.

"You know, I take that back, Kelly. I'd love to have that beer."

Especially if you and Jessica go get it...

My host's face drooped ever so slightly—if he'd bet that shoulder slap was going to scare me off, he'd bet wrong. "Ah, sure thing. Lucina, would you go get a couple of Coppertail from the beer fridge?"

Damn it.

Lucida's green eyes sparkled, and she grabbed Cathy's hand. "Come on, you can give me a hand."

Cathy clearly wanted nothing to do with the buxom college kid, but she was my daughter, and knew how to play along. "Sure."

Plan B, you have an apprentice, use him...

I fired off a quick text to Adam.

There are Birds of Paradise in the front yard, right?

Adam's response arrived almost immediately.

No birds here, just plants.

"So, Gene. What do you do?" Kelly asked, taking a seat at one of the oversized chairs on the covered portion of their pool deck. Jessica followed and sat in his lap. In that moment, he looked for all the world like a modern-day conqueror sitting on his throne with a concubine.

My stream of texts with Adam continued, forcing me to hold two conversations at once. I wasn't sure which was more painful—Kelly the Tanned or Adam the Forgetful.

Birds of Paradise ARE plants.

Oh.

"I do a little of this and a little of that. I'm in the construction business—"

"That's great," my gracious host said, slipping a bronzed hand around his wife's waist. "It's so good to see people still out there working with their hands. You know—good honest everyday work—even if it doesn't pay."

Break the orange flowered head off.

Um, okay. Like this?

A bright orange and blue flowered head appeared on my screen, caught up in my apprentice's stubby fingers.

"Thanks, I try."

Kelly nodded. "Sounds like you set a good example for your daughter. Do your best even if it's not financially rewarding—it's good for the soul."

Do you even have one of those, Kelly? If your niece is wearing Ten Spins' tramp-stamp, she's squirreled her soul away somewhere...

I nodded and fired off a text to Adam.

Perfect. Now get the last of the powdered black acorn.

Why? Where is it?

"It's good to lead by example, even when you might want to wring their necks."

"True," my host said, running his fingers over Jessica's knee.

It's in your damn bag, check under the dried-out toad skins.

Found it. Now what?

"Here come the beer maidens," Kelly said, pointing to Lucina and Cathy. My daughter trailed the taller and more elegant brunette, her eyes solidly on the Spanish-tile floor.

Sprinkle the acorn on the flower and toss it on the Escalade.

Ah...

The black SUV in the driveway, other side of the gate. And get ready, you're about to give me one heck of a distraction.

"Thanks, sweetheart." Kelly accepted the cold glass of golden-yellow beer from his niece as I did the same from Cathy—something was eating at my daughter and I wasn't sure what, but I needed her to snap out of it, and quick.

Got it! Holy crap the squirrels are going crazy!

Get in your car and pull around the block, the squirrels will do the rest.

Bird of Paradise is a beautiful flower that, if you look at too quickly, resembles brilliant orange and purple plumage of a tropical bird. Few people know they're an excellent spring-board for small-mammal Magick. Packing that colorful musket full of enchanted acorn dust was just what the doctor ordered: instant chaos, in a thousand furry little packages.

Squirrels everywhere, going after the SUV.

I clicked the screen off and turned my attention to the grey squirrels now streaming between the magnificent oaks that filled the yard beyond the pool. They raced up the trees and launched onto the roof in the hundreds. Jessica's car alarm burst to life and filled the back porch with its high-pitched wail.

"What is that sound?" Mrs. Shelldeck said, getting up from her husband's lap and looking toward the front of the house. "Kelly, my Escalade!"

Jessica raced into the house, her crispy husband right behind her.

I fished the Walking Liberty out of my pocket and flicked it in the air. It was time to get some answers.

Silver for your thoughts?

38

OLD FLAMES

I caught Lucina's pale hand and slammed the Walking Liberty down into her palm. "Anima emptio!"

Boom!

Magick erupted from the coin and from my hand, the swirling power catching the young woman's voice in her throat. I knew I had her, but the immediate question was just what that meant. Her soul wasn't what I'd expected; there was something dark and seductive twisting beneath that porcelain skin.

Demon?

Ten Spins Infernal Lock meant that twisted soul was stuck in a permanent half-state just outside her body, and I'd just thrown down a mint silver Walking Liberty half-dollar for half that broken soul.

Magick demands sacrifice, but it also totally digs on irony.

Black wings and long claws shifted in that half-soul—Lucina wasn't human, at least not entirely.

Succubus!

"Dad! What are you doing?" Cathy screamed, seeing some serious Deep Magick for the first time in her life.

Lucina's alabaster skin rippled, and a faint second version of her gothic-bombshell body floated just outside the frame of her curvy real one. This Lucina brought a whole different definition to angry and was not pleased to have been caught by a stodgy, old, dad-bod Magician. "What are you doing?"

"Half-dollar, half-soul. No one teaches the classics these days."

"You idiot," Lucina hissed, her broken soul shifting furiously between that of a beautiful young woman and a black and twisted Demon. "The Infernal Lock keeps my halves in balance."

Shit, now that I had not considered.

Lucina's translucent fingers swiped at my face, but passed right through it.

"Dad, you're hurting her!" my daughter shouted, her voice breaking.

Just a few more seconds...

Lucina's soul was two parts, a hybrid of Demon and human lineage. Trapped by the Walking Liberty, that dark half was gaining power over the human half by the second. Black and gossamer wings unfolded from the back of her twisting spirit.

Make it quick, Gene.

"I'm not hurting her, and I won't, provided she tells me what I want to know," I said, squeezing the coin and Lucina's palm harder. "You sent New Dead after my wife and I want to know why."

Lucina's demonic spirit growled and pulled at my fingers with translucent claws.

"Stop!" both ladies cried.

"I will, but only if you tell me the truth," I said, rooting Lucina to the spot as if I'd driven a tent-stake through her hand. "Why did you send New Dead after my wife!"

The soft voice of 69 Mallory Lane returned—this time it came from my daughter and cut me to the core. "Yes, now that's the Gene Law I wanted to see. I knew you had it in you."

Lucina's half-soul flickered like a match in the wind; her

Demon half was getting stronger. "New Dead? I don't understand. Please let me go," Lucina cried.

"You're lying," I said, the coin's sharp edges digging into my skin. "Who taught you Ten Spins' Infernal Lock? You don't just wake up with that knowledge. Someone is screwing with my family and I want to know who!"

"Go, Gene," the Cathy-shaped house said, her voice soft and supple. "This is exactly what I've been looking for. I knew you had it in you, I just knew it."

"Get out of my daughter," I growled.

Cathy smiled, her eyes practically sparkling. "Happy to. I'll see you around, Magician."

"I told you," Lucina cried, her black wings expanding. "I don't know what you're talking about."

"Don't play with me. I'm old, and I'm cranky, and I tired of dealing with wannabe monsters trying to screw with my family."

I cranked down on the coin with all my might. Lady Liberty's gnarled edge drew blood against my skin, but it was a small price to pay to see the Demon hybrid squirm.

"Dad! You are killing her!" Cathy shouted, her voice no longer that of Mallory Lane.

"I didn't touch your family!" the half-soul screamed.

"But you know something. Stop stalling and tell me."

Lucina squirmed and pulled, twisting her human and Demon halves in a hundred directions while her body remained perfectly still—like a fly trying to escape the spider's web, the woman's half-soul could not escape the pull of Walking Liberty silver.

You could finish this right now, just squeeze a little harder...

The coin shuddered in my palm. The Magick wanted to go further, it wanted to tear the hybrid soul apart and revel in it, but did I? My face reflected in the young woman's panicked eyes, and I didn't like what I saw.

"I can always buy the rest," I said, easing back, and patting my other hand on my pocket. It technically wasn't true, but if Lucina didn't know about Walking Liberty, there was a good chance she wouldn't know that I was lying either.

"I don't know anything about New Dead, or Asaroth the Defiler. I'm here to keep an eye on my aunt and uncle while Mom is in town on business," Lucina's twisted soul shouted.

"What sort of business?"

I pumped a little more Magick into the coin and Lucina's half-soul. If I'd been paying more attention, I would have wondered where my own daughter was at this moment; instead, I was far too focused on the squirming catch about to snap my line.

"Agh!" Lucina shouted, her Demon soul's black wings snapping. "I told you, I don't know. I only know I have to stay here a few more nights and pretend to make nice with the relatives, then she'll have what she's looking for."

The Cadillac's car alarm was still going strong, which meant the squirrels were doing their thing, but that wouldn't last. I would have loved to see my little 'var-my' going to town on that woman's high-priced land yacht, but I only had seconds before the Demon half would slip free of my grasp. I needed an answer, and I needed it now.

"Who is your mother? And what is she looking for?" I shouted, pulling the half-soul toward my face.

A new voice spoke up behind me, soft as crushed velvet and as sharp as a razor's edge. It was a calm and sultry sound I hadn't heard in more than twenty years, and hadn't ever expected to hear again.

No, she's dead. I saw her die.

"Let go of my daughter, Gene. Or you'll find Cathy in far fewer pieces than you can stomach."

Morgan Crowley.

Didn't I tell you? Magick loves irony.

39

MA' SIGIL

I didn't turn around, I was too afraid of what I might find.

It can't be her...

But that voice was impossible to forget. It came with the smell of clove and incense, with innocence lost and never found again, and with a whole crap-ton of baggage. My fingers practically twitched at the thought of lace, leather, and crushed velvet. Only one woman had ever made my heart beat with equal parts excitement and sheer terror, and her voice was unmistakable.

Morgan Crowley.

The first woman to introduce me to Deep Magick, and to teach me the secrets to unlocking the cosmic power swirling inside me. I'd made mistakes, so many mistakes, chasing the bright eyes and crooked smile of that terrible woman. Flashes of memory filled my mind: the fiery doors of an ancient library, Morgan's screams, and the rush of Magick. I shook them away.

It can't be her. Morgan Crowley died.

"I don't know who you are, but Morgan Crowley is dead," I said, yanking back the Lucina half-soul trying to escape my fingers and the Walking Liberty. "Let go of my daughter now, unless you want me to do the same thing to you."

"Have you really come that far, Eugene Law? The man I remember lacked that killer instinct—at least right up until the end."

The end.

More memories washed over me, too many to count, and all of them digging up a pain I'd done my best to keep long buried. "You can't be her. Morgan Crowley died."

"Look at me, Eugene Law. Do I look dead to you?"

I couldn't turn around. Lucina's Demon-half flapped its translucent wings, the monster's power growing by the second. The Succubus side of that broken soul was winning, and soon it would overpower the coin and me.

"Oh, you can't, can you?" Morgan's voice said, the same velvety tone that had twisted me in knots all those years ago. "Gotta stay focused on the problem at hand, eh Gene?"

"No one survives that place."

Morgan chuckled, her voice filling with venom. "No one but me."

Lucina freed a finger and her green eyes lit up. There was no way I could hold the Half-Succubus much longer.

"It's not possible. Ed promised me it wasn't possible."

"Your old roommate? Please tell me you don't hang around that moron anymore. What could he know about the other side of those doors?"

Lucina pulled another clawed finger free. The Succubus half of her soul was winning. I'd be in for a lot more problems when that half broke free. Those bright green eyes were already drawing me into a raw and powerful sexual energy just beyond the flickering half-soul.

Damn it.

"Dad!" Cathy's cry shattered my concentration and sent two more Lucina fingers slipping off the coin.

Cathy! Stop, Gene. Focus, don't lose the coin.

"Let go of my daughter," I cried, sweat stinging my eyes. I couldn't hold the half-soul much longer.

"You know something, Gene, when I clawed my way out of the hole, I didn't come back to the world I'd left. A lot had changed since that day."

Lucina's half-soul pulled harder at the stinging coin. It took all I had to keep her from slipping free. "I... don't... care..."

"So what do I discover? I find I have a half-sister. I find that you can look up anyone now. It doesn't take Magick, it's all online. Imagine my surprise when I discover just what happened to Eugene Law and his *wife* Porter." Morgan's voice seethed with anger.

Cathy's cries vanished and my gut sank with them. Still I tried to muster what little bravado I had left. "This is just between us, Morgan. Let my daughter go."

"I plan to, but would you like her with or without her face?"

"If you hurt her—"

"You'll do what? Send a pack of squirrels to irritate me to death? Come on, Gene. You used to have power, real power, but look at you now. Walking Liberty coins? Squirrel packs? It's a shame, but that's what happens when you choose the wrong path. You could have had me, together we would have been unstoppable. I mean, look at you. Khakis? Really?"

"Cathy!"

That wasn't Morgan's voice, that was Tristan—a very concerned and altogether distressed boyfriend of the month.

"What are you doing to her? Stop!"

Morgan's voice cut like daggers. "You want to think very carefully about your next move, nephew."

"Let her go or I'll shatter it!" Tristan shouted.

Deep Magick flooded the room and knocked the air clean out of my lungs. When I had been crouching in the hallway at the Old Tampa Hotel, I'd had a taste of it, but that was just the tiniest drop, and even then it'd been enough to clamp my butt cheeks tight.

This was a thousand times worse.

Lucina stopped struggling, and her eyes told me why: the Half-Succubus was terrified. This wasn't the House—this was corrupted evil. The House was like a shark, an apex predator, but still a cog of the supernatural order. This was different, this was wild and unpredictable, this was Old Dead. It didn't follow rules, it broke them, and people, and even half-demons.

"Don't be stupid, Tristan. You know whose skull that is," Morgan said, her voice no longer brimming with confidence.

"I don't care. If you don't let her go right now I swear I'll smash this into a thousand pieces."

Way to go, Triscuit!

"And kill us all? I hardly think you'll do that. The Wild Magick alone would be enough to bring this whole place down around your ears, and what about your girlfriend?"

"Tristan," Cathy cried, her voice ragged. "Help me!"

Ten Spins' sigils, Morgan was always a fan. She had the patience for those tiny little lines and excruciating details. Morgan must have designed Lucina's Infernal Lock, and probably the Brighton 8's summoning circle too. She must be the one calling in Asaroth. She must have done the same thing to the skull, and that's what she's drawing her power from. Morgan Crowley had finally found her battery.

The Lucina-demon flickered in my grasp; the much younger and more energized half-soul had almost gained the upper hand. At any second, it wouldn't matter what I did—that soul-sucking she-devil would be free, and all I'd have would be nothing but a blackened Walking Liberty to show for it.

Think, Gene!

"Give me the skull, Tristan, before you do something monumentally stupid," Morgan hissed.

I couldn't hold Lucina any longer, and I knew the instant I

did let go I was going to need to get away fast. One touch and the Half-Succubus would have me in her clutches.

All right, Magick man. On the count of three we toss the coin and give the young woman back her soul, then turn around and let Morgan have it with all you've got. This is what you get for going off half-cocked. One... Two...

"Nobody move! I've got an Imp and I'm not afraid to use it!" shouted my favorite non-family-member apprentice of all time.

Way to go, Adam, you big man-bun of awesomeness. I never doubted you.

40

THE GOOD, THE BAD, AND THE
IMPISH

*I*mps can really screw with Magick—aside from being pink, rubbery, and annoying, they know how to turn a spell up one side and down the other. Trying to Magick up some thicker hair with an Imp around? Get ready to have it come out your ears. Working on that spell to freeze time? Be prepared to be pelted by frozen dimes.

Simply put, Magickal contamination was one of their most well-known and least understood traits—mainly because the Magicians that elected to study them often ended up blown to tiny bits by their own Magick.

Minor Demons do not suffer boredom.

I let go of Lucina's hand, along with the scorched remains of a blackened Walking Liberty, then spun around to find out what I'd missed.

Cathy!

I was suddenly very happy I hadn't been watching—Morgan had my daughter bound by the Rubick's Cube. It was one of her specialties from college. That infernal cube would split apart her victim's body and shift it into impossible positions. My stomach rolled at the sight of Cathy as a cubist's painting. Her eyes which were now somewhere near her knees, told me all I needed to know—my daughter was in pain.

Morgan stood behind her, smiling. That same smile might have won over an innocent young Magician away at college all those years ago, but it didn't do a damn thing now. The slender and well-endowed Morgan didn't look much older than the last time I'd seen her. She'd moved on from the brightly colored locks of her college days, but hadn't shed the signature corset, and was still making sure the casual observer got more than an eyeful. Those eyes still twinkled, but now they did it with a vengeance I'd never noticed before.

Behind her, Tristan held one of the scariest-looking skulls I'd ever seen. Wrapped in complex sigils, it was sure to be Morgan's link to the Old Dead. Even though the power rolling off of it was immense, it was contained by my ex-lover's complex designs.

As much as I hated to agree with her, destroying the skull would be bad—very, very bad.

Even with all that was going on, I was surprised to find the Half-Succubus and I weren't the center of attention anymore—not even close, really. That title was currently held by my apprentice.

Adam had the Imp perched on his shoulder, finger-guns blazing, and drawing more than a few incredulous looks.

Any sane Magician in the room would have held their breath or made a run for the hills at the thought of banting about an unbound Imp, but none of that appeared to have formed as fruits on my apprentice's decision tree—he'd gone full Minor Demon and wasn't backing down.

"Now that we have your attention. Put Gene's daughter back together and let them both go, or…"

Nice work, Tonto!

Morgan kept a hand on Cathy and pressed the Rubick's

Cube against my daughter's skin. "Or else what? Do you know what this is?"

He doesn't.

"I've got a bigger question for you," Adam said, zipping up his hoodie. "Are you willing to try it with a loaded Imp pointed at your head?"

The Minor Demon flicked his tail, and I swear I heard that gun duel whistle from *The Good, the Bad, and the Ugly.*

"Don't be crazy, Morgan," I said, taking a step toward my daughter. "Let Cathy go and no one gets Imp'd today."

The hesitation in my ex's eyes was palpable. No Magician liked being cornered, but a power-hungry monster like Morgan *really* didn't like it.

"How do I know once I let her go you won't come after me—"

"Stay back!" Adam yelled, but it was too late. Lucina's fingers closed over my shoulder. Waves of pain and exhaustion rolled down my back, seizing the muscles and twisting me like a contortionist.

"I've got him, Mom!" the Half-Succubus shouted, her hand drawing life from my body like a vacuum hose.

"Lucina, stop—"

Her daughter might not have understood the perilous implications of trying to drain my life energy in the presence of an Imp, but Morgan did.

The Minor Demon snapped its tail like a whip and Lucina screamed. Her hand disappeared from my shoulder, and I turned back to find her writhing in pain on the ground. The arm that had been draining my essence was now blackened and withered like an old prune.

"What have you done to me!" the Half-Succubus screamed, clutching the now-useless appendage to her ample chest.

The Imp showed off his impressive array of razor-sharp

teeth and giggled. "You should see the look on your face! Hurts to go from suck to blow, eh?"

The little pink Demon was right—he'd just pumped me full of Half-Succubus energy. It swirled around in my chest like a double-shot of espresso, and one look at Morgan told me she knew it too.

"Kids, right?" My ex said, backing up.

"You can keep your demon-child, Morgan. Just give me back my daughter!"

Magick crackled around my hands—bright rings of gold and yellow that threw sparks on the cold pool deck. Oh, I would have given anything to see myself in a mirror—you typically don't get to run at double-power, and I knew it must have looked damn impressive, even with khakis.

"Fine," Morgan said, letting go of Cathy and untwisting the Rubick's Cube. My daughter re-assembled to her beautiful young self before falling into my outstretched arms.

"I can't feel my feet..." she whispered, her properly configured face tired and afraid.

"It happens, she'll be fine," Morgan said, setting the cube down and keeping her hands up.

I raised a still-glowing fist toward my ex-girlfriend. "Give me one good reason why I shouldn't—"

Morgan spun around and placed a hand on the sigil-covered skull in Tristan's hands. "I'll give you one really good reason."

The arcane swirls and lines glowed under Morgan's fingers, and the wave of energy they gave off was immense—even running hot I was no match for Old Dead, and I knew it.

"Adam!"

"What?"

"Think about the car," I said, backing up with Cathy in my arms.

"Huh? I left it around the block."

"My car..."

"Isn't it in the shop?"

"Gah! My wife's car—just do it!"

"Imp, you don't want to screw with me on this," I said, backing away from Morgan and the skull.

"Then I'm gonna need a name."

"Good—wait, right now? I'm a little busy."

The Minor Demon's tail flicked from side to side. "A name, Magician."

How did I get myself in this mess...

"Stewart."

The Imp jumped up with excitement, then immediately frowned. "Excellent—wait, what? Stewart? What the hell kind of Demon name is that?"

"Right... Stewart *The Annoying*."

I spun around and latched a glowing hand onto Adam. "Let's blow this popsicle stand, Tonto!"

"Wait, Dad—Tristan!"

The gangly youth shot past his aunt, the Old Dead skull still solidly in his hands, and rammed into the three of us.

Great, nothing like piling on...

"Ianuae Magicae!" I shouted, closing my eyes and holding tight to the people I loved—and Triscuit.

Teleportation is about the craziest thing you can try as a Magician. It's insane when you think about it, reconstituting matter in another place—which was why I was having someone else do the thinking for me. I just hoped Adam did a decent job remembering what Porter's car looked like.

Magick demands sacrifice. Holy hell, this one's gonna hurt.

PART III
SACRIFICES MADE

41

SPILL THE BEANS

*a*dam had my wife's car zipping along the expressway en route to my house. I'd tried Porter's phone multiple times, with no answer, and now that I could see clearly enough to work the tiny keyboard, I fired off a few texts as well.

Big problem. You home? Don't leave the house! On my way.

I waited for a response and found my legs bouncing against the floor mats.

Come on...

"She answering?" Adam asked, changing lanes.

"No."

My apprentice didn't have to respond. I could tell by the look on his face he was just as concerned as I was—that may not have been his wife on the other end of the phone, but Porter had always treated him as a friend.

Cathy stretched out in the backseat, her head tucked against Tristan's chest.

"You think she'll be okay?" Adam asked, rubbing his beard.

"Yeah—I hope so."

Morgan... alive. How did she do it? How did she survive? That doesn't matter, what matters is she's here, and that means no one is safe. She may not have the Old Dead skull battery, but she was still more than enough to handle without it.

We raced along the elevated expressway, rooftops rolling past like the backs of great brown turtles. At one point a large pelican dipped down to fly in line with the car. The wide-bodied bird kept in perfect formation with our motley crew for a few miles, then headed toward the inner bay—I knew it was largely symbolic, but I still appreciated the escort.

Adam pulled us off the expressway and into some heavy surface street traffic—through it all the Imp continued to read out loud the contents of Cathy's English book.

"So that's how…"

The Imp looked up and nodded. "It's the bourbon of languages."

Adam guided us through traffic, and I turned around to face Cathy's current boyfriend.

"Okay, as much as I appreciate what you did back there, I'm gonna need to know a lot more before I even begin to consider trusting you, starting with, what's Morgan doing here?"

Tristan was a tough read. Sure, the kid had just gone toe-to-toe with his Magickal aunt, and until just recently held an Old Dead skull in his lap practically overflowing with evil Magick, but also was just a kid, and clearly not sure what to make of his life choices so far.

Tristan shook his head. "I don't know."

I sighed. "That's not good enough. You've got to give me something or we'll let you out, and we won't stop the car first."

Porter's car chose that moment to roll to a stop at the light and Adam gave me an apologetic look.

"Unless there's a stop light—"

"Or a stop sign!" my apprentice said, trying his best to come across tougher than his marshmallow exterior implied.

"Gah—I'm trying to get some details here."

Adam quickly turned his attention back to the street.

"So, where was I?"

"You were asking me what my Aunt is here for?" Tristan said, his eyes drifting to the window.

"Oh, right—and?"

"She's here because of me..."

"What did you do?"

Tristan brushed stray hairs out of Cathy's face. "You know what it's like to have something in your head?"

"Excuse me?"

"Do you know what it's like to have something in your head, all the time, always there, and always pushing on you? You question everything, every thought, every desire," Cathy's boyfriend said, his shoulders visibly tense.

"I—"

"Of course you don't. You are Eugene Law, Aunt Morgan told me about you. You're the real deal—the incorruptible."

Hardly.

"I—"

Tristan let out a long breath and slumped against the seat. "It started a few months ago, on a field trip to the Old Tampa Hotel."

The Old Dead...

"That was the first time I heard the voice—dark and raspy, like dragging a rusty chain through my head. It told me things, terrible things."

"Didn't you leave?"

"Sure, but so did the voice. It followed me everywhere. It drew me back. It made me dig that out of the wall," Tristan said, his eyes on the sigil-covered skull.

"How did Morgan—"

"I called her, okay? Look, I don't know anything about this insanity." Tristan waved his hand in the air. "But I know my aunt, and I know she understands this stuff. I just wanted it out of my life, don't you understand?"

235

"What happened then? Why didn't she just take the skull and leave?"

"Well, everything changed after she got here. First it was the skull, but then she found out about Cathy."

Now it was my heart's turn to ramp up. "What do you mean?"

"Once Aunt Morgan found out about Cathy, she got very interested in her—reading posts, checking her timeline, you get the idea."

Shit.

Tristan nodded. "Yeah, from there she went to Cathy's mom's page and looked through all of her friends."

Porter's friends—Tabby! No, she can't work any Magick at Tabby's, not without some power I don't know about.

"Gene, what do you want me to do?" Adam asked, bringing the car to a stop at the next light.

"If Morgan's been digging into our life, then Porter's not safe —no matter what Magick I put over the house."

Adam took the next right and gunned the car's modest engine. Even though it was less than a mile away, my house, and my love, had never felt more distant.

42

REAL MOTHER

*W*e reached our street without incident and found the house still standing. Adam pulled into the driveway and I hit the garage button. The large aluminum door rose slowly, giving me ample time to see the legs, shorts, top, and then folded arms on the other side.

"What the hell, Gene!" Porter shouted, stomping out to meet me. "You've been gone all day!"

"Imp, get under the seat—now. Take the skull with you!" I said, still in the car and hoping Porter hadn't seen the rubbery demon yet.

"It's Old Dead and it stinks."

"Do it!"

The Imp dragged the skull and his tiny frame under my seat.

Satisfied he was hidden, I threw open the passenger door and caught Porter before she could step onto the driveway. "Stop, don't move."

"What?" my wife said, barely able to contain the frustration in her voice.

"Don't leave the house!"

"God damn it, Gene. I've been cooped up in this house all

day—worried sick mind you—and now you're telling me I can't stand in my own driveway?"

"I sent you a bunch of texts," I said, pulling out my phone.

"I lost my phone at the damn restaurant, or did you forget that?"

If lightning had come down from the heavens and split me stem to stern I would not have been more shocked than I was at that moment.

Someone's getting those texts, and whoever has your phone would know all about... Kris!

I scrolled for Tabby's number as Tristan poured Cathy out of the backseat of the car. She leaned against him for support.

"Cathy!" my wife shouted, shooting past me and down the driveway toward our daughter. "Are you okay?"

"Hey, Gene," a perky and bubbling Tabby said on the other end of the phone. "What can I do for you?"

"Tabby, is everything alright?" I held my breath.

"Yeah, it's fine."

"Oh, thank God—"

"That sweet young woman Porter texted me about just swung by just a few minutes ago to pick up Kris. It was so nice of you guys to take on a disabled babysitter—frostbite on her arm as a kid, amazing story—anyway, I loaned her one of our old car seats, so she's good. Nice and safe."

My guts collapsed, and in doing so, made sure my lungs wouldn't pull in air. It was like being dragged under by the tide, but without an ocean wave in sight.

"Gene?" Tabby said.

I felt my knees hit the pavement.

"Gene? I think we got disconnected."

I tried to speak, but no words came out, and if they had Tabby wouldn't have heard them; she'd hung up.

Porter placed an arm under Cathy and with Tristan and Adam's help they carried our daughter into the garage.

"What is she saying?" Porter asked over her shoulder as she opened the door and directed Tristan and my apprentice toward the couch. "Are you going to get Kris?"

"I..."

"Oh my God, Gene," Porter said, seeing me on my knees, her voice breaking with panic. "What is it? What happened?"

"Kris is gone."

"What do you mean he's gone? He was at Tabby's house. She wouldn't just let him go. What—"

"She used your phone."

It was Porter's turn to come up short of breath. "Who—"

"They used your phone to text her. They had all my messages, how could they not know? They sent Lucina there to get him and texted Tabby ahead of time like it was coming from you."

Every ounce of color drained out of my wife's face. She clutched at my workbench to keep herself upright.

"Who is Lucina?"

"I'm going to find him and get him back," I said, reaching for Porter.

My wife pushed me away and steadied herself. "Who is Lucina?"

Before I could respond, my phone started ringing, the warbling vocals of Black Magic Woman filling the hot garage. It was a number I didn't recognize—the bright green answer button flashed.

"Answer it!"

"Hello?" I said, switching the phone to speaker.

Morgan's sultry voice oozed out from the other end. "Hey there, sexy."

Porter grabbed her chest, the air escaping from her lungs like a burst balloon. "Gene..."

"It's her."

My wife had done her best to hide it, but since college she'd lived in fear of that voice, and the woman attached to it. Morgan's evil had fueled an untold number of nightmares, but all this time that had been the extent of it. The sun would rise and the darkness would vanish. My wife could go about her day safe in the knowledge she was protected, and that Morgan Crowley was no more.

Porter's fingers drifted to the spot where her engagement ring once sat. Morgan had returned, and there was nothing for my wife to wake up from. "How is she alive? You told me no one comes back from that. Ed said as much. Gene, how is she alive?"

"I don't know…"

"And a warm hello to you, too, Porter," Morgan spit the name out like it was spent gum. "Hold on, someone wants to say something. Go ahead…"

"Hi, Mom!"

My wife slammed her hand down on the workbench. A momma bear enraged, whatever fear she had of Morgan got pushed into the backseat at the sound of her son's voice. "Give me back my son, you bitch!"

Any air left in my wife's lungs was expelled in a single burst. It was like she'd been kicked in the gut and couldn't recover fast enough to speak.

"Mom?"

"Hi, Kris," I said, trying to keep our youngest from getting worried. "I'll be there in a little bit. Are you okay?"

"Oh yeah, there's popcorn and snacks and—"

"He's fine," Morgan said, returning to the phone. "And he'll stay that way, provided you bring me what I want."

My wife regained her composure enough to respond. "What do you want?"

"Tell her, Gene. Tell her what I want."

I looked back at the car, and the sigil-covered skull tucked under the seat.

"She wants the skull."

"What skull?" Porter said, then ripped the phone out of my hand. "You touch my son and I'll tear off your skull and hand it to you."

"That's sweet, Porter, but your threats still ring hollow—just like in college. Gene, you sexy Magician, get me the skull—and who knows, perhaps I can convince you to come back to the winning team."

"Morgan—"

"Meet me at the theater in one hour, just you and the skull, and I'll have Lucina return your son to you."

Movies and television are so good at telling you all the rules for a hostage negotiation—smart things like choosing the place, asking for proof of life, and calling the police, but what they forget to tell you is just how hard all that is to remember all that when your son's life is on the other end of the line.

"Fine."

Porter pushed past me and stormed toward her still-idling car.

I clicked off the phone. "Porter, where are you going?"

My wife yanked the passenger door open and tore into the glove box. She retrieved a small, matte-black handgun with trembling fingers. "I'll find her and make her give me my son back—or I'll show her what a *real* mother is capable of."

43

THE UNHOLY HAND GRENADE OF PORTER

I approached my wife slowly, her hands still shaking. "Where did you get that?"

"You think you're the only one that worries about the family? I worry too—a lot." My wife ejected the magazine and checked the contents like a well-practiced pro.

"I see you've done that before."

Porter rammed the magazine home, the gun giving off a satisfying click as the metal locked into position. "Terrible things follow you, Gene. They find you wherever you go. I learned that lesson in Miami a long time ago. Since that time I upgraded to heavier artillery. You remember Miami, don't you?"

"I do…"

"Yeah, well, I got tired of being helpless."

"I'm sorry."

Porter checked the safety. "We can worry about that later. Right now, I have a son to find."

"Damn, Magician—this one is tough as testes!" the Imp said, crawling out from under the seat and dragging behind him one sigil-covered skull.

A startled Porter jumped and fumbled with her gun before training it on the Minor Demon.

"What the hell is that?"

"Don't shoot!" I yelled, not so much for the Imp as for the barely contained mass of sigil-locked Magick currently inhabiting the skull between the tiny monster's legs. "Porter, meet the Imp. Imp, this is—"

"One mighty fine specimen of raw female power—and she's packing, to boot. I gotta say I'm impressed, Magician. I took one look at your khakis and didn't figure you for much of a ladies man, but was I ever wrong."

"What's he talking about? Actually, you know, I don't care. What is an Imp and what the hell is it doing in the back of my car?"

"An Imp is a Minor—"

"Hey, I thought we talked about that," the Imp said, cutting me off.

"He's a Demon, but the small and mainly concerned with screwing things up kind."

"You mean, like a 'from Hell' sort of Demon?"

"Yeah, but—"

"What's he doing in my car?"

"He is guarding that Old Dead's skull. It's jacked up with Magick that Morgan wants to draw from—ostensibly to destroy you and get me back or, barring that, usher Asaroth the Defiler into this world. Or if all else fails, just turn us into hosts for the most vile New Dead she can find."

The Imp nodded. "That does sort of cover it really well. Nice work, Magician."

"And why is this skull battery thing on the floor of my car?"

The Imp shrugged. "It seemed better than putting it on the seat." He reached out and ran a hand over the leather. "I mean, this is nice leather, and I just figured..."

"It's a long story—"

"That I don't have time for," my wife said, waving her gun toward the driveway. "Get the hell out of my car—now."

"Wait, Porter, you don't understand. Morgan will kill for that skull, and if she gets it back, then she'll use the power inside to—"

"The bitch wants the skull, huh?"

"Yes, but—"

Porter grabbed the Imp's tiny wings and tossed him on to the driveway, then kicked the door shut with her foot.

"You don't even know where they are," I said, pleading with my wife to stop.

Porter didn't listen, instead she climbed into the driver seat and jammed her handgun in the cup holder. "They're at that stupid movie theater over by the Karate school."

"Wait! What are you going to do?"

"I'm going to *do* something. I'm not going to sit around for an hour while God knows what happens to my son."

"Honey, get out of the car, we need to put together a plan. Trust me, I've done this before, I've gone off half-cocked and it doesn't end well."

My wife pulled the skull out of the back and set in on the seat next to her. "I've got a plan—either she gives me my son, unharmed and in one piece, or I'll smash this thing into a million pieces in front of her."

"That's a terrible idea—"

"You got a better one?"

"Yes! Please come inside. I don't like the fact that Morgan has our son any more than you do, but driving over there and threatening her is going to get you killed. You don't have any protection. Your ring is gone, remember? Unmade! That means whatever she wants to throw at you, she can, and there's nothing you can do to stop it."

My wife paused for a second, one hand on the wheel and the other on the gear shift. "How did you handle her the last time?"

"Adam aimed an Imp at her head and threatened to unravel any Magick she performed, but it was insane; the unraveling could have just as easily undone the protections on that skull."

Porter unlocked the passenger door and pushed it open. "Hey, pink-demon-thing, you want to take a ride?"

The Imp looked at me. "Ah?"

"No, you don't." The tiny Demon shook his head.

My wife slammed the door shut.

"Don't do it, Porter, you've got a damn Magickal hand grenade in your front seat. You shatter it and we'll have a lot worse problems on our hands."

Porter put the car in reverse. "Magickal grenade, huh? Sounds to me like Morgan better get her shit in order, cause if I don't get my son back I'm going to fuck it right the hell up."

My wife tore out of the driveway and down the street, leaving the Imp and me alone.

"You sure know how to pick 'em," the Minor Demon said, rubbing his head with a tiny clawed hand. "Are all your women, so... expressive?"

Porter's car tires squealed as she rounded the corner, leaving a trail of smoke behind them.

"Yeah, I guess they are."

44

HOME BOUND

The Imp and I entered the house to find Adam and Tristan standing over a slowly waking Cathy.

"Give her some room," I said, pushing the two men to either side. "You okay, honey?"

Cathy blinked her eyes a few times. "Yeah, ugh—I feel like I was hit by a garbage truck. What was that, Dad?"

"That was some seriously shitty Magick—I'm just glad you're okay."

"Where's Mom?"

"She left."

"She what?" at least two of them said in unison.

"Morgan has Kris and wants the skull. Porter, it turns out, has a loaded gun in her glove box. She's trucking the Old Dead skull to the Brighton 8 in exchange for Kris."

"You can't let her have the skull back," Tristan said, his eyes pleading. "You don't know what she'll do to me, or my family."

"Trust me, Morgan being reunited with a Magickal battery at nigh-full charge is basically the last thing I want, but she dragged Porter into this, and now there's no telling what'll happen."

"She'll get possessed again, I know she will," Tristan said, running a hand through his thick young-man hair.

"Wait—how did you know she was possessed before?" I said, turning my attention to the boyfriend of the month.

"Because I drove the van. The skull is more than a battery, Morgan uses it to control these ghost things—"

"New Dead," Adam and I said for him.

"Yeah, something like that. Anyway, she uses the skull to summon and command them."

"I figured as much. We've got to get there before my wife does."

Adam rubbed at his beard. "How are we going to do that? We don't have a car."

Shit.

"Let me figure out that. Tristan, you stay here with Cathy—"

"Dad!"

"Don't even start with me, young lady. You've had a more than a full day and I don't want to go into this worried about you."

"But I can help," my daughter said, struggling to pick herself up from the couch.

"I know you want to but honestly, right now you're a liability, along with Tristan. It's damn hard to possess an experienced Magician, and the New Dead know that. Adam and I will go, I need you and Tristan here and safe."

"But I *am* a Magician!"

It was my turn to raise my voice. "Not yet you aren't. Right now, you are a sweet young woman with a flair for speaking to the dead. You don't know the first thing about what it takes, what it really takes, to be a Magician. There are sacrifices, Cathy. Hell, the whole damn thing is a bunch of sacrifices. You aren't ready for that."

"I'm not ready? There's a whole stack of books in there that says otherwise. I think you're the one who isn't ready."

So much of her mother.

"Cathy—"

"No, Dad, this is my family, too, so I deserve some say in what happens."

I threw my hands up. "I don't have time to argue with you. Stewart The Annoying, do not let my daughter or Tristan leave this house."

"It is done—gah, that's a terrible name," the tiny Demon said.

"Dad!" Cathy cried, pushing herself up from the couch. "What are you doing?"

"I'm keeping you and Tristan safe, the best way I know how."

"Gene, what have you done to him?" Adam asked, taking a step back from the once-jovial Minor Demon now perched on the coffee table like a trained attack dog.

"I've given him a purpose. Now he'll do what I say, exactly how I say it, until I release him."

"But he looks so... dark?"

"The Imp is fine—which is more than I can say for us. Adam, go into my closet and get the red duffle bag from on top of my safe. Don't worry, but it might squawk."

"You got it—wait, what? Did you say squawk?"

"Yes. Is there a problem?"

"What's in it?" my timid apprentice asked.

"Spare socks and underwear—what the hell do you think? It's a bit of Magick I keep secret for rainy days. I'd say this counts as a rainy day, wouldn't you?"

"What does it do?"

"Adam—red duffle, top of the safe, behind an ill-inspired tan suit. Do *not* shake it!"

Adam hesitated, then raced off into my bedroom.

The bag wasn't going to be enough, Morgan had become far too powerful since her college days—it was the skull. What had Porter called it? A Magick battery?

I stared at Kris's toy cars. Even though the rug was back

down and covering the Seal of Ariadne, my son's cars and the few batteries I'd removed from them remained pushed up against the wall where I'd left them what seemed like forever ago.

Pull out the battery and the toy dies—but that move is textbook insanity. Still she's got Kris, and by now Porter too. Desperate times...

I pulled my phone out and scrolled through the texts until I found Rob's last message. I mashed the dial button, and the compact mechanic answered on the second ring.

"Hey, Gene. What can I do for you?"

"I need a couple of favors—like right now."

Rob's voice switched to serious mode. "What do you need?"

"First, I need a ride."

"I think the guys are all done with the Dad Wagon. I was going to roll it around the block a few times to make sure—"

"I need it here."

"You got it. What else?"

"Is Justine around?"

"She's over at the precinct right now, but I think she's going on a break shortly. Is everything okay?"

"It will be. Can you give me her number?"

"Sure," Rob said, then rattled off Justine's phone number. "You sure you're okay, buddy? You don't sound like yourself."

"Porter's in trouble, Rob—or at least she will be unless I take care of a major problem. Now, when can you get here?"

"I'm on my way."

"Great, see you in a few."

I clicked off the call as Adam rounded the corner with my red duffle. The mission-oriented Imp continued to guard my frustrated daughter and her boyfriend. I punched up the digits for Justine and was pleasantly surprised when she answered on the second ring.

"Justine, hi, it's Gene Law. Yes, from earlier... I'm so happy for you too. Now, I hate to do this, but I have a favor to ask—and it's a big one."

* * *

TRUE TO HIS WORD, the best mechanic in West Florida was at my house in less than ten minutes. The Dad Wagon purred in the front yard, ready for action.

After a few last-minute admonishments to the Imp and my daughter, I joined Adam and Rob on the old concrete driveway in the dusky half-light of early evening.

"All good to go, Gene."

"Thanks, Rob. Listen, I need you to stay here. I don't have time to drive you back, and it's really not safe where we're going."

The compact mechanic waved me off. "I talked to the crew—we want to help."

"We?"

A second car pulled into my driveway—a large truck with six monster wheels and a rich black paint job. All in all, it was not unlike the ill-fated Banshee-shredded vehicle from the other morning, but this one had far fewer fairies and a lot more tough-looking dudes.

"Yeah, I got the whole crew to come along. They know you and your wife. You guys have been coming to us for, what? Seven years?"

"Yeah, but it's—"

"Right, you're practically family. So I told them your wife was in trouble and they all decided to come."

The driver of the Mack Truck of manliness waved to me from behind the glass. His five o'clock shadow appeared to be a semi-permanent fixture, but it went well with the scar along his chin, and expertly complemented the tattoos on his neck.

"Rob," I said, guiding my mechanic away from the lynch-mob-on-wheels. "I appreciate the offer, I really do, but these aren't *people* problems, these are *Magick* problems."

"I figured as much, but the guys want to help. They're tough as nails, Gene."

I don't doubt that for one minute.

"They've all done their time and they're good people. People you *want* on your side."

Rob was right. I did need people on my side, and his crew were some of the toughest-looking guys to ever grace my driveway, but what was tough when compared to the spirits of the damned?

"Rob, let me be blunt. This is New Dead, a lot of them. These are the spirits of the damned, summoned up from Hell to possess the bodies of the living. I don't care if your guys are swinging tire irons and lug wrenches, it's not going to make a difference."

"But—"

"They're ghosts, Rob. It's not like you can hit them."

I hated taking the wind out of his sails, but what could I do? If I let his crew roll in, there was just as good a chance they'd turn into rides themselves, and we'd have an even bigger problem on our hands.

"I understand," my mechanic said, turning back to the truck. "I'll get the guys to drive me back to the shop."

Rob walked past my apprentice, who was lost in thought staring at the rippling man-muscles in the black pickup. He unconsciously ran a hand along his waist and grazed an already overloaded belt.

I should get him one of those jiu-jitsu belts—wait, that's it!

"Rob, wait! I've got an idea. Tell your crew to follow me."

45

TIRE IRON PHYSICS

*I*t was good to be back in the Dad Wagon. Even with everything that was happening, it somehow felt right to be driving to near certain-agony and death in the Mazda. The Lone Ranger had his horse—I had my car.

"What's the plan?" Adam asked.

"The plan? The plan is simple: save Porter and Kris, and don't get killed, maimed, burned, or possessed in the process."

I kept an eye on the black truck behind us. Rob and his crew of prison-grade mercenaries hugged close to our tail.

"I meant for the... the help you have coming with us."

"Oh, you mean the muscle?"

"Yeah."

"Back when this all started I had a particularly vicious New Dead come after me at Cathy's jiu-jitsu school."

"What'd you do?"

"Dragged it out of the guy and into the bathroom—gave it enough substance so I could actually fight it."

All the color drained out of Adam's face. "Isn't that dangerous?"

"Well, only if you consider giving a bloodthirsty spirit of the damned that would love nothing more than to split your skull a corporeal body dangerous."

Adam fidgeted with his seat belt. "Ah…"

"But that wasn't even the most dangerous part."

My apprentice let go of the seat belt and hugged my bag a little tighter to his chest. "Then which part was?"

"The part when I opened a gate to Hell."

"What?!"

"It's not that bad—just have to watch out for the fleas."

"The fleas?"

Before I could answer, we pulled into the parking lot with the black truck right behind us. Bright yellow light spilled out from the long windows of Cathy's jiu-jitsu school. It appeared to be in session, and there were enough cars out front to have me more than a little concerned—an army of trained fighters possessed by the spirits of the damned would really be a pain in the butt.

Why couldn't it be the Yarn Barn that stayed open on Saturday night on the far side of town? It had to be skilled fighters.

"There's your wife's car!" Adam shouted, pointing at Porter's slick new ride parked in front of the theater. "I don't see her."

"Neither do I."

I also don't sense the Old Dead. Neither of those things make for a good sign.

I parked the Dad Wagon next to Porter's car. There were no signs of a struggle, and a small flashing red light on the dash told me she'd taken the time to lock the car.

The muscle truck pulled in next to us, its powerful engine rumbling to a stop.

"What are we going to do?" Adam asked, keeping an eye on the darkened entrance to the Brighton 8.

"We'll start with getting out of the car," I said, taking my red duffle from Adam and pushing open the door. I stopped to get a look at the Honda's back seat—no skull, and no Porter.

Am I relieved? Or just a different form of concerned?

I gently placed the duffle on the hood of the still-warm Dad Wagon.

Rob and his crew piled out of their truck like murdershriners, each one just a tiny bit scarier than the one before them, but all looking to the world's best mechanic to lead them.

"Thanks for offering to help guys," I said, trying to look tough in spite of my ashen-faced apprentice. "I don't know what Rob told you..."

One of the larger and more heavily muscled mechanics pounded a fist into his palm. "He said your wife was in trouble."

"Aside from the kidnapping of my son, yes, that about sums it up. Wait, I forgot to mention the unholy spirits of the damned."

"Huh?"

"He means ghosts," Adam said, puffing up his chest.

Muscles started, then froze mid-nod. "Wait, did you say ghosts?"

"Sure did."

The large man conferred with a lanky face-tattooed individual next to him before returning to me. "So you know how to get rid of ghosts?"

"I do."

A wave of relief washed over Muscles. "Oh hell yeah. Let's bust some ghost shit up!"

Rob placed a hand on Muscle's shoulder. "Thanks, Charlie. Now, Gene, is that the place?" the lead mechanic said, pointing to the theater.

"It is. Remember, though, this woman has my son, and potentially now my wife. I can't have you guys go barging in there—"

The disappointment on their faces was palpable.

"—until we have a plan. I can't have you guys getting

possessed by sprits of the damned and then deciding our heads would look better detached from our bodies."

A smattering of nods and neck rubs told me I still had at least half my audience. "Just give Adam and me a minute to figure out the best plan, then we'll go."

Rob nodded and conferred with his team of human-sized action figures.

I unzipped the duffle, splitting it from stem to stern across the car's hood like a gutted fish. "Adam, remember when you made love jerky?"

My apprentice turned away from the darkened strip mall long enough to cock his head to one side and look at me like I'd gone crazy. "Yeah... but I don't think being a goat would really help us, and it was so itchy..."

"I don't want you to make love jerky, but I want you to apply some of that skill of yours toward concocting potions."

"What kind of potion?"

Jingle.

One of the strip mall doors opened, bringing with it a sour bouquet of rot and burnt flesh that caught the breeze and wafted over us.

"Where did that come from?" I said, my back to the shops.

"From the school; they're coming this way!"

"Shit—"

"There's like two dozen of them..." Adam said, his voice cracking. "Is that what New Dead smell like?"

"Yeah. Lovely isn't it? Now help me, we've got to get them out of those innocent people before our mechanic muscle bashes someone's skull with a socket wrench."

"What do you want me to do?"

"I want you to work up a spell to get the spirits out of their bodies and subjected to the laws of tire-iron physics."

Adam wrung his hands. "I don't... I only..."

"There's a pump sprayer in the trunk, go grab it."

My apprentice popped open the Mazda's trunk and returned with a white plastic pesticide sprayer, its black nozzle dangling above the ground behind him like a scorpion's tail.

"There's nothing in it…"

"Crap."

Adam crunched up his face. "We need something earthy, right? Something with salt in it?"

Salt of the earth—great equalizer when it comes to spirits.

"Yes."

My apprentice turned to the tattooed tag-team wrestling squad. "Any of you guys have like an energy drink or something?"

Muscles nodded. "Yeah, I got a Monstero, but I drank some —is that okay?"

Adam grabbed the oil-can-sized beverage. "Oh yeah, these are good. Have you tried the Gorilla Grape?"

"No, I'll ask my mom—err, my housekeeper to get me some," Muscles said, looking around furtively, as if checking to see if anyone had noticed his slip-up. If anyone had, they'd taken into account the size of his biceps and decided it wasn't worth following up on.

Adam dumped the can into the pump sprayer. "One thousand milligrams of salt per serving."

"How many servings?"

"Three in this can."

"Holy crap, it's amazing your heart still works," I said, shaking my head.

"All part of a balanced diet," Adam said as he screwed the lid back on the pump sprayer.

"I'm pretty sure no one—literally no one ever—considered Monstero part of a balanced diet."

Adam ignored me. "What now?"

"Now, before they get here, I need you to enchant that Monstero to extract the New Dead from those," I said, pointing to the dozen plus smoldering souls of the damned closing in on us.

Adam hesitated. "I don't know if..."

"You've got the skill to do this. I know you can do it, but more than that, I *believe* you can do it."

Magick is all about belief—it's time to put mine to the test.

"Wait, Gene! What are you going to do?"

I gently dug my hands into the duffle, coming back with a slightly oversized bright-pink plastic yard flamingo. I zipped the bag shut and cradled the yard art under my arm like a football, then turned to face the darkened doors of the Brighton 8. "I'm going to go save my family."

"Gene? Where'd you go?" Adam asked, as if looking right through me. Which, as long as I held the flamingo, he was.

I set the small plastic bird back on the hood. "The Flock, it's a long story, and honestly, one you would do good to not emulate."

My apprentice smiled and pumped air into the sprayer. "I won't let you down, boss."

"I know you won't. You're a great apprentice, and if I survive this, beer's on me."

"Really?"

I didn't have time to answer him before the first wave of the martial art monsters were upon us.

Yes, really—now don't make me regret thinking that.

46

FLARES AND FLAMINGOS

*T*hey didn't stop to talk. Then again I don't know what the New Dead would say that I hadn't already heard before. The refrain was pretty much the same every time. "We are terribly unhappy at the current state of our existence. We wish you ill will and would like to take your life as our own."

They don't use those exact terms, but the *soul* of the message was always the same.

Adam gave that pump sprayer one last thrust, then spoke the incantation. Magick popped and clicked like a cheap keyboard from my apprentice's fingers. "Format c colon!"

I almost dropped Gertrude the Flamingo. I'd always taught that incantations should be in a language other than your tongue, but I hadn't expected Adam to go with a command right out of the nineteen-eighties DOS manual.

It worked, though, I could feel the Magick flow down his arm and into the frothy green energy drink in the tank.

I'll be damned. You did it. I never doubted you... Okay, just a little.

Adam turned the spray nozzle on the fiery horde of compression-shirted possessed. Bright green energy drink infused with enough sodium to stop a horse—and more than a little Adam-brand Magick—rained down on the New Dead in a faint mist.

The burning spirits of the damned writhed in pain before being forced out of their hosts.

Now visible, and supremely pissed off, they made for one heck of a target.

Muscles was the first to pull a lug wrench out of the back of the pickup and start swinging. I'd have expected more fear, but these guys had been raised on worse in video games; for them, this must be just the next logical progression. His forged-steel wrench smashed into one of New Dead, blasting a hunk of ashen bone and withered flesh from its face.

Nice!

My excitement was short lived, however, as the creatures missing flesh restored themselves in seconds with a vibrant green glow.

What the hell else was in that energy drink?

Rob didn't waste any time. He organized his crew, and they went on the offensive. Adam kept the spray on until the pump ran out, then followed up by swinging the plastic tank with wild abandon. He made contact more than once, but all he succeeded in doing was making the creatures angrier.

The newly freed jiu-jitsu students didn't know what to make of the situation, but to their credit when one of the New Dead got the better of Rob's guys those ground-fighting experts immediately latched on and went for broke.

It was a full-on melee, and I had to use my best moves to weave between the fighters. The lanky mechanic with the impressive neck ink swung a well-timed crowbar and blasted one of the New Dead in the leg; but since he didn't see me, he didn't know he'd only missed my ducking head by inches. The parking lot was a minefield of tearing claws and blunt force trauma.

Holding the flamingo under my arm like a football, I

launched myself into the fray. With that beautiful piece of yard art in my hands I was invisible, but that didn't mean I couldn't get hurt—it just meant they wouldn't get to see me writhing in pain. That little bird and I had been through a few dust ups, and each time we'd come out on top. I just hoped she had a little more luck tucked away in those plastic feathers. Fists swung for my head, and I ducked, only to tumble to my knees to avoid being blasted by Rob's foot.

The more the New Dead fought, the more they regenerated. Something was keeping the them fresh as a daisy. They weren't going to go down with flesh and steel—we needed to open a Hellgate.

I crossed another few feet, only to skip to the side when a lug wrench blasted a dent in the pavement where I'd been standing. It was then that it opened up: a clean shot to the door. I squeezed the plastic bird under my arm and took a deep breath.

"Geronimo!" I shouted, racing through the fray, dodging fists and claws, leaping grapplers and the damned.

I burst free and into the narrow drive in front of the theater, only to slam right into the side of a black and white police cruiser.

Boom!

The impact knocked the air out of my lungs, and shattered my companion, sending tiny shards of the once-Magickal bird raining down on the dark pavement.

No!

I laid what remained of the tiny bird's head gently on the pavement.

I'm sorry, little one.

"Gene?" Officer Justine's squad car blocked my path to the door. "What the hell is going on?"

I sucked in a deep breath. "A lot... Did you bring it?"

Justine appeared far more concerned about the fighting going on behind me. "Yes, but... what are those?"

"New Dead—long story. Did you bring the bones?"

Justine reached for her radio, then stopped. "Shit—do you know how much trouble I'd be in if my captain knew I was doing this?"

"Immense amounts is my guess."

"Hell yeah. Are you sure you know what you're doing?"

"Nope."

Justine popped the trunk on her cruiser. "They're in the evidence box. We don't have the whole skeleton, we're missing—"

"The head."

"Yeah, how'd you know?"

"Because it's inside there," I said, pointing to the ominous doors of the Brighton 8. "With the woman holding my wife and son captive."

"This is a kidnapping, Gene. You should have called the police."

I removed the brown cardboard banker's box from the trunk of Justine's cruiser. It was lighter than I'd expected it to be, but then again, I guess I really didn't know what I'd expected it to be. It wasn't like I carry around boxes of bones every day.

When your daughter becomes a Magician, you'll get more experience with it. Just think of all the weekends at the graveyards. So. Much. Awesome.

"I did. You're here."

Justine caught sight of Rob and his muscle across the parking lot, and her jaw tightened. "I told him not to do anything stupid."

I held the box under my arm and let the trunk close. "Rob? He couldn't do anything stupid even if he wanted to, he's like the smartest guy I know."

"He has a tendency to go off half-cocked from time to time..."

What's the chubby bearded guy doing?" Justine leaned out her window and stared past me at Adam.

"He's my apprentice," I said, turning to see what Adam was doing. "It would appear he's trying to open a gate to Hell and doesn't remember he needs brimstone—can we borrow one of your flares?"

Justine hesitated. "Borrow?"

"Thanks!" I yelled, pulling one of the bright red flares from her trunk. "Adam, catch!"

I launched the unlit flare end over end toward my apprentice.

Please catch it.

As it would turn out, my kindergartener possessed more catching acumen than Adam—a lot more. My apprentice dropped the pump sprayer and reached out for the flare, only to have it pass through his fingers and slam headlong into his face.

Ouch.

"I got it!" Adam cried, rubbing his face while feeling the ground for the dropped flare.

Before he could get his hands on it, though, New Dead pounced on him, sending Adam and the flare spinning across the pavement.

"Shit!" Justine unhooked her seat belt and kicked open the door. The tough-as-nails future detective left the squad car running and raced across the parking lot, nightstick in hand.

"Go! Save your family—I got this."

CRACKER BREAK

J had my bag unzipped and was ready to fill it with the dusty bones of Old Dead still sitting in Justine's squad car, when a familiar voice stopped me cold.

"I told you I'd be back, Magician."

The New Dead...

I grabbed for the first thing in the trunk I could find that wasn't Old Dead, but sadly Justine must have been on traffic duty, as all I could put my fingers on was a scuffed-up orange traffic cone. I swung the cone in a wild arc, missing the possessed Claudia Wilson by mere inches.

"Whoa—" She pulled back, surprisingly spry for her age thanks to the New Dead. "Being inside your wife was so good. Then again, you already knew that."

The New Dead's ashen face taunted me, its tongue licking those burnt lips.

"I'm done sending you back to hell."

"Good, cause I'm done going back. You can't stop The Defiler—not now. He's coming and—"

The New Dead must not have gotten the memo—don't go into any diatribes until you've got the advantage, and certainly don't do it when you've got a traffic cone pointed at your head. I slapped the possessed woman across the face with the wide base of the rubbery orange barricade. It was a largely symbolic gesture, but it sure as hell made me feel better. "Would you just cut the bullshit?"

The possessed theater owner snarled and lunged at me like a jungle cat. In hindsight pissing it off might not have been the smartest move. Energized by the possession, Claudia's sinewy body hit me like a bag of iron rods. My knees buckled against the squad car, and I tumbled into the trunk, my back landing hard alongside the box of Old Dead bones.

"Maybe I should pay your wife a visit again?" Claudia said, her ashen face inches from mine. "I think she liked it."

I reared back to take a swing at the old woman, and hesitated. Claudia had to be in her eighties; if I broke her body the New Dead would just move on, and where would that leave her?

Damn moral compass...

The New Dead proprietress made sure I paid dearly for that moment of hesitation, launching herself on top of me and raining down a hailstorm of highly energized fists.

This plan isn't working.

I pushed back against Claudia, but the New Dead was too strong. Her body clung to mine, and she kept the punches coming—even though she was old, the New Dead was more than making up for it with unholy rage. I wasn't going to hold up long under this sort of punishment, but I couldn't hurt Claudia.

I need to change the venue.

"I'm not letting you get my wife," I said, only half defending against the spinning blows. "Not again."

As expected, the monster came in harder, slamming fists and yanking me close. "You will, and you'll love it."

I needed a fair fight, and I wasn't going to get that out here in the real world.

We Magicians have a few innate defenses when it comes to New Dead, the chief of which being we are typically a lot more difficult to possess. The reasons for this aren't exactly understood, or well-studied, but I believe it comes from a sort of base conditioning you have as a practitioner of the Magickal Arts. So, what better thing to do than willingly drop those protections and draw the New Dead inside.

Now this is more my jam—reckless seat-of-the-pants style combat with the forces of evil.

Sensing his opportunity, the New Dead left Claudia Wilson and dove head first into me.

Welcome to my jungle.

* * *

I'D LET the New Dead inside me with the express intent to use whatever I had available to me to defeat him from the inside, and my subconscious had selected… my office.

What, did it expect me to staple him to death? Put him in an HR report?

Standing in front of me, the New Dead's spirit was far bigger than I'd expected. In fact he made Rob's muscle-men look small by comparison. His ghostly form loomed in the frame of my office door, barely squeezing between the imaginary jamb.

"That was a stupid move, Magician."

I believe the exact term is 'brain-dead stupid move,' thank you very much.

The New Dead stepped into my office, his wide hands flexing. He took a deep breath. "Yeah, there's some power here, I can smell it. I'm going to enjoy destroying your life."

"I'm pretty sure I've already beat you to that."

My old desk was the only piece of furniture between me and

an unhealthy mental beatdown, and it didn't last long. The New Dead grabbed the wooden edge and yanked it aside, knocking its imaginary contents across the floor. Pens, papers, files, and a half-eaten package of the saltiest crackers I'd ever tasted skidded across the cheap carpet.

Salt crackers!

I grabbed the seat back of my green chair and swung the broken duct-taped mess at the spirit—in my mind I'm a damn good bit stronger than in real life, and I have lots of great wrestling moves.

Butt-spring beatdown!

The spinning legs of the world's worst chair smashed into the New Dead's face, shredding his burnt skin and sending a splatter of black ichor across the wall. As easily as it would snap a dry twig, the monstrous spirit grabbed the chair by its wheeled base and ripped it out of my hands, then sent it crashing into the wall.

I really hate that chair.

The New Dead lunged at me with his catchers-mitt-sized hands aimed for my neck. I pushed off the back wall and dove for the half-eaten package of salty peanut butter crackers. I got a hand on the plastic package, but not before the New Dead had his own crushing grip on my leg.

He pulled me back across the floor like a cat playing with its meal.

"You should never have let me in here, Magician. Now I'm going to make it mine."

Bold words, but not entirely accurate. This was my imagination, my mind, and therefore it ran on my rules. These weren't just the saltiest crackers I'd ever tasted, these were the best exorcism crackers ever created—my mind, my rules.

I crushed the flimsy plastic in my hands, letting the pulverized bits of salty goodness accumulate in what remained of the sleeve.

The New Dead flipped me over like an overcooked pancake and pulled me toward him. "This ends now," he said, his burned and blackened face leering.

I unloaded the sleeve of salt-coated delight into that mug and covered him with the burning goodness of 'Eugene Law's Finest Exorcism Crackers—now with extra *salt*.'

"Agh!"

The spirit tried to cover his eyes, but I didn't give it the chance. I plunged my thumbs into those soulless sockets and pushed the salt in deeper.

"No trips back to Hell this time!" I shouted, my fingers deep within the inky blackness of his head.

It's cracker time!

"Oblivio!"

48

BIG GUNS

*C*laudia Wilson didn't look so good, but after what she'd been through the poor woman should have looked a lot worse. I placed a hand under her nose and confirmed she was breathing, then gently laid her in the trunk of the car next to the box of Old Dead.

I shoved those dusty bones in my duffle—when you get right down to it, shoving dirty old bones into a bag really puts your life into perspective. It's one of those 'what am I doing with my life?' sort of moments where you inevitably end up with a mixed bag of emotions—and bones.

With the duffel loaded I took one last look at the New Dead battle still raging in the parking lot.

This is on you, Magician.

I pulled on the door and let the cool air ruffle my shirt.

Yeah, this might be my fault, but I'm sure as shit going to end it.

* * *

THE LOBBY of the Brighton 8 wasn't much different than I remembered it. The furniture was still wrapped in plastic, at least the pieces I could see. Someone had left the lights off, leaving me with only the dim beams breaking through the tinted glass doors to guide my way.

"Porter?" I asked, half hoping to hear my wife's voice complaining about me following her, or mucking up her perfectly good 'crazy-woman' plan.

Nothing.

I hefted the bag of bones on my shoulder and felt around the walls for a light switch.

You got this far without a real plan—impressive. What did Justine say? Going off half-cocked. Yeah, that sounds about right.

My fingers traced the outline of a switch.

Aha!

Click.

The entry lobby remained dark.

Damn it, too busy raising the dead to get the stinking power turned on? Come on, Morgan, get your shit together.

Using what little light there was I found the couch and ran my fingers along it. I figured I could trace a path along the furniture and find my way toward the concession area. If I remembered correctly, Claudia's office wasn't too far away.

My fingers rolled along the smooth contours of the couch, dipping down the cushions and then back up again. That was until they traced something else entirely—something smooth, soft, and altogether feminine.

"Porter?"

"Oh no, sexy—far better."

Lucina!

Strong yet supple fingers grabbed my wrists and yanked me into the crushing darkness of weaponized sexuality—my world went black.

* * *

269

DIM RED LIGHT filtered through half-open blinds and played across the wall in alternating bars. I stretched and let my hand slide over to the other side of the bed—still warm.

Where is she?

I slid her pillow toward me and buried my nose in the luxurious aroma. The mixture of roses and something more, something I couldn't put my finger on, only served to excite my lesser half further.

"Hey there, sexy," Lucina said, her voice drawing me to the outline of that curvaceous body back-lit by a flickering candle. "You like?"

What wasn't to like? Her all-but-transparent white lace left little to the imagination. The ripe fullness of her chest pressed against that gossamer fabric and drew me to them like a thirsty man in the desert. Smiling, she slid one finger down the center of her alluring top and pulled it aside to reveal a tantalizing seam of silvery-white in the flicking candle light. I pushed myself up in the bed, but found my legs didn't want to move.

"Oh, don't get up on my account," Lucina said, placing a knee on the bed and leaning forward, her chest scant millimeters from breaking what little containment the soft fabric offered. "Besides," she murmured, running a soft hand up my leg, "it would appear the most important part is already up and ready to go."

I was lost in her green eyes, somehow able to see them between the candle and the bright red bars covering the back wall. It was a small apartment—one of those efficiencies—but that hadn't stopped us from using every part of it. I was still hazy on the details, but I was sure we'd been together for next to forever—the sex was too amazing not to be.

Lucina crawled up onto the bed and let the ends of her plunging top graze my hips. I tried to reach for her, but I found my arm restrained. I was tied to the bed post with what looked like a white strip of silk.

Odd, I wasn't tied up a second ago...

"Did you forget? You promised me we could try something a bit more... exotic," the green-eyed vixen said with a subtle bite to her words.

That sounds like something I'd say—I'd say anything for more of her.

"I..."

"Shh." Lucina straddled me with her hips—warm and sensual hips that pressed against mine so perfectly. She leaned forward and let her breasts brush across my face. Still covered in the barest hint of fabric, they tickled my cheeks.

"Now," she said, leaning in to place her lips just above mine. "Kiss me."

I opened my mouth and let my eyes close, the soft whisper of her breath teasing my lips.

"Get your demon hands off my dad!"

Cathy! My daughter? I have a daughter!

TINY TWISTING

Catherine Law—my daughter.

It took a few seconds for that thought to pierce the gossamer veil of Lucina's sexpot enchantment, but by then her Half-Succubus lips had touched mine. The soft flesh lips dragged me down like a boat anchor, pulling me deeper into an abyss of ecstasy and oblivion. The Succubi fed on lust, and Morgan's daughter had found a way to tap into a rich vein of desire hidden in the recesses of my soul.

"Dad!" Catherine shouted.

Part of me wanted to swim to her, to fight back against the waves of unrelenting pleasure, but another part of me just wanted to let go. The tide was strong, and all I had to do was give in, then drift away to annihilation on the lips of Lucina.

I slammed into the wood floor, the bag of bones landing next to me, and blinked my eyes in the dim light. I was back in the lobby, with a ring-side seat to one hell of a cat fight.

Lucina, no longer draped in sexual prowess, but still dressed to kill in a flowing black gown—fought back against someone with more than a little grappling talent—my daughter.

Cathy's body wasn't solid; instead it was some spiritual

manifestation of my tiny twister. She had her hands wrapped around Lucina from behind, and was pulling and yanking at something.

Rip!

The Half-Succubus's soul pulled free from her body sending the sexy young woman collapsing to the ground next to me, while a demonic and grotesque version of her forced my daughter's back against the couch—and then through it.

"Cathy!"

The two women appeared on the other side. My translucent daughter was outfitted stem to stern in her favorite jiu-jitsu gi. With her ghostly hair pulled back, Cathy had come to fight. Lucina's Succubus half was a black and twisted thing, with long snake-like hair and spindly arms. Her naked breasts hung low and flapped against her body like cheap saddle bags. Using long claws, she slashed at my daughter's gut. The gash didn't draw blood—Cathy was pure spirit, after all—but it did slice into her and leave glowing white tears.

My daughter caught Lucina's claws and yanked her forward, twisting the demon-girl's rubbery body and latching onto her back. That was when I saw it, the glowing silver string that seemed to stretch on to eternity behind Cathy. Somehow, my daughter had figured out how to project her spirit from her body; Ariadne's Thread was the only link between the two halves of Catherine Law now. Cut that cord, and Cathy wouldn't be able to make it home—home, where her body lay in a near coma right this instant. This was some seriously dangerous and damn advanced Magick.

My seal and the safe... she'd gone past the beginner book—way the hell past.

Cathy had clamped down on the Demon's back and tucked her ankle under her opposite knee—a jiu-jitsu trick that made my little grappler nigh impossible to dislodge. Sadly, that move only worked when your opponent didn't have hidden wings.

Lucina's demon-soul flared out long bat-like wings, knocking Cathy backwards and forcing her to unhook her feet. The monster swung around and clamped its claws down on Cathy's cord.

"Oh no you don't!" I shouted, grabbing the bag of bones and hurling it at Lucina's dark-half like a hammer.

Crack.

The Old Dead's remains rammed into the demon-girl and crushed one of her wings against the hard floor. My daughter wasted no time and immediately mounted the rubbery black Demon and rained down a hailstorm of wild punches. Darkness spilled out of Lucina, but still my tiny twister poured it on.

"This is for my brother," she cried, her fist cracking the demon-girl's already crooked nose.

Lucina swung her claws wildly trying to fight off the ferocious Magician-in-training, but all this did was open her up for one of my daughter's favorite submissions.

Cathy caught the beast's arm and clutched it to her chest, then in a graceful and nigh-artistic fashion she swung her body around it like a fire pole. My daughter's back hit the wood with Lucina's arm bent between her legs. Cathy's knees flexed and her ankles squeezed against the Demon's head.

Arm bar. Finish it, sweetheart.

Cathy threw her hips forward and the spindly black arm snapped with a gut-churning wet crack.

Lucina screamed, a violent and terrible shriek that made me clutch at my head.

Cathy raised one of her legs and drove her heel hard into the Demon's face, ending the shriek with a single blow.

The black and bulbous body faded away beneath my tiny twister, along with the human form that lay unmoving on the floor.

"Dad... are you okay?" Cathy asked, trying to catch her breath.

"What part of don't leave the house didn't you understand?"

My daughter got to her bare feet and brushed back a few translucent hairs. "I haven't left the house. I'm still sitting in the Seal of Ariadne."

"Catherine Jude Law, you know exactly what I mean. You went in my safe—damn it, Cathy, that's dangerous Magick, and nigh insane at your skill level."

Cathy beamed. "Admit it. I did it. I found a way to help—"

"No, you found a way to put yourself in even more danger," I said, pointing at the silvery thread that faded into the darkness behind her. "Even now you're like a magnet to all the dark and evil things that dwell just beyond the veil. What happens if they cut that cord? What happens if you get lost in between?"

My daughter opened her mouth to respond, then closed it.

"Exactly. You didn't even think of that, did you?"

Of course she didn't, she's just like you and Porter—the Pixie dander doesn't fall far from the Magician.

"What should I do?" Cathy asked, crossing her arms and trying to look tough, but her face was now acutely aware of the dangerous situation she'd put herself in. I took a step toward her, but found my knees barely functional. I wobbled a bit and leaned against the couch. Lucina's kiss had drained my strength.

Had it drained my Magick too?

"Give me a second, I'll think of something. First, we've got to find your mom—"

Morgan's deep, velvety voice shattered my focus. "She's right here. Let me turn on a light…"

50

DEM BONES

*L*ight flooded the room, forcing me to cover my eyes. Always one for the dramatics, my ex-girlfriend had the Old Dead's skull once again solidly in her fingers.

"Where's Porter?" I shouted, pushing myself up from the couch and limping toward the counter.

Morgan tucked the skull under her arm. "I see you ran into Lucina. I made sure to tell her what you liked. I'll admit I find it hard to believe you found a way to turn that down—I thought I knew you too well."

"She's gone."

"Oh no, my daughter is lost forever." Morgan placed the back of her palm against her head. "Holy Hell, Gene. You really think it's that easy to fight off a Half-Succubus as powerful as Lucina? No, she's not gone—temporarily reforming in some lower Hell, sure. But gone? Hardly."

Morgan hadn't brought up Cathy once. Either she couldn't see her, or my daughter had found a way to hide herself; I didn't know whether to be proud, or even more terrified, but either way I dared not look for her.

"Where's my wife and son?"

"Why so direct, Gene?" Morgan asked, taking a step away from the counter. "You used to be so much more mysterious—married life really has blunted your sharp edges, hasn't it. I miss the *old* Law; he was darker, and a hell of a lot more fun." She pushed open the steel casket that was part of the display for *Demon High*. "Come on up, you two, time to join the party."

Porter sat up from inside the coffin with Kris clutched tight to her chest, and her gun pressed against his head.

My heart stopped and bile flooded the back of my throat. My wife's eyes were bright red and her face was awash in tears. For his part Kris, simply appeared too tired to follow much of what was going on. This far past his bed time I hoped I was right.

"Gene..." a shaky Porter said, her finger on the trigger. "I... can't... stop."

"Right, right... 'I can't stop.' Could you at least try to do this with a little more passion? Honestly, Gene, what did you see in this woman? Flat chest, flat hair, no personality, and worst of all, no Magick—I just don't get it."

"Morgan," I said, taking a step forward and stealing a glance at my bag. She was clearly drawing from the skull, but the bag of bones was too far out of reach. "What are you doing?"

"You don't get it?"

"No," I said, taking a small step toward the bag. I had no idea where Cathy had disappeared to, but I hoped she wasn't going to try anything stupid. "Asaroth the Defiler? Why would you want to bring him here? That's not your style."

Morgan tilted her head to one side. "Asaroth? Who the hell said anything about the Defiler?"

I moved a little closer to the bag. "Funny thing. You know he gave himself that nickname? No matter—you can't fool me. I saw the summoning sigil in theater eight—I was here the other night. I know you are going to use the Old Dead's Magick to summon him. What I don't know yet is why? Why the horde of New Dead? And why do that to Claudia Wilson?"

"I have no idea what you're talking about. Summoning circle? Asaroth? New Dead?"

That makes no sense. I saw the circle. I know Asaroth when I see him, and I know New Dead...

"I hate you, Gene. I mean like, complete abject hatred, but I don't mess with Asaroth. If I recall correctly, communing with higher powers is *your* thing."

The book... The book sitting in my safe... The safe my daughter opened.

"You ruined me, Gene."

It was my turn to be confused. "I don't understand."

Morgan squeezed the skull tighter, causing its sigils to glow a sickly green. "You will."

Porter cocked the gun. "Gene!"

"Do I have your attention now?" Morgan shouted.

"Morgan, you've had my attention ever since you got back into town," I said, not entirely lying, but hoping I could stall her long enough to reach the bag. "I'm guessing you're still angry with how we left things—"

"Guessing!"

"Let me finish," I said, taking another step toward the duffle. "When I saw you at the Shelldeck house it brought back a lot of emotions, you know that."

"You let me go!" Morgan shouted, forcing Porter to push the gun barrel against Kris's head. "I told you I loved you, and I did. We had so much potential, don't you remember? We were going to make the world a better place. Why, Gene? Why did you throw it all away?"

"I wasn't the person you thought I was."

"But I gave you so much. I taught you Magick. Eldero's Seven Seals, the Velcurses Conundrum, even the Jacobean Prefect."

Just a few more feet.

"I'm sorry for what I did to you, Morgan. I really am. No one should have ever had to endure that."

My foot brushed against the bag. The bones inside practically hummed—they must have been able to sense the close proximity of the skull.

Am I sure I want to put these two together?

"You broke me, Eugene Law—and now I'm going to break you, person by person, and you're going to watch."

"Mom!" Cathy cried, appearing inside the casket, Ariadne's thread hovering just behind her.

"Catherine?" Porter said, tears in her eyes.

"Do it, Cathy!" I shouted, ducking down to unzip the bag.

My daughter threw herself at Porter and Kris, tackling the souls clean out of their bodies as the gun barrel exploded. The bullet missed Kris's head by inches, but it was still enough to burn the side of his cheek. The kindergartener didn't feel any of it, though, as he and his mother were now hovering with my daughter just outside their bodies.

Morgan didn't waste time on words. She held up the Old Dead skull and gathered her Magick.

With the amount of power swirling around her it was clear to see this one was going to be the game ender. As long as she had that skull, Morgan Crowley was too powerful—that's why the skull needed to go back to its prior owner. I just hoped to hell he appreciated it.

"Get them back in their bodies!" I shouted, directing my junior Necromancer to get the souls of her brother and mother safely back to where they belonged.

"Gene!" astral Porter shouted. "What's happening?"

"Family reunion—do it now, Cathy!"

"Cathy?" Porter said, laying an astral hand on her daughter's translucent face. "How?"

"Another time, Mom. I'll see you on the other side." My

daughter gently placed her mother and brother back in their limp bodies that still lay in the coffin.

Morgan's Magick ramped up. Armed with the skull, she was pulling in power—a lot power—and the second she chose to release it we'd all be toast.

Pull the battery and the toy stops.

"Reformacione," I cried, throwing the bag of bones for a second time tonight, and really hoping I could get lucky enough to have them land close.

In the end, it didn't matter. With the bag unzipped, the bones tumbled out like spilled popcorn, littering the floor as they spun.

Dem bones, dem bones gonna rise again. Holy Hell—What have I done?

51

OLD DEAD

The dusty bones tumbled out onto the floor, but they didn't stay there. They pulled together, piece by piece, bone by bone, reforming the Old Dead's skeleton. Just like the song, the leg bones connected to the thigh bone, and the thigh bone connected to the hip bone.

Dem bones gonna walk around.

And walk around they did—right at my Magickal ex-girlfriend.

The Old Dead's body was on a collision course with its head, and I sure as hell didn't want to be the one that got in its way.

Morgan gripped the skull tighter, amassing what Magick she could, and just like me at the Shelldecks' pool, Morgan's hands glowed and crackled with power.

"Cathy—"

"Hide? You got it," my spectral daughter said, diving into the coffin beside her unconscious mother and brother.

Morgan unleashed a furious blast of multi-colored lighting at the advancing bones, but she might as well have shuffled her feet to whip up a static charge for all the good it did her. The Old Dead aren't deterred by Deep Magick—it's their jam.

Old Dead are Magicians that go in for the amazing-cosmic-powers-to-cheat-death plan. The actual process was not well known, and for good reason; once complete, those dusty old bones are near impossible to destroy and tend to be about as warped as bent nickel.

The skull tore free of Morgan's fingers and hurtled across the room to its rightful position on the shoulders of the shuffling undead.

And now you've gone and done it.

Tendons erupted from the Old Dead's joints, tendrils of sinewy tissue that snaked like ivy and joined the arms, legs, and skull to the rest of the body. A thin layer of plastic-wrap-like skin stretched across bones in a haphazard pattern, covering only bits and pieces of the old Magician. Its eye sockets sprung to light with burning fires that smoldered like spent coals.

Morgan's controlling sigils burned away to reveal a smooth and polished skull.

So much for someone's battery.

Not one to stand in the face of defeat, my ex-girlfriend made a break for the exit—only, she didn't make it much more than a few feet. The boney vise-grip of the old dead grabbed Morgan's wrist and pulled her toward it.

"Where do you think you're going?" it said, with a deep and penetrating voice that made my gut do a few somersaults. "You like the power, don't you?"

Morgan froze, her eyes wide as saucers and stuck in complete panic mode. It was hard to watch. While I hated who she'd become, there was still a part of me that didn't want to see an old love suffer—and that was a good thing.

"Hey!" I shouted, waving my hands in the air like an idiot. "Over here!"

Way to go, Gene—get the hundreds-of-years-old dead Magician to turn his gut-churning gaze on you. Brilliant.

The Old Dead pulled Morgan toward him, bringing her face

next to his. He took a deep breath, or at least it looked like a breath. It was hard to tell without a nose or any other real internal organs.

"It's not you," he said, tossing my ex-girlfriend to the ground like a discarded toy. "Where is that choice Medium I tasted earlier?"

Choice Medium? Oh hell, Cathy!

The Old Dead took another pseudo-breath. "It's like a spring day. Fresh and inviting—untouched and innocent."

"Cathy! Get the hell out of here!"

My daughter's head popped up from the top edge of the casket. Then, taking one look at the Old Dead, reached for her silver cord.

Good, give it a pull and it'll bring you back to your body.

My daughter wrapped both hands around that translucent umbilical cord and pulled, but instead of being dragged back to her body, Cathy found herself holding the cut end of her one-way ticket home.

What the hell?!

There was only one person left in the house who could have done that.

Tristan had lied—every last ounce of his story had been utter bullshit. That boy wasn't afraid of Morgan—he was using her. Cathy's boyfriend was hellbent on summoning The Defiler, and my daughter had just unlocked the safe and given him a road map to finish it.

Those weren't sparkler burns on his arms, those were Hell Flea bites. Son of a bitch.

The Old Dead stretched out his sinewy fingers and my daughter floated toward him; she tried to stop herself, but like a swimmer being dragged down by a gator she couldn't fight the monster's pull.

"Dad!"

If I'd been a better father, we wouldn't have been in this

position, and if I'd planned before diving into things, my first-born daughter wouldn't have become the main course for an undead Magician.

Sometimes, though, you don't think, sometimes you just do —and hope to hell it doesn't mean your undoing.

I removed the simple metal flask from my pocket, the same flask I'd filled with bourbon earlier—it didn't need to do much, but maybe it would be enough to give Cathy time to break free.

And go where? Her cord has been cut—from the other side!

"Quia mortui sunt fratres!" I shouted, dumping the bourbon on the rich red carpet.

It was old Magick, so old very few people even thought of it as Magick anymore. Pouring out that expensive bourbon and sending it to my dead brothers and sisters wasn't going to make for a big display of power. There were no lightning bolts forth-coming, and I certainly wouldn't have the fiery hands of kickass power I'd enjoyed at the Shelldeck pool, but if it worked, I wouldn't need any of those things.

The Old Dead turned away from Cathy, just long enough to focus his burning-eyes on me.

"Go, Cathy!"

My daughter swam through the air, trying to pull away from the temporarily distracted undead Magician. "I can't get back to my body!" she cried, her ghostly form frantically clawing at the air.

Thin and wispy tendrils of mist reached up from the small puddle of premium liquor, snaking and twisting to wrap around the boney legs of the Old Dead. Long-dead Magicians really don't like those undead ones that try to stick around—think of it like cheating on your taxes.

The mist pulled on the Old Dead's legs, driving those bones to the ground and the undead Magician with them.

"Cathy!" I shouted, crossing the lobby to get to my spiritually detached daughter. "You need to find your way back, I can't do it for you."

"Dad, I don't know how!"

"And this is why we don't jump ahead in the books, right?"

"Dad!" my daughter cried, turning end over end in the air like a lost astronaut.

"Right. Close your eyes, Catherine. Focus on my voice. Think about home, think about your family. Think about what's important to you."

My free-floating daughter squeezed her eyes shut and clutched the sliced end of her silvery lifeline, then slowly started to fade from view.

"There, you've got it—"

Cathy's spiritual body crashed into the floor, pulled down by the same tendrils of Magicians past that were crushing the Old Dead. I'd spoken too soon—the spirits of my dead brothers and sisters in Magick had decided they'd like to have my daughter too.

Crap.

5 2

SPECIAL DELIVERY

*I*n the blink of an eye I'd gone from beating back a true Old Dead, to watching my daughter's untethered soul being dragged away by the unbridled anger of long-dead Magicians.

Yeah, Magick is like that—*exactly* like that.

"Dad!" Cathy yelled, fighting for her freedom against the misty strands trying to drag her down. "Help me!"

The Old Dead was in the same predicament as my daughter, but being corporeal meant he had a lot more time than my untethered high-school spirit.

Crap, crap, crap!

Undoing it now was sure to mean problems later. Magick was like a top, and once you got it spinning it was next to impossible to stop without it smacking your hand or it whirling off to smack someone else's.

"Dad!"

Not the time to stand around and debate it, full stop!

I spit in the small pool of spilled bourbon, dropping a perfectly grotesque wad of Magician saliva right in the center of that golden-brown puddle. The crippling mist vanished, releasing my untethered spirit-child, and the ancient Old Dead now hellbent on my wanton destruction.

Go me.

For a Magickally animated skeleton without much in the way of muscle, the Old Dead was faster than I anticipated. Its sinewy fingers wrapped around my neck and slammed me into the carpet. Not one to waste time on long-winded speeches or proclamations of superiority, the undead Magician squeezed my throat while at the same time drawing out my Magickal essence.

This wasn't like the sexy-fun-time experience with a Half-Succubus—that would have been bliss compared to this. This was a tortuous burn, like peeling back my skin one layer at a time while using the business end of an acetylene torch to do it.

I screamed, and not just because of the pain—which was near soul-rending—but because of what I'd lost.

Somewhere just beyond the edges my conscious vision, Cathy fought back against the Old Dead, but her shade was too weak. Without the tether to draw strength from her body she was no more effective than a plastic bag in the wind. On top of that, Kris and Porter were unconscious, and I didn't know the extent of their injuries, or even if they'd ever be the same again.

Face it, Gene. You've lost.

My vision started to fade, and my Magick with it. I closed my eyes and lost track of my own screams.

Then it stopped.

I cautiously opened one eye, then the other. I was still pinned beneath the sinewy, crushing force of the Old Dead, and I still had my neck intact, but everything else had stopped. Cathy and the undead Magician were frozen in place. My daughter had wrapped the cut end of her silver cord around the boney neck of the monster, for what little good it did, but neither of them moved. In fact, nothing moved. It was as if the rest of the world were stuck in some unending moment.

There came the sound of shoes on the soft carpet. I tried to turn my head, but when you've got your neck pinned to the ground by a hundred-year-old monster that's really hard to do.

"Hello?" I said, but in my current state it came out more like 'heh whoa.'

"Someone's got a delivery."

The House!

A skinny old man shuffled into view, his comically wispy hairs drifting gently in the cool evening air. He tightened an old bathrobe around his waist and paused a moment to pull a pair of lightly tinted glasses down from his eyes. A rusty metal railroad spike dangled from his fingers like frozen cod. "Gene, Gene, Gene. John Henry's Spike? Did you really think you could end me? I mean, I am eternal. You know that."

"Uh..."

The old Magician-shaped House shook his head and held the railroad tie up to the light. "Pretty creative though, I'll give you that. But don't you think Viktor would have thought of this? I mean, he was old, but he wasn't a moron."

"I had to try..."

The House dropped down next to me, his threadbare robe flapping open enough to give me an anatomically correct eyeful, just like the man whose likeness he wore had been prone to. "You had to? Here I am, still trapped in that stupid house, so many complex plans spiraling out of control, and all along you've been plotting my destruction?" The old man sighed and set the spike on the ground beside my head. "I'm starting to think you don't want to work together after all."

"Sounds... about... right..." I said, fighting to get words past my undead neck tie.

The old Magician frowned, then stood, cinching his robe tight. "Oh well, there's always your daughter..."

No!

I grabbed the spike, but the House was gone, and with him

went my stay of execution. The writhing pain of the Magick stripping resumed with righteous fury.

I clutched the spike in my fingers, its power cold in my palm. The House would have to wait, I suddenly had more important plans for this single-use piece of problem-ending Magick.

I couldn't speak the words, but I don't think I had to—what tiny Magick was left in me knew what I wanted. It could see Cathy hovering just above the Old Dead, fighting for her father, and it knew damn well what slept in that casket.

The undead Magician crushing my throat hadn't been back for more than a few minutes, but it was time for him to reach a very timely end.

Using what little coordination I had left, I drove John Henry's last spike clean into the side of that Old Dead skull.

53

WILD MAGICK

*B*oom.

Hundreds of years of pent-up Magick, natural and stolen, exploded in a brilliant wave of light and sound. This was Wild Magick, exactly the sort of thing that Morgan had been concerned about back at the Shelldeck estate. Wild Magick was just as it sounds, all but uncontrollable, and more often than not deadly as a heart attack.

"Cathy!" I shouted, bracing myself against the surge of cosmic power roaring through me.

"Dad!"

The kid was already spinning end over end away from me, her translucent body caught in the crest of a searing wave of Wild Magick.

Get the cord, you fool!

The remains of Ariadne's Thread shot past my head like a kite tail in an autumn wind. I lunged for the end, catching it with my tired hands before I lost my one and only daughter to oblivion.

"I've got you!" I shouted, a hand on her cord, but the Wild Magick was too strong. It was like drinking from the fire hose—

too much and too fast, an unrelenting flood of energy. It had to go somewhere, and right now that somewhere was inside me. My heart pounded like a jackrabbit, and my hands throbbed. Cathy's cord slid through my fingers as she spun farther and farther away from me, carried on the torrent of untamed Magick.

"Dad!"

"I'm trying!"

I tightened my fingers down against the silver thread, but those numb digits had already become next to useless. The cord was still spinning out, and I couldn't stop it. I closed my eyes and fought the urge to vomit. My guts twisted and my head spun—it was too much Magick, too much to control.

You can't control everything, Gene. Sometimes you have to just let go.

But I couldn't. I couldn't let go of the fear, the worries, or the regrets. I couldn't let go of them, because I hadn't known a life without them. Cathy spun helpless on that silvery thread, tears streaming down her translucent cheeks. "Dad!"

You have to do it.

I reached out for the Thinning, for the bare patches in the veil where the Wild Magick flows freely, and I sent everything I could straight into them. "Hold on, Cathy!"

The Wild Magick coursed through me like a laser light show. It streamed up and out of the building, taking the roof off with it, and filling the Florida night with a spectacular display of light and sound. Old concrete and busted rebar rained down around us. Large chunks smashed into the newly restored concession counter, shattering glass and crushing displays.

Porter, Kris!

Sheets of torn steel slammed the casket shut, then bounced off, leaving deep gouges and dents. In the aftermath of the Wild Magick outburst, John Henry's Spike vanished, its forged steel rusting away in the cranial cavity of that undead Magician.

Fragile bones collapsed on the red carpet, breaking apart like fine parchment paper until all that remained was the shattered skull that landed in my lap.

"Cathy," I cried, coughing in the dust and grit, my hands still tight to Ariadne's Thread. "Are you okay?"

Through the hazy air, my daughter's translucent hands gripped the edge of the concession stand, while all around her lay broken concrete, steel, and rebar.

"I... I think so," she said, pulling her translucent body toward me using the silvery cord like a tow-line. "Is it over?"

"Yeah." I pushed the crumpled bones aside and tried to stand. "We just need to get your mom and Kris, then we can figure out a way to—"

Whoosh!

"Dad!"

Cathy's lifeline snapped out of my hands, an unexpected gust of strong and supernatural wind pulling her up and out the roof.

"Cathy!"

"Gene," Adam cried, throwing the front door wide and coughing into his sleeve in the thick air. "Gene, we've got a problem!"

"Cathy's Thread has been cut, she's—"

Adam rubbed at his red eyes in the stinging dust. "Gene, I can't close the Hellgate. Something happened, and it's too strong—things are trying to come through!"

Cathy!

* * *

THERE WAS HELLFIRE, and lots of it—the parking lot had become a modern-day Inferno. Rob, Justine, and the rest of the jiu-jitsu school were deep in it, fighting off the Minor Demons of the netherworld. Hell Fleas by the thousands streamed out into the night sky like malevolent embers of a raging campfire. The Hellgate itself was monstrous. Easily two stories tall, it engulfed the parking lot. The forces of evil marshaled on the other side. Black and twisted shapes crawled across that bleak landscape— Hell was on the move, and it was coming straight for us.

"There she is!" Adam shouted, pointing to my daughter, who was currently clinging to the burning edge of the swirling vortex.

"Cathy! Hold on. I'll coming. Adam, where's the flare?"

My apprentice held up a burnt-out and empty flare casing. "I tried that."

"Crap."

Cathy's silver thread whipped past her like a ribbon streaming into the burning Hellscape.

Rubbery Minor Demons, Imps and the like, poured out of the gate like a class of pre-schoolers on free candy day. With bulbous noses and spindly arms, they clawed their way past the ring and into the parking lot. Most of them didn't make it far before meeting the business end of a crowbar or lug wrench. Justine, Rob, and the rag-tag crew of *The Qwik Fix* had stuck around, and along with a smattering of jiu-jitsu students they were doing everything they could to stop the horde of wailing evil.

"Gene!" Rob shouted from across the fiery parking lot. "What the hell is going on?"

"You're doing great, Rob," I shouted back, giving my confused mechanic a thumbs up. "Adam, you've got to help me, I've got nothing left. I just channeled a hundred years of pent-up Magick out the top of the movie theater like it was the climax of a firework show erupting from my skull."

Adam zipped his hoodie and pushed up his sleeves. "Let's do this," he said before turning to face to fiery vortex. "Gene…"

"Yeah."

"What do I do?"

Ariadne's Thread snapped and spun like a fishing fly inside the terrible darkness, its tantalizing dance drawing a rapidly growing audience of devilish admirers.

"We've got to pull her back," I cried, my voice barely carrying above the swirling pull of the fiery portal.

"But what about the gate? We can't let it stay open."

As much as I hated to admit it, Adam was right. The longer the gate stayed open the more people we put at risk, and the more evil things we gave access to our world in the process.

"Then we need to move. Give me a hand."

My apprentice took my hand, and together we plowed our way toward Cathy. We hadn't made it a few feet before a familiar voice and a bright pink Minor Demon slammed into us.

"Hey, guys," Stewart The Annoying said, flapping his wings to keep himself aloft. "I figured this was your doing."

"What are you doing here? I gave you an order not to let Cathy leave the house."

The Imp shrugged his tiny pink shoulders. "I tried, but it's hard to do much when you get banished."

"What? How?" Adam asked, his hands holding tight to my whipping shirt.

Stewart shrugged. "Tristan. Who would have guessed that kid's a damn decent Magician—fooled me, that's for sure."

My daughter's silvery cord went taut—something had a hold of Cathy.

"Something's got her," I cried, the broken edge of Ariadne's Thread dragging me away from Adam and the Imp.

The rubbery-pink Minor Demon spun around in the air and squinted into the churning flames. "That's Asaroth the Defiler. You can't let him get her."

Adam grabbed my arm and together we skidded toward the swirling gate. "What do you think I'm trying to do? Certainly open to ideas."

"On it," the Imp said, beating a path toward my flagging child. The Minor Demon latched on to Cathy's arms and pulled, pumping the air with his diminutive wings, but she wasn't moving.

"Kick, Cathy!" I shouted.

"I am!"

My daughter swung her feet wildly, but the pull of damnation was too strong. Her silvery cord cracked like a bullwhip and my daughter's fingers slid on the portal's fiery edge.

"Let go," the Imp said, fighting with his wings to keep her from vanishing into Hell.

"No, don't, Cathy!" I pushed off of Adam and lunged for the tiny monster, grabbing a hold of his foot. "I've got you guys."

"No, you don't," he said, grunting out his words. "It's too strong. She's got to let go. Order me to keep her safe and the gates of Hell itself will not prevail against her."

"I'm not letting my daughter go!"

Tears streamed down Cathy's shimmering cheeks. "Don't let me go, Dad!"

"I won't!"

Whatever was on the other side of that thread pulled again, and this time it yanked me forward enough for me to graze the fiery edge of the gate.

"Agh!" Hellfire melted my shirt sleeve to my arm.

Cathy slipped deeper into the swirling darkness—and that's when I saw them, the inky black and soul-sucking eyes of Asaroth the Defiler, hungry for the succulent soul of an innocent Catherine Law.

"Order me," Stewart cried, his wings beating hard against the fiery vortex.

"Don't let me go, Dad!"

"He won't stop with her, Magician," the Imp shouted, his wings failing. "He'll come for the rest of you—order me and I'll keep her safe."

"Cathy!"

"Dad, I don't want to die!" My daughter's eyes burned red with tears as the flames of Hell licked at her face.

"I'll find you. I promise!"

"Dad, no!"

"I hereby order you, Stewart The Annoying, to safeguard my daughter from here to eternity."

The Imp shuddered, his skin turning purple. He broke free of my tenuous grip and threw himself onto my terrified daughter. Thick black tendrils stretched out from the Defiler, but the Imp bit down on the remains of Cathy's cord, snapping it like a fishing line and holding tight to her.

"Dad!" Cathy screamed, her ragged voice cutting me to the bone. My knees buckled and and my stomach rolled, but I couldn't look away. Stewart tucked my only daughter's frail body close, and together they vanished into the fiery depths of Hell.

"He's coming," Adam shouted, yanking my arm. "The Defiler is coming, and he's really pissed."

I couldn't move, nor did I want to.

Part of my soul had vanished into Hell, and the rest of it wanted nothing more than to join her.

My apprentice shoved the spent flare into my weak hands. "Magick demands sacrifice, right? Well you just gave it one hell of a fucking sacrifice, so make it your bitch and close this damn gate."

"She's gone."

"No, you said it yourself—Stewart will keep her safe, and you'll bring her home. You are the most amazing Magician and father I know, but none of that will matter if you sit here and let the rest of the world burn."

"But—"

Adam pulled me to my feet. "Do it for your wife—for your

son! Do it for everyone you've ever cared about. Close the damn gate!"

My apprentice was right—Magick demands sacrifice, and I'd just given it my firstborn.

The Defiler's black tendrils reached out through the yawning portal, spreading into the parking lot and withering whatever they touched—cars rusted, asphalt turned to dust, and somewhere Justine's sidearm barked out rounds.

"Do it!" Adam cried.

I pulled back the melted remnants of my shirt and dragged the darkened tip of the spent flare along my bleeding arm.

"Et ignis vitae!"

The flare ignited, a strong and vibrant golden fire that roared defiant in the face of Hell itself.

I stared into the abyss, hoping for one last vision of my daughter, one last look that would tell me she would be all right.

You've lost your daughter to the gates of Hell—she'll never be all right again.

"Close the gate!" Adam shouted, his hoodie flapping.

I held up the glowing golden flare and wrapped my hand over the flame.

"Finis."

54

FALL OUT

I wish I was able to say I got to see the gate close, and that the look on Asaroth's disappointed face had been worth the third-degree burns on my hand. But, if I did, I didn't remember any of it. The newspaper loved the whole thing; in fact, Claudia Wilson quickly became a local legend with her amazing pyrotechnics display cleverly timed with the release of *Demon High*.

The best Magick is the kind you'd never guess was Magick in the first place.

Adam and Porter were in the hospital room with me when I woke. A few days had gone by, and the doctors had done a nice job fixing up my hand, but even with my Magick I'd still have a scar—Hellfire is a right bastard.

My apprentice had found Porter and Kris, and with Justine's squad car running point, had deposited us all at the hospital. In fact, it was Adam who had found Cathy's unconscious body on the floor of our living room.

The burned-out sigil scored into the floorboards and an empty chest told me what I needed to know—Tristan had banished my Imp and stolen Ten Spins Infernal Constructs.

298

That little thieving bastard...

It was another day before the doctors cleared me to leave, but life didn't begin to return to normal—how could it? My wife spent day and night in Cathy's hospital room, praying for a miracle—our daughter needed all the prayers she could get where she was now, I was certain of that.

We found the white van, and inside plenty of missing pieces. Tristan and Morgan had been working together, but on what, I didn't know. They were both lost in wind, and try as I might, I couldn't find either of them.

Even after my Magick beat down, I tried to reopen a small gate to Hell. It didn't need to be big, just enough to communicate with Cathy, to tell her I would find a way to bring her back.

It took days before I could manifest even the tiniest portal, and even then all I received for my efforts was a dusting of Hell Fleas.

Wherever Cathy was, she was too far away for me to find her.

More time passed and the tension continued to rise between Porter and me. I suppose we each blamed ourselves for what happened, for what little good that did us. Caught in the crossfire, Kris became a violent and distant version of his once goofy self. While we were in the hospital watching over Cathy's body, we were also dealing with a young child hellbent on his own destruction.

That's how I found myself sitting here, in the Dad Wagon, or what was left of it, outside of the last place I ever wanted to be, waiting for one of my least favorite people.

The Lincoln town car pulled in behind me. Oddly enough, while there was plenty of room, the lawyer didn't park directly in front of 69 Mallory Lane—the House made sure of that.

"Damn, Gene, this is one tough place to find," Sharon said, stepping out of her car and retrieving her briefcase. "Now, what the hell is so important that you had to call me out here on a Sunday night?"

"Did you get the document?"

Sharon pulled a stack of papers out of her leather briefcase. "Yeah, listen—I'm not your lawyer, but this is some kind of crazy employment contract. Ten lifetimes? That doesn't even make sense."

Maybe to you it doesn't...

"I have something to add to that stack," I said, handing her a small white envelope. "Inside you'll find my resignation, effective immediately."

"What?!"

"You heard me. You said it before, you want me out. Well, here's your chance."

"Are you under duress?" Sharon asked, shifting her eyes to take in the surrounding street, but—except for the House—we were completely alone.

"No... but in a manner of speaking I guess we all are. Is the contract legal?"

Relieved to be talking about something mundane, the lawyer laid the document out on the hood of her car.

"Yes, essentially. If you throw out all the strange quid pro-quos, this is a pretty straight-forward employment contract, but it's a little odd."

"How so?"

Sharon paused to frame her words. "Well, I've never seen one where you have to give up something to get the job."

"Sacrifices—yeah, they're a bitch."

She stacked the papers back together and handed them to me. "I don't like you, Gene, but I hate what happened to your daughter. If this gives you some closure, then I'm happy for you."

I handed her the signed resignation letter, ending my term with Kinder. "Tell John I appreciated the job."

"I will."

I gave one final nod and stepped off the street and onto the curb. It took every ounce of willpower to not turn around right then.

Do it for them...

"Gene?"

I stopped and fished a key out of my pocket, a key I'd promised someone I'd never use. The cold metal lay heavy in my hand.

"I don't believe any of this shit, but if that contract is real, then in two weeks I'll forget I ever knew you."

I slid that cold steel into the lock of 69 Mallory lane, twisting it gently until the deadbolt thumped against the aging frame. A non-existent breeze ruffled the gossamer curtains inside.

I took a deep breath and hoped I wasn't making the worst decision of my life, then pushed the door open.

"Goodbye, Sharon."

* * *

"Dad?" my daughter asked, leaning against the ice cream display case. "What flavor?"

"You know me..."

"Don't make me guess."

I smiled and squeezed Cathy against me, willing this moment to last as long as I could. "Geez—don't make a scene. Just tell me what you want."

"Cookies and cream, honey, you remember, right?"

My daughter hesitated. "Yeah, that's right, I remember now."

Cathy collected our ice creams and walked them back to the table. Kris was already face deep in his tiny bowl of chocolaty goodness, and even Porter—who staunchly avoided deserts— had made an exception and nibbled on a kiddie cone of vanilla soft-serve.

The Law family was celebrating.

It'd been two weeks to the day since Catherine Law had miraculously awakened from her coma. The doctors—being doctors—kept her around for observation, but in the end they had no other choice but to return her to us. In short, they'd grown tired of her stir-crazy antics and the constant wrath of Porter.

Smart choice.

Once I was alone with my daughter, I asked her about what she remembered, but true to the contract, she remembered nothing. In fact in all their minds it was as if Cathy had been injured in jiu-jitsu and was restored to health.

With his sister returned to him, Kris reverted back to the fun-loving and good-natured kid we'd known was there all along. Even Porter was different with Cathy home. Sure, they still bickered—show me a mother and daughter that don't from time to time—but there was a level of wholeness I hadn't noticed before.

I noticed a lot of things now.

I spent my waking moments trying to pack in as many memories as I could. I used those two weeks to haul the kids to theme parks, to take my wife dancing, and to do all the things I should have been doing all along.

But, no matter how hard I tried to stem the tide and slow the seconds, they kept coming—an unrelenting march of moments leading to this, my final day.

"Cathy, you're dripping," Porter said, pointing to the thin dribble of cookies and cream rolling down our daughter's fingers. "Get a napkin."

"It's empty," Cathy said, fumbling with the dispenser.

"I'll get some," both of the women in my life said, heading to different tables.

"Goodbye, Kris."

"Bye, Dad!"

I set my ice cream down, and with a heavy heart pushed open the glass door and stepped out into the light chill of a late fall evening. I stopped to take a seat on one of the park benches outside, turning my head so I could watch the final moments of what had been my family.

After a few agonizing seconds they cleaned up the table and walked out the door. They rolled right past me, talking and laughing as if I wasn't there—because for them, I wasn't.

True to the contract I'd signed with 69 Mallory Lane, my family would now be safe. Safe from the dark things that wanted nothing more than a succulent bit of innocence to snack on and, most of all, safe from me.

Family demands sacrifice.

55

BATHROOM BLOODIED

*B*lack blood speckled the bar's cheap bathroom mirror. I wiped what I could with my hands, but Demon blood is a pain in the ass to get off basically anything.

How many was this now? A dozen? Two? Have I really lost count?

I turned the faucet on and let it shudder a few times before unleashing a blast of water into the tiny sink, then jammed my hand against the soap dispenser—empty.

Damn it.

Cold water poured over my hands.

The soap didn't really matter; it would take a lot more than crappy pink goo to wash away my inequities—or the monster blood.

Working for the House had become a full-time occupation, and judging by the feral Imp whose lifeblood was oozing into the floor drain, I wasn't half bad at it. So far, the requests—I felt better calling them that—had been centered on removing any competition that had settled into the Sunshine State.

I picked at the fleshy bits of Minor Demon gore stuck under my nails.

Let's see, five Imps, two Incubuses... that's not right... The plural of Incubus is Incubi, right? Where's Porter when I need her?

I knew exactly where my wife was—far away from me. That had been part of the deal, along with restoring our lost daughter and broken family.

I'd told myself it was worth it, and repeated those words in the mirror each and every night, but truth be told even I wasn't sure I believed them anymore.

The bathroom door banged against the dead-bolt.

"Somebody's in here!" I shouted over the splashing water.

Somebody who's gonna have to figure out how to haul away a dead Imp...

"Gene?"

I froze—I wasn't in a part of Florida where anyone would know me. Worse yet, my deal with Mallory Lane meant most of the people I loved wouldn't know me even if I wanted them to.

"Who said that?"

My words bounced off the dingy tile, but received no response. I stepped over the fallen Imp and placed a hand on the door—secretly hating the fact that now I'd have to wash my hands again—and threw open it in a single motion.

The twangs of a blisteringly fast banjo thundered down the hall, carried on smoky air and blending nicely with the voices of a raucous crowd. It was ladies night at this backwater middle-of-the-state watering hole, and what ladies there were had already drawn the rest of the sweaty masses toward the stage.

I was alone.

I pushed the door closed and locked it again, then rolled up my sleeves, content to scratch my head and think through ways to maneuver what remained of the Imp out the exhaust window.

"Whoa... I knew that guy. We did some milk curling and cattle mutilations back in the early 1400s... Tough way to go."

An Imp—or more accurately, my Imp—stared back at me from the blood-smeared glass.

"Stewart?"

"Yeah—boss, you don't look so good."

I waved him off. "I've been better. What do you want?"

"I... I screwed up. You told me to protect her and—"

I folded the dead Minor Demon's wings over its bloodied face. "I'm a little busy right now."

"But—"

"Look, it doesn't matter. You did what I told you to do. Cathy's spirit is back in her body—that was part of my deal with the House."

"What?!" the mirror-bound imp practically fell through the glass. "When did that happen?"

"Six months, three weeks, four days, and..." I looked at my phone, "two hours ago."

"Something doesn't make sense..."

I dragged the body toward the window.

How am I going to get it up and out without covering myself in Imp gore?

"What doesn't make sense?"

"I lost her just now."

My heart seized in my chest, and not from the cheese fries I'd eaten earlier. "What do you mean 'just now?'"

The Imp turned away from the glass. "Damn it. They're coming—"

"What do you mean *just now*?!"

"I mean, she never left."

The bathroom door banged again.

"Damn, they're fast," Stewart said, pulling away from the glass. "I've got to go! I'll find her—I made you a promise." The tiny purple creature vanished into the hazy streaks of grime.

I stood transfixed, staring into the mirror, and then right

through it. The door banged again, but my knuckles remained white against the cheap porcelain sink while a broken record refrain rolled in my head.

She never left...

MARTIN SHANNON'S WEIRD FLORIDA

Short Stories

0 - Danderous Delivery (Newsletter Subscribers Only)

1 - Hook, Line, and Slinker

2 - Ballroom and Chain

3 - Bahama Blues

4 - Plasma Pistols

5 - Lights Out

6 - Mourning Paper

7 - Ignorance and Unleaded

8 - Black Valentine

9 - Soulless

10 - Ten Turns (Coming Soon)

Novels

1 - Dead Set

2 - Gathering Gloom

3 - Beaten Path

4 -Bloody Deed

5 - No Fury (Coming Soon)

GATHERING GLOOM

TALES OF WEIRD FLORIDA

Will Gene see the truth in time, or will he be lost deep in the heart of a Gathering Gloom?

Not much matters to Eugene Law, a young and naive Magician more concerned with fun and friends than the hard road to Magickal proficiency. Yet when a seemingly chance encounter shows off the true depth of Gene's power, he'll find himself in the crosshairs of deadly ambitions where spindly legs stir and hungry fangs glisten beneath the eternal twilight.

Innocence lost is wisdom gained, but for Eugene Law, is the juice worth the squeeze?

Enjoy this look back at Gene's college days in the exciting book two of The Tales of Weird Florida. Available at Amazon.

AFTERWORD

I've done my best to paint Florida in a unique and Magickal light, but don't take my words as gospel. I encourage each of you to come down to this strange slice of Americana and see it for yourself.

If you do, don't be surprised if a little Florida Magick rubs off on you, the Sunshine State has a habit of doing that—just don't say I didn't warn you.

Martin
Somewhere under the Cypress
October 2019

ACKNOWLEDGMENTS

Books don't happen on their own, nor do they grow on trees—okay well, they sort of do—but you get the picture.

This book and all of its Magick could not have happened without the help of the following people:

Dawn Ius, my first coach—thank you for lighting the fire.

Faera Lane, my cover artist and confidant—thank you for believing in me, and for making my books shine.

Amber Townsend, my beta reader—thank you for countless calls and texts. So much of Weird Florida only exists because of you.

Denise Koehler, Font Artist Extraordinaire—thank you for bringing my vision of Florida Magick to life.

Kira Butler, Graphic Artist to the Stars—thank you for bringing martin-shannon.com out of the nineties.

KA Miltimore, Cass Kim, Edison T. Crux, and the rest of my anthology buddies—thank you all for believing in me, and for the kick in the pants I so desperately needed.

Last but not least, thank you, reader. To know you've made it this far warms my heart more than you can imagine.

ABOUT THE AUTHOR

Martin Shannon's been using his imagination to avoid weeding since he was in short pants. His first series, *Tales of Weird Florida*, is an homage to the Sunshine State he knows and loves, and spent countless hours riding his bike through as a kid. It's got mystery, mayhem, and more than a little Magick. He hopes you enjoy the supernatural side of the upside down state, but if not, he's got a banjo, and he knows how to use it. You can find out more at www.martin-shannon.com.

ON NEWSLETTERS, WRITING, AND REVIEWS

Thank you for making it this far. It is my sincere hope you enjoyed the story, and the opportunity to slip into the sometimes too tight shoes of Eugene Law and company. If you did, please take a few seconds to help me spread the word, and in exchange I promise to send out free short stories as well as keep you up to date with each new novel in the Tales of Weird Florida world.

Writers live on reviews, newsletter sign-ups, and tiny scraps of praise. The writing life can get rather lonely, as evidenced by my social-media presence. So, drop by, say hello, sign up for the newsletter, and if you feel strongly enough, write a review or tell your friends. Remember, every time you write a review, an angel gets its wings.

Made in the USA
Monee, IL
27 November 2020

49712815R00192